BUTCH CASSIDY
THE LOST YEARS

D0972023

Also by William W. Johnstone with J.A. Johnstone

A Rocky Mountain Christmas

Luke Jensen, Bounty Hunter

A Lone Star Christmas

The Family Jensen

MacCallister: The Eagles Legacy

Support Your Local Deputy

Phoenix Rising

WILLIAM W. JOHNSTONE
With
J.A. JOHNSTONE

BUTCH CASSIDY
THE LOST YEARS

Kensington Publishing Corp.
http://www.kensingtonbooks.com

KENSINGTON BOOKS are published by

Kensington Publishing Corp.
119 West 40th St.
New York, NY 10018

Copyright © 2013 by J.A. Johnstone

All rights reserved. No part of this book may be reproduced in any form or by any means without the prior written consent of the Publisher, excepting brief quotes used in reviews.

All Kensington titles, imprints and distributed lines are available at special quantity discounts for bulk purchases for sales promotion, premiums, fund-raising, educational or institutional use.

Special book excerpts or customized printings can also be created to fit specific needs. For details, write or phone the office of the Kensington Special Sales Manager: Kensington Publishing Corp., 119 West 40th St., New York, NY, 10018. Attn. Special Sales Department. Phone: 1-800-221-2647.

Kensington and the K logo Reg. U.S. Pat. & TM Off.

ISBN-13: 978-0-7582-9457-9
ISBN-10: 0-7582-9457-3

First Hardcover Printing: May 2013
10 9 8 7 6 5 4 3 2

Printed in the United States of America

For our friend James Reasoner

Zephyr, Texas, 1950

After the hot, bright sunlight outside, the grocery store was dim and pleasantly cool. Electric fans sitting here and there in open spaces on the shelves stirred the air around and blended the smells of pepper, vinegar, cinnamon, coffee, and a thousand other items into an aroma that intrigued the senses of Nathan Tuttle. The irregular slap of ivory against wood drew him toward the rear of the store. A bluish-gray haze of cigarette smoke hung in the air above the scarred wooden table back there, past the meat case and the counter where the cash register squatted.

Four men sat at the table playing dominoes. One of them, a stout man wearing a white apron, was probably the store's owner. Another wore jeans and a grease-stained mechanic's shirt with the name "Howard" stitched onto an oval patch sewn to it. The overalls and dirt-encrusted work shoes of the third man indicated that he was a farmer.

The fourth man, who had a brown, hand-rolled cigarette dangling from his lips, was lean almost to the point of gauntness, his leathery face a study in planes and angles. He wore a straw cowboy hat tipped back on his head, revealing crisp white hair. His faded blue shirt had snaps on it instead of buttons. He sat with his back to the wall, facing the door, Nathan noted, so he would be able to see anyone who came in.

The man glanced up at the newcomer, and even though he had to be at least eighty years old, his eyes were those of a younger man, blue and piercing and intelligent. He had a small scar under the left one.

The old man looked down at the dominoes in front of him again, obviously dismissing Nathan from his thoughts. That came as no surprise. Tall, slender, and bespectacled, with a natural awkwardness about him, Nathan knew he wasn't a very impressive physical specimen. He liked to think he made up for that with his mind, but the jury was still out on that.

The storekeeper looked up at Nathan, too, and asked, "Something I can do for you, son?" In the middle of a hot afternoon like this, the store wasn't busy. In fact, Nathan was the only potential customer at the moment.

"I'm looking for Mr. Henry Parker," he said.

The glances the other three players shot toward the man in the cowboy hat told Nathan he had come to the right place.

"This here's Hank," the storekeeper said with a nod toward the old cowboy.

The man added a domino to the arrangement on the table and said, "Makes fifteen." A rectangular piece of board with holes drilled in it lay on the table near his left hand. The holes were arranged in five columns, with ten holes in each column. The cowboy took a small wooden peg and moved it up three holes. He didn't look at Nathan.

"Hello, Mr. Parker," Nathan said. "I was wondering if I could have a word with you."

Parker drew on the cigarette and let the smoke trickle out his nostrils.

"Go ahead."

"In private, if we could," Nathan said.

The farmer chuckled and said, "Sounds like you might be in trouble with the gov'ment, Hank. This boy looks like he might be a gov'ment man."

Parker finally looked up at Nathan again and asked, "You come from Washington, son?"

"No, sir. Dallas."

That brought more chuckles from the other three men, as if being from Dallas was almost as bad as being from Washington.

"We're right in the middle of a game here," Parker said. With a graceful motion, he gestured toward the dominoes on the table. "I'm ahead, and I only need thirty more points to go out."

The mechanic said, "The lousy dominoes I'm gettin' today, it might take me three hands to score that much count."

"Jim Strickland told me to look you up, Mr. Parker," Nathan said.

Parker's face looked like it might have been carved from old wood. Without changing expression, he said, "Jim Strickland, eh? How is ol' Jim?"

"Very interesting," Nathan said.

The storekeeper asked, "Don't think I know a Jim Strickland. He any relation to the Stricklands up at Blanket? I recollect one named Mose, and another boy, called Alvy, somethin' like that."

Parker shook his head and said, "Jim's no relation, as far as I know." He turned his dominoes face down. "You fellas go on without me."

"You're quittin' in the middle of a game?" the farmer asked. "That ain't like you, Hank."

"Well, hell," Parker said as he got to his feet, "there'll always be another game, won't there?" He pointed to the store's entrance and went on to Nathan, "We'll go sit on one of the benches on the front porch and talk. You got to buy me a cold soda pop, though. It's hot out there today."

Nathan reached into his pocket for a coin and said, "Sure. How much?"

"Soda pop's a nickel," the storekeeper said.

Nathan handed him a dime.

"I'll get one for myself, too," he said as he went to the red metal drink box. He paused with his hand on the lid and looked back at Parker. "What would you like, sir?"

"Co'-Cola will be fine, son," Parker said as he stepped around the table and the other players.

Nathan took two bottles of Coca-Cola from the bed of half-melted ice on the bottom of the box, let them drip for a few seconds, and then popped the caps on the opener attached to the side of the box. He handed one to Parker, and the two of them strolled outside together.

It was warmer out here, but at least the awning over the sidewalk put the wooden benches in the shade. The single block of businesses that constituted the community's downtown was all but deserted. No cars hummed past on the highway.

The two men sat down. Parker stretched his legs out in front of him and crossed them at the ankles. His plain brown boots showed signs of long wear.

"My name is Nathan Tuttle, sir."

"Am I going to be pleased to meet you, Nathan?" Parker asked with a faint smile on his face. "Or am I going to regret it?"

"I suppose that depends on our conversation."

"Ain't that always the way?" Parker lifted the bottle to his lips and let a long drink slide between them. When he lowered it, he went on, "What brings you to Zephyr besides a hankerin' to act all mysterious-like, Nathan?"

"I work for the Pinkerton Detective Agency." Nathan had intended to be very forthright and open, putting his cards on the table right away, so to speak. But something about Henry Parker was intimidating, despite his mild appearance and soft-spoken manner. After admitting that he was a Pinkerton, Nathan fell silent.

Parker took another drink of the soda and said, "Go on."

"My father was a Pinkerton agent," Nathan said. "So was his father before him."

"It's not a job that's usually handed down from father to son, from what I hear," Parker said.

"That's the way it worked in my family. My father and grandfather were both devoted to the idea of upholding the law."

"Most fellas who feel like that become cops, not strikebreakers and railroad goons."

Nathan bristled with anger, unable to suppress the reaction.

"That's not all the Pinkertons do. They pursue criminals all over the country."

"Is that what you're doin', Nathan?" Parker drawled. "Pursuin' a criminal?"

Nathan felt like the man was making fun of him. He knew that he ought to be used to that by now, but it still rankled him.

"As a matter of fact, I am," he said. Warming to his subject now, he continued, "A couple of years ago, not long after I went to work for the agency, I came into the possession of my grandfather's trunk. Inside it were a lot of his notebooks and papers concerning the cases he worked on. I found them to be fascinating reading, especially the ones about his search for one outlaw in particular: Butch Cassidy."

"When was this, when your grandpa was lookin' for Butch Cassidy?"

"Around the time of the First World War."

Parker shook his head slowly and said, "I hate to break it to you, Nathan, but he was wasting his time. Butch Cassidy was killed before that down in South America, in one of those countries that's even hotter than Texas. I remember hearin' all about it. Seems like it was . . . 1906, maybe. Somewhere around in there."

"1908," Nathan said. "In Bolivia, at a little town called San Vicente."

"See, there you go, you know a lot more about it than I do."

"That's where Robert Leroy Parker and Harry Longabaugh, better known under their aliases Butch Cassidy and the Sundance Kid, supposedly were killed in a battle with the Bolivian army."

"Well, two men against an army . . . It don't sound very likely they would have come through that alive."

"The Pinkertons have never officially declared them dead."

"I don't reckon you have to be declared dead to *be* dead."

Nathan ignored that comment and went on, "My grandfather, Newton Tuttle, believed that while Longabaugh was indeed killed in Bolivia, Robert Parker survived the shooting, although he was wounded, and escaped from the Bolivians. A week after the battle at San Vicente, an American who appeared to be ill— or suffering from a gunshot wound—appeared in a coastal village in Chile and bought passage on a trading ship that took him to Lima, Peru. From there he was able to secure a berth on a liner bound for Liverpool. He traveled under the name Leroy Michaels."

"Now, I can see why you might think I'm related to Butch Cassidy, since my name's Parker and you say that was his real name, too . . . even though there are a whole heap of people with that last name. I don't recall that I've ever known anybody with the last name of Michaels, though.

"Robert Leroy Parker started calling himself Butch Cassidy after he met a rustler named Mike Cassidy," Nathan said. "The connection seems obvious to me."

"It's your story, Nathan," Parker said softly.

"Actually, it's my grandfather's story. He's the one who traced Leroy Michaels to England, where he recuperated from his wound and eventually traveled to France and Spain, only by then he was using the name Jameson Lowe. Jim Lowe was another name Butch used as an alias for a while."

Parker sipped from the soda bottle and said, "Go on."

"Eventually Jameson Lowe sailed to New York and disappeared. There's speculation that Etta Place, Harry Longabaugh's lover, was in New York about the same time, so it stands to reason that Cassidy wanted to see her and break the news of the Sundance Kid's death himself."

Nathan's eyes were keener than they looked behind his glasses. He didn't miss the way Henry Parker's hand tightened on the bottle when he mentioned Etta Place. Parker didn't say anything, though.

"Jameson Lowe dropped out of sight after his visit to New York. My grandfather actually hadn't been assigned to track down Butch Cassidy and determine once and for all if the outlaw was dead or alive. That was just a tangent off another investigation, but he became so interested in it that he continued to follow up on his own time after his superiors insisted that he drop the matter. He came to believe that Butch Cassidy was living in Texas under the name Jim Strickland and had become a successful rancher."

"What made him think that?" Parker asked.

Nathan hesitated, then said, "I don't really know. There are . . . gaps . . . in my grandfather's documentation of his investigation. I know at one point he planned to travel to Texas to meet this fellow Strickland and see if he was right. But I haven't been able to find any indication that he ever made the trip."

"And why do you think I'd know anything about Strickland?"

"Well . . . you agreed to talk to me after I mentioned the name, didn't you?"

That brought a slow chuckle from Parker. He said, "I just wanted to see what sort of burr you had under your saddle, son. I could tell as soon as you came in the store you were fit to bust about somethin'. You've spun an interestin' yarn, but what does it have to do with me?"

"I suppose I've talked around it for long enough, haven't I?" Nathan took a deep breath. "I've taken up the challenge where my grandfather left off, sir. I've been trying to find out what happened to Jim Strickland, and I've traced the man I believe was using that name through several more identities until I arrived at a conclusion. I believe that you are the man who was once known as Jim Strickland, Mr. Parker. Or should I say . . . Mr. Cassidy?"

For a long moment, Parker didn't say anything. Then he tipped his head back and let out an easy laugh.

"Son, you've been out in the sun too long," he said. "It's done somethin' to your brain. Do I really look like a famous owlhoot and train robber to you? I'm just a stove-up old cowboy."

"You seem rather spry for your age, sir . . . which, if I'm not mistaken, is just about the same age as Butch Cassidy would be if he survived that shootout in Bolivia. Mid-eighties, am I right?"

"Be eighty-five my next birthday," Parker said. "Just what the hell would you do, kid, if I said, yeah, I'm Butch Cassidy?"

Nathan was prepared for that question. He said, "In all likelihood, I wouldn't do anything. There are no charges still on the books against Butch Cassidy. I just want to know the truth. I want to know if my grandfather was right."

Parker still seemed amused. He took another drink and said,

"Well . . . I'm not admitting anything of the sort, mind you, but folks around here seem to think I'm a pretty good storyteller. Tell you what I'll do. You've spun me a yarn, so I'll spin you a yarn of what it might have been like if I really was Butch Cassidy. How about that?"

"I'm more than willing to listen to anything you want to tell me, sir."

"All right, then." For a moment Parker squinted as if in thought, then resumed, "If you're right about that wild idea you've got in your head—and I ain't sayin' you are, mind you—then the story you're lookin' for begins on a cold night in West Texas in 1914 . . ."

CHAPTER 1

When I saw the blue norther coming I would have found a place to hole up and wait it out, except there didn't seem to be any such a thing in these parts. It was a damn fool stunt to begin with, starting from San Antonio to El Paso on horseback in December. But I had never spent that much time in Texas, and I wanted to take a gander at some of the country. You hear Texans bragging about the place all the time, as they're in the habit of doing, and after a while you want to see it for yourself.

So I bought a couple of good horses and some supplies, figuring I'd use one of the animals as a packhorse and the other as a saddle mount and switch back and forth between 'em, and set off across country. I figured I'd probably run into some fences along the way, at least until I got farther west, but . . . well . . . fences have never bothered me all that much, if you know what I mean.

I could've bought a car and driven to El Paso, I suppose—you could do that, even that far back—but while I could handle one of the contraptions if I had to, I'd never been comfortable doing so. The worry that the damned thing might blow up on me always lurked in the back of my mind.

So it was horseback for me, and that's how I came to be out in the middle of nowhere when the sky turned so blue it was almost black and the wind began to howl out of the north, bringing with it a bone-numbing chill. I lowered my head, hunkered deeper in my sheepskin coat, and kept going. Wasn't nothing behind me, so I knew it wouldn't do any good to turn around.

At least it wasn't raining or snowing, even though a thick overcast hung above me. I knew there had to be a ranch house somewhere ahead of me, and if I kept moving I'd find it. I knew that because if there wasn't, I stood a good chance of freezing to death before morning.

The light was starting to fade when I heard popping sounds. With the wind blowing so hard and making such a racket it was hard to be sure, but I thought they might be gunshots. It was hard to tell exactly where they came from, too, but I turned my horses in what I hoped was the right direction.

Now, you may think it was foolish of me, riding toward gunfire rather than away from it, but I looked at it like this: whoever was shooting that gun probably had a place to get in out of the weather, and that was what I needed more than anything else tonight.

The last of the gray light disappeared, and I was left to plod along in darkness. There had been only a handful of shots, and the shortness of the volley could mean almost anything, so I didn't see any real point in speculating about it. Keep going and I might find out, that's the way I looked at it.

My horse stopped short and shied back a step. I said, "Easy there, fella." I couldn't see what had spooked him.

I wasn't carrying a handgun, but I had a Winchester in a scabbard strapped to the saddle. I drew it out and worked the lever to throw a cartridge into the chamber. Then I swung a leg over the saddle and slid to the ground. The packhorse's reins were tied to the saddle horn. I hung on to the reins of the animal I'd been riding as I moved forward cautiously.

It only took a couple of steps to tell me why my horse had stopped. The ground fell away into a gully. I could barely make it out as it twisted across the plains like a snake.

If the gully wasn't too deep and the sides weren't too steep, the horses and I could climb down into it and get out of the wind, at least. I might find enough wood to build a small fire. It was a slender hope but better than nothing. Ever since night fell I'd been looking all around, searching for a yellow pinpoint of light that marked the window of a ranch house but I hadn't seen anything except endless darkness.

I put the rifle back in its sheath and hunkered on my heels at the edge of the gully. I reached into my coat and fished a match from my shirt pocket. It lit when I snapped the head with my thumbnail, but the wind snatched the flame right out. Trying to get one burning up here was just going to be a waste of matches. I slid a foot over the edge and used it to explore the slope. It wasn't a sheer drop-off, so I had hopes of being able to get the horses down there.

The prairie was dotted with mesquite trees, their limbs skeleton-bare at this time of year. I tied the saddle horse's reins to one of them and went back to the edge of the gully. I was going to have to explore it by feel until I got down out of the wind.

I turned around so I was facing the slope and started climbing down. The gully wall was rough enough that there were plenty of places to brace myself. When I got down low enough that my head was out of the wind, the night was still plenty cold but not as breathtakingly raw.

My right foot came down on something soft that let out a loud groan.

I like to think my nerves are pretty steady, but I'd be lying if I said I didn't let out a holler and jump up in the air. When I came down I lost my balance and started rolling.

I was lucky that gully wasn't very deep. I only turned over a couple of times before I hit bottom. Even so, I landed hard enough to knock the wind out of me and send my hat flying.

"What the blue blazes!" I yelled when I got my breath back. I probably said a few things that were worse than that, too, but I disremember.

Whoever or whatever I'd stepped on groaned again.

That pained sound, mixed in with the howl of the wind, gave me the fantods. I sat up and scuttled backward a little, well aware that I'd left my Winchester up on the flat with the horses and cussing myself for doing such a foolish thing. I hadn't expected to find anything in this gully, but I'd been around long enough to know that whatever you expect in life usually ain't what happens.

I didn't know if my companion could answer me or not, but I said, "Who's there?"

The answer came back in a weak voice.

"You have any . . . whiskey . . . amigo?"

Despite calling me amigo, he didn't sound like a Mexican, but I'd already discovered that in that part of Texas, most people, white and brown alike, spoke a mixture of the two lingos. And as a matter of fact, I did have a flask in my saddlebags. But before I fetched it, I wanted to find out more about what was going on here.

"Are you hurt, old son?" I asked.

The man tried to laugh, but it came out more like a pained grunt.

"You could . . . say that. Got a couple of . . . bullet holes . . . in my guts."

Well, that was bad, and a damned shame to boot. One bullet hole in the belly was enough to kill a man. Two and he was a goner for sure. But I said, "Hold on, I'll see what I can do." I started to crawl toward the sound of his voice, then paused and asked, "You ain't fixin' to shoot me, are you?"

"No reason to," he said. "You ain't . . . one of the varmints who shot me. They've long since . . . took off for the tall . . . and uncut."

I found another match and lit it. This time I was able to keep it going by cupping my hand around the flame, although the wind caused it to dance around quite a bit. The feeble, flickering glow from it revealed a stocky man with a close-cropped white beard lying against the bank like he'd slid part of the way down it. His coat must have hung on something and stopped him. He had both arms crossed over his belly.

A glance over my shoulder told me that the gully was about a dozen feet wide, with a sandy, fairly level bottom. Clumps of brush grew here and there.

"Let me help you lay down, old-timer," I said, "and I'll take a look at those wounds."

"I told you . . . I want whiskey. Ain't nothin' you can do . . . about the other."

I figured he'd be more comfortable stretched out, though, so when the match burned down I shook it out and got hold of him, lifting him as gently as I could and easing him down so that his legs were in front of him on the gully floor and his back was leaned against the bank. He muttered some things I didn't understand, most likely complaints because I hadn't fetched that flask yet.

It took me only a few minutes to find my hat, gather some dry branches from the brush, place them in a heap, and get a fire burning. Once the flames were going, they gave off enough light I could see a broken-down place in the bank where I thought I could get the horses down.

"I'll be back," I told the gut-shot old man.

"I ain't . . . goin' nowheres."

I brought the horses down one at a time and tied them to a sturdy-looking bush. They were close enough to the fire to draw a little warmth from it. Then I got the flask from my saddlebags and knelt next to the wounded man.

I uncapped the flask and held it to his mouth.

"Here you go."

He sucked at it greedily as I tipped it up. I didn't give him too much. The stuff was going to burn like fire when it hit the holes in his guts. He might pass out from it, and I wanted to know what happened to him.

Whoever shot him might still be roaming around, I thought, and I was curious just how trigger-happy they might be.

I set the flask aside and asked, "Who shot you, mister?"

"Abner . . . ," he struggled to say.

"Somebody named Abner ventilated you?"

"No . . . damn it! That's . . . my name . . . Abner . . . Tillotson. Don't want to . . . cash out . . . without somebody knowin' who I am."

"All right, Mr. Tillotson. What happened?"

"Thought you was gonna . . . try to patch me up."

"I decided there wouldn't be a whole lot of point to it," I told him honestly. His coat was open enough for me to see how black with blood his shirt was underneath it.

He chuckled and said, "You're right . . . about that. I'll tell you . . . what happened . . . I was shot by three . . . no-account rustlers . . . that's what."

"You've got a spread hereabouts?"

"We're on it . . . the Fishhook."

"You have family there?"

"Naw . . . no family anywhere . . . just me. Three or four Mex hands . . . work for me part-time. None of 'em there now. I knew there was a norther comin' . . . so I rode out to . . . check on my critters. That's when I come across . . . them rustlers . . ."

"Who'd be out wide-looping cattle in weather like this?"

"Those no-good Daughtry boys . . . Stealin' comes as natural . . . as breathin' to them. They don't care . . . what the weather's like. They were pushin' . . . a dozen of my cows . . . toward their place. I yelled for 'em to stop . . . and they turned around and started . . . burnin' powder at me." Abner paused. "I could do with . . . another drink."

I gave him one. He winced, but he got it down.

"Where's your ranch house? I'll get you back there."

"Two miles . . . due west of here. It backs up . . . against a butte. You'll find it." He raised a blood-smeared hand and waved vaguely in the direction he'd mentioned. "But you'll have to . . . come back and get me later . . . if the coyotes ain't dragged me off. You got . . . somethin' else to do tonight?"

"I wasn't planning on doin' anything except trying to keep from freezin' to death," I said.

"No . . . you're gonna go after . . . them Daughtrys . . . and settle accounts for me."

"Why the hell would I want to do that?"

The words came out of my mouth a mite harsher than I'd intended, but he had startled me with that flat pronouncement.

"Because I'm gonna . . . give you my ranch in return for . . . avengin' me."

I started to say something else, but he held up that bloody hand again to stop me.

"I've seen . . . a thousand drifters like you . . . in my time, son."

I doubted very seriously that he'd ever seen anybody exactly like me, but I wasn't going to argue with a dying man.

"I know what . . . you need," he went on. "You need a home. You ain't . . . as young as you used to be."

Well, he was right about that, I thought. I was pushing middle age, pushing it pretty hard, when you come right down to it.

"You're bound to be . . . gettin' a mite tired. You need a good place . . . to settle down . . . and the Fishhook's a fine spread. I'll sign it over to you . . . right here and now . . . if you give me your word you'll settle those rustlers' hash."

"You said there were three of 'em. Three against one ain't very good odds."

"Yeah, but I can tell by lookin' at you . . . You still got the bark on you, boy. I'm bettin' my ranch . . . you can do it." He laughed again. "Of course . . . I'm losin' one way or the other . . . ain't I?"

To this day, I don't know what made me do it. Maybe I just wanted to ease his way from this world into the next. But I said, "All right, Mr. Tillotson, I'll do it. I'll go after those rustlers. Can't promise you I'll kill all of them, but I'll do my damnedest."

"That's all . . . anybody can ask of a man. You got paper and . . . a pencil?"

"Yeah."

"Get it. Write out a bill of sale . . . I'll sign it. But gimme . . . another drink first."

I did that, then took out a book I'd bought in San Antonio. I'd picked it up because it was a story about a cowboy named Cassidy who had a bum leg, and that struck me as funny. The book had a blank page or two in the back, so I tore one of them out, flattened it on the cover, and after pausing to build up the fire a little and make it brighter, I used a stub of a pencil to scrawl a bill of sale transferring ownership of the Fishhook Ranch from Abner Tillotson to . . .

Until that moment I hadn't thought about what name I was

going to put down. I had gone by several different names in my life. Sometimes it came in handy for a man in my line of work to be somebody else. I'd used the name Jim before, and to be honest I just plucked Strickland out of thin air. I didn't recall ever knowing anybody by that name.

So I wrote down "Jim Strickland," and then I read what I'd written to Abner. He managed a weak nod and said, "That'll be fine. You're a good man . . . Jim."

I don't know if he just ran out of breath before he said the name, or if he was telling me in his own way that he knew it wasn't real and didn't care.

He held out his hand and said, "Gimme the pencil. Afraid I'm gonna get blood on it."

"Don't worry about that," I told him.

He took the pencil. I held the book where he could sign his name on the page. His hand was shaking some, but I could read his signature. I didn't think anybody would dispute the bill of sale, since he didn't have any family, and anyway I wasn't sure I would ever use it. While the idea of settling down held some appeal, I didn't know if I could do it. I'd been on the drift for a long time.

When he was finished his hand fell back in his lap. He said, "You better . . . get after 'em now. They got a shack . . . couple miles north of here. Ain't much more than a lean-to . . . built against a little rise. Don't trust 'em . . . they're tricky bastards. I never should've . . . give' 'em any warnin' . . . Should've just started shootin' first myself. You might want to . . . bear that in mind."

"I sure will, Abner," I told him. "You better get some rest now, hear?"

"You think you could . . . see your way clear to leavin' that flask with me . . . while you go after those skunks?"

"Sure, I can do that." I pressed the silver flask into the hand that had held the pencil. He had dropped it on the ground beside him.

"Much . . . obliged."

He seemed to be having trouble keeping his eyes open now.

His head rested against the dirt wall behind him. His chest still rose and fell, but slow, slow.

I knew if I piddled around a little before riding out after the Daughtrys, Abner would be dead and I could forget the whole thing and go find the ranch house. His horse was long gone, doubtless having run off after the shooting, but I could pack his body in on my extra animal. I could even toss that bill of sale into the fire and watch it burn. A part of me wanted to. If I'd wanted to live the life of a rancher, I could've stayed in Utah when I was a kid.

Anyway, I couldn't rightfully condemn the Daughtry boys for rustling. My own past was not without blemish in that respect, and I never cared for the idea of being a hypocrite.

But shooting an old man in cold blood . . . well, I had to admit that rubbed me the wrong way. I didn't really know a blasted thing about Abner Tillotson, but I like to think I'm a pretty good judge of character, and my instincts told me he didn't deserve to go out like this.

I folded the page with Abner's signature on it and stuck it in my hip pocket. Then I went over to my horse and put the book back in the saddlebags. I looked at Abner but couldn't tell if he was breathing or not.

"I'll be back, Abner," I told him anyway.

Then without thinking too much about what I was doing, I untied the reins, swung up into the saddle, and rode off into a dark, bone-chilling night in search of a trio of murdering rustlers.

CHAPTER 2

If you were to ask me about the coldest I've ever been, you probably wouldn't think that it would be when I was in Texas, what with me spending so much time in Utah, Wyoming, Idaho, and places like that. But all these years later, even on the hottest day of the summer, a shiver still goes through me when I think about that night ride across the Texas plains.

I left the packhorse in the gully with Abner. I left the fire burning, too, which went against the grain because of the danger of prairie fires. My hope, though, was that it would keep the scavengers away from him for a while. Maybe I would get back before the fire burned down completely.

He had said the Daughtry place was a couple miles north of the gully. It was too dark to be sure how much ground I was covering, but I was counting on spotting a lighted window to steer by. Until then I had to rely on instinct to keep me going in the right direction.

After a while, just when I started to worry that I was lost and wouldn't even be able to find my way back to the gully, a faint yellow glow appeared in the distance ahead of me. It was tiny at first but got bigger as I rode toward it. Eventually I was able to tell by its roughly rectangular shape that it was the window I'd been looking for.

From what Abner had told me, I felt confident that I was approaching the Daughtry place. He hadn't mentioned anybody else living around these parts.

With the wind blowing out of the north the way it was, I didn't think they would hear my horse's hoofbeats. Just to be sure, though, I reined in when we were about fifty yards away. I didn't see anything close by where I could tie the horse, so I let the reins dangle and left him ground-hitched. I pulled the Winchester from the scabbard and started toward the light on foot.

When I got closer I could make out more of the details, even on that dark night. The shack looked like a jumble of boards piled against the face of a little bluff. It had a tin and tar-paper roof with the iron stovepipe sticking up through it. With the bluff to block the wind and a fire going in the stove, it might be halfway comfortable in there, I thought.

Off to the right was a shed that actually looked more sturdily built than the shack. I saw several bulky shapes huddled together in there. I guess the Daughtrys knew how important it was for a man to take care of his horse. Beyond the shed was a corral. The stolen cattle stood stolidly inside it with their back ends turned toward the wind.

It would have been easy enough to kick the door down and go in shooting. They wouldn't know I was anywhere around until it was too late for at least one of them, and probably two. Maybe, if I was really lucky, all three of them. I mulled it over for a minute or so and came mighty close to doing it that way.

But something stopped me. As I mentioned, I've had what you might call a checkered past, but for most of that time, even in my wildest years, I had managed not to kill anybody. There had come a point where that changed—sometimes there's just no other way out, and to be honest, there are some evil bastards in the world who just need killin'—but I still didn't want to ventilate anybody who didn't have it coming.

As I stared at that lighted window, I realized that I didn't know for an absolute certainty it was the Daughtrys in there. Even if it was, I didn't know who else might be in the shack with them. Wives, kids, maybe even an old dog or two. I didn't want any of them getting in the way of a stray bullet.

What I needed to do was draw them out some way, and I thought I saw a way to do it.

That stovepipe poked up through the tar paper fairly close to the bluff. I circled around and climbed the bluff well away from the shack. Even though I was only about eight feet higher than I had been, the wind felt even harder and colder up there. I tried to ignore it as I cat-footed toward the shack.

When I was behind that haphazard assemblage of lumber, I took off my coat. Under it I wore a thick flannel shirt and a pair of long underwear, but the wind cut through both garments like they weren't there. Shivering and trembling, I hung the jacket on the end of my rifle barrel and extended it toward the stovepipe. It almost reached. I gave the Winchester a flick of my wrist. The jacket jumped in the air and settled over the top of the pipe.

It wasn't blocked off as well as if I'd been able to get out on the roof and stuff something down the pipe. From the looks of that roof, though, if a pigeon landed on there it might fall through. Doing it this way, some of the smoke was going to escape, but I thought enough of it would back up into the shack to do the job.

I crouched there on the bluff waiting for something to happen. I didn't have to wait long. Somebody started yelling and cussing inside the shack. The door slammed open and three men stumbled out, coughing.

The Winchester held fifteen rounds, so I figured I could spare one. I put it into the ground near their feet, making them jump. They had made the mistake of all standing close together instead of spreading out, which told me they were pure amateurs when it came to being ambushed. I didn't want to give them a chance to realize that mistake, so I yelled, "Stand right where you are! I'll kill the first man who moves!"

Well, they moved, of course. They twisted around toward the sound of my voice. One of them even started to reach under his coat. He stopped when I worked the Winchester's lever and he heard that sinister, metallic *clack-clack*.

It was a dramatic touch and I shouldn't have done it. I should have already had a fresh round chambered. I have a liking for those little flourishes, though, and even though I've been told that they'll get me killed someday, a man's got to entertain himself from time to time.

Still coughing from the smoke that followed them out the door, one of the men shouted, "Who in blazes . . . are you?"

"Never mind about who I am," I yelled back at him. "Is your name Daughtry?"

"What the hell business is that of yours?"

I pointed the rifle at him and said, "Just answer the question." I tried to make my voice as cold and deadly as the wind.

"I'm Ned Daughtry," the man admitted. "These are my brothers Clete and Otto. You satisfied now, you son of a bitch?"

"Anybody else inside?"

A wracking cough bent the man forward. When it was over he said, "No, just the three of us."

"In that case," I told him, "Abner Tillotson says you should all go to hell."

That threw them. One of the others said, "Who's Tillotson to you?"

"A friend," I said. What else could you call somebody who was giving you a ranch?

That decided it. They knew they'd gunned Abner, and they knew I'd come gunning for them in return. Wasn't nothin' left but to get to it.

So that's what I did.

I already had the Winchester pointed at one of them, so I went ahead and shot him as soon as they started to reach. The slug bored through him at a downward angle, bent him back, and dropped him to his knees. I worked the lever as I swung the rifle and fired two more rounds as fast as I could crank them off. Muzzle flashes lit up the night, but despite them I still couldn't see much. They returned fire. I went to one knee as a bullet whistled over my head.

For a couple of heartbeats the night was filled with fire and lead from both sides of the fight. A second Daughtry brother stumbled and fell. I tried to locate the third one so I could shoot at him some more, but he was gone.

I couldn't see him, but he might be able to see me. I flattened out on top of the bluff.

A part of my mind kept up with the shots even though I wasn't really thinking about it. So I knew I'd fired nine times and had six rounds left. That ought to be plenty, I thought, but first I had to have something to shoot at.

I couldn't see anything, couldn't hear anything except the wind. But I knew somewhere out there was a fella who wanted to kill me, and I didn't like the feeling. Not one bit.

He was a slick bastard. Got around behind me somehow. If he hadn't stumbled a little in the dark and made a tiny noise, he might've plugged me. As it was, I rolled over just in time to feel his shot whip past my ear and hit the ground instead of blowing off the back of my head.

A Winchester's not real good for close work. I got a shot off, but it must've gone wild because he was on me, kicking me in the side and screaming curses at me. I dropped the rifle, grabbed his leg, and heaved on it. He fell and landed on top of me, and we both went off the edge of the bluff and dropped two feet to crash onto the shack's roof.

It was just as flimsy as it looked. We broke through it and fell another few feet, landing on a table this time. He was still on top of me, and the impact was enough to knock the breath out of me for the second time tonight. I was half-stunned and my muscles didn't want to work, but I forced them to anyway. I shoved him off the table onto the floor.

The smoke had cleared out some with the door open, but there was still enough of it in the air to sting my mouth and nose and eyes as I rolled off the table the other way. I put one hand on the table to steady myself as I looked around for a weapon of some sort. My rifle was still up on the bluff, and I didn't know if the last Daughtry had managed to hang on to his pistol when we fell through the roof.

He had. The damned thing blasted again as he rose up on the other side of the table. But he hurried his shot and it went into the wall behind me. I didn't give him a chance to get off another one. I grabbed the handiest thing I could and flung it at him.

That was a kerosene lantern sitting on a shelf against the wall. It hit him and broke, and fire leaped up on his chest and set his beard on fire. He got so worked up about that, yelling and jumping around, that he forgot about trying to shoot me again. I leaped onto the table and pushed off of it into a diving tackle that took him off his feet. The back of his head hit the hard-packed dirt floor with a sound sort of like what you hear when you drop a watermelon. He didn't move after that, just lay there with the fire consuming his buffalo hide coat, his beard, and his face.

I knew that was really going to stink, so I picked up the revolver he'd dropped, tucked it behind my belt, and grabbed his ankles so I could drag him outside.

I hadn't forgotten about the other two brothers, so as soon as I had the burning one out of the shack, I dropped his legs and drew the gun, even though I didn't know whether it still had any bullets in it. Turned out it didn't matter, because neither of the other Daughtrys were moving and never would again unless somebody picked them up and carried them. I didn't intend to waste that much effort.

From the corner of my eye I saw some other flames and looked up to see that the heat from the stovepipe had finally set my coat on fire. I let out a heartfelt, "Son of a *bitch!*" That coat was a good one, and without something to break the wind I might still freeze before morning.

Stay here tonight, I told myself. The shack was pretty drafty, but there was a fire in the stove. I could make my way back to the gully in the morning.

But by then coyotes and maybe even wolves would've been at Abner's body for sure, and they might have gone after my pack-horse and supplies, too. Sighing, I looked around the inside of the shack for something I could wear.

I found another buffalo-hide coat. It stunk to high heaven when I shrugged into it, but it was better than nothing. I found a box of cartridges, too, and reloaded the Colt I had picked up.

I stood by the stove for a few minutes to warm up as much as I could before venturing out into the night again. When I knew I couldn't postpone it any longer, I climbed up onto the ridge, got my rifle, and then went in search of my horse.

He had wandered off but hadn't gone far with his reins dangling like that. The whole affair had spooked him some. I hadn't had him long enough for him to be used to such violent ruckuses. Hell, *I* wasn't used to such ruckuses, and I'd been in the middle of plenty of them over the years. I had to whistle a little tune and talk soft to him for a few minutes before he settled down enough for me to catch him.

Maybe he just didn't want somebody wearing a coat that stunk that bad on his back.

Soon I was riding south again, hoping I could find the gully where I'd left Abner Tillotson and my other horse.

CHAPTER 3

At least the wind was at my back during that ride, instead of try-ing to scrape the flesh off my face with knives of ice, like it felt when I was going north. I had to use my bandanna to tie my hat on and keep it from blowing off.

The fire was still burning by the time I reached the gully. Abner's body was undisturbed. Cold as it could be, too. He'd ei-ther been dead when I rode away earlier or had crossed the di-vide soon after. The packhorse was still there, too, and if a horse's neigh can be said to sound disgusted, the one he let out when he saw me sure did. It was like he was asking me what the hell I was thinking, going off and leaving him alone in a gully with a corpse.

"At least I came back for you, old son, instead of gettin' myself killed, too," I told him as I took one of my extra blankets from the pack. I spread it out on the ground, laid Abner's body on it, and rolled him up in it.

He was heavier than he looked, and I could've used some help getting him onto the horse. Everybody I'd ever relied on to give me a hand was either dead or in prison, though, or else dropped off the face of the earth so I didn't know what had hap-pened to them. I was on my own and had been for several years. I didn't like it much—I'm a friendly cuss by nature and enjoy having people around to compliment me on how clever I am—but that was the hand life had dealt me.

I finally got Abner loaded. I led both horses out of the gully. The wind had actually died down a mite, the norther having expended some of its force. I saw a few stars overhead through gaps in the clouds, and they helped me steer a westward course.

By morning the wind would die down all the way, I knew, and the clouds would break up and clear off, and the temperature would drop like it had fallen in a well. I could have tried to ride it out in the gully, but it would be better if I could find the ranch house.

The starlight helped, and so did the good sense of direction I'd been born with. Some hills rose to the north and south, and smack dab in the middle of the valley between them I found Abner's ranch house. It was an adobe in the Mexican hacienda style, with a good-size barn, a couple of corrals, a cook shack, a small bunkhouse, a blacksmith shop, and a smokehouse. Of course, I didn't know all that at the time. I could see some buildings scattered around, but I didn't explore them. I just put the horses in the barn, unloaded Abner's body, and carried it into the house. It was dark as sin inside, so I laid him on the floor until I had fumbled around, found a lamp, and got it lit. Then as the yellow glow filled the room I picked him up again and placed his blanket-wrapped corpse on the bed in the back corner.

There was a fireplace on the other side of the room with a supply of wood piled up beside it. I got a good blaze going so the place could warm up while I was tending the horses.

It was still chilly but reasonably comfortable in there when I came back in from the barn. I stopped outside long enough to hang that buffalo-hide coat on one of the vigas sticking out below the roof. I didn't want that stinking thing in the same room with me all night.

The adobe had one main room with the fireplace and a table and chairs on one side, an old sofa and a couple of rocking chairs on the other side, and the bed in the back. A bookcase full of books stood against the wall between the rocking chairs. It appeared that Abner was an avid reader, like a lot of men who live alone. The lamp was on a small table beside one of the chairs. It had a green glass base and a ceramic top with roses painted on it, not exactly the sort of thing you'd expect to find in an isolated ranch house where a rough old cattleman lived alone. I suspected there had been a woman in Abner Tillotson's life at one time or another, and this lamp was a memento of their time together. That was a story I'd likely never know.

I had brought in my supplies, so when the flames in the fireplace died down a little I boiled some coffee, fried some bacon, and ate it with a couple of leftover biscuits I'd had wrapped up in my saddlebags. It was meager enough fare but satisfied my hunger. I didn't mind preparing a meal with a corpse on the other side of the room, and I wasn't going to be bothered by sleeping in the same room with him once I stretched out on that sofa. I had occupied closer quarters with dead men before.

After I'd eaten, the weariness hit me. I didn't try to fight it off. During the night I got up a time or two and put more wood on the fire, but I just wanted to keep the chill off. I didn't want to warm things up too much with Abner in the room, but I wasn't going to leave him outside where varmints might get at him, either.

I was up early the next morning, and it was as cold as I'd figured it would be. I'd never felt a witch's teat or a grave-digger's ass, but I didn't see how they could be any colder than that December morning on the Texas plains. My breath fogged up like a thunderhead in front of my face when I went outside. But the wind was still so it didn't feel too bad.

It hadn't been cold enough, long enough, to freeze the ground. Once I'd looked around and found a suitable spot for a grave, I didn't have much trouble digging it. My side was a little stiff and sore where that Daughtry brother had kicked me, but some shovel work loosened it right up.

The place I picked was on a little rise off to the south that overlooked both the ranch headquarters and the little creek that ran nearby. The view wasn't all that much just then, but I figured it would be pretty nice come summer.

There was a buckboard in the barn, along with a couple of mules and two horses besides my pair. I hitched the mules to the buckboard, loaded Abner on it, and drove out to the hill where I'd dug the grave. When I got there, I found a strange horse waiting. The saddle he wore told me he was likely Abner's mount, come home after spending a cold night wandering around. I said, "You're lucky you didn't freeze to death, hoss."

He tossed his head in agreement, then stood there watching solemnly while I lowered Abner into the grave and shoveled dirt back into the hole.

When I finished I took off my hat and said, "Lord, it's been a while since we talked, but I'm hopin' you recollect who I am. This man was named Abner Tillotson. You're probably better acquainted with him than I was. I didn't really know him, but he struck me as a good sort. He didn't cut down on those rustlers when he could have and probably should have. So maybe you'll have the same sort of mercy on him and welcome him home up yonder. That'll do it, I guess. Amen."

When it warmed up some, I'd make a marker and put it out here on the grave. For now that was all I could do. I led the horse back to the barn, and after I'd unhitched the mules I unsaddled him, broke up the ice on the water bucket in the stall where I put him, and dumped some grain in the trough.

I went back in the house and started fixing some breakfast. Funny thing, the night before I'd felt like this was still Abner's place and I was just a guest. That feeling had stayed with me while I was burying him. But now when I looked around the room it was different.

It surprised the hell out of me, but I realized that I was home.

CHAPTER 4

Later that day I put my saddle on the horse I'd been using as a pack animal and rode back to the Daughtry place. I didn't have any trouble finding it. It didn't look any better in broad daylight. The three bodies lying scattered around in front of the shack didn't help its appearance any, especially since the buzzards and coyotes had already been at them. In fact, a couple of the black-winged scoundrels abandoned their feast and flapped off lazily as I rode up. They squawked in annoyance at me. I ignored them and rode on to the corral.

Abner had said the brothers were hazing off a dozen of his cows when he came upon them. I counted the critters in the corral and came up with eighteen. I couldn't be sure where the other six came from without examining the brands, but I figured there was a good chance they were Fishhook stock, too, so I opened the corral gate and drove out the whole bunch. They were mine now.

That left the three horses in the shed. There was no telling when somebody else would come along. Might be days or weeks or even months. I opened the gate on the front of the shed and let them out, too. I didn't want to be caught with horses that had belonged to three dead men, so I took off my hat, waved it in the air, and yelled at them until they ran off. It was a hard thing, turning them loose to fend for themselves that way. But life has a habit of giving us hard choices sometimes.

I drove the cows back to the Fishhook. This couldn't be all of Abner's herd—my herd, now—but I didn't know yet where he had grazed the others, so I let them stop along the creek. There wasn't much grass there, but enough to keep them from straying, I hoped.

With that chore taken care of, I spent the rest of the day exploring the ranch, including all the buildings around the main house. I didn't know the boundaries of Fishhook range, but I rode a good distance north, south, east, and west, making a big circle around the place. I had the Winchester with me, plus the Colt revolver I had taken from the Daughtry brother who'd kicked me in the side.

I found another couple hundred head of stock scattered along the base of the hills to the south. They were branded with a crooked mark I took to represent a fish hook, plus the letters *AT*. I might change the brand later on, I thought, to something that fit better with the name I had chosen, Jim Strickland. Or I might not. It all depended on how ambitious I was feeling. After I'd been here a few months I might decide to sell the place and move on. But I wanted to give it a fair chance, although I had already honored the deal I'd struck with Abner. All three of the men responsible for his death were dead.

I also found a small herd grazing in a pasture to the east, not far from the gully where I had run into Abner. The rustled stock had to have come from that bunch. When I got back to the house I took the cows in the corral and drove them out to join the others. I checked the brands first, though.

Sure enough, the extra six animals had Fishhook brands on them, although the Daughtrys had tried to rework them into something else. It was such a clumsy effort I couldn't even tell what the new marks were supposed to be. Those boys had picked the wrong line of lawbreaking to get into. It's a pretty sorry owlhoot who can't even rustle cattle and use a running iron properly.

That was a full day's work. After supper that evening I pulled out an old trunk I found in one of the small back rooms while I was looking for clean bedding and went through its contents.

The first thing I found was a sober black suit that looked like it hadn't been worn for years. It was dusty and smelled of mothballs. Too small for me even if I'd wanted to wear it, which I didn't, so I set it aside. I found some dish towels with fancy stitching on them, another indication that there had been a woman in Abner's life at one time.

Wrapped up in one of the towels was a photograph in an oval gilt frame. It was the sort of picture you saw a lot back in those days, with a man sitting in a chair while a woman stood just behind and to the side of him with her right hand resting on his left shoulder. The man was a lot younger and his hair and beard were dark, but I could tell he was Abner. The woman had fair hair that fluffed prettily around her head. She wasn't a great beauty, but she was pleasant enough looking. Both of them were dressed in their best duds and had pinched expressions on their faces like they needed to go to the outhouse. I don't know why photographers always insisted on folks looking like that when they had a portrait made. I had my picture taken once with some pards of mine in Fort Worth, and the whole thing tickled me so much I couldn't help but smile a little when the flash powder went off.

I turned the photograph over, but nothing was written on the back. I wrapped it up in the dish towel again and set it with the suit, which I had a hunch might be the same one Abner was wearing in the picture.

Some more digging around in the trunk turned up a big, thick, heavy book. It was a family Bible, and knowing that people often kept important documents in such a book, I sat down cross-legged on the floor, put it in my lap, and carefully opened it.

Sure enough, several folded documents were right in the front of the Bible. One of them was the deed to this property. That was what I'd been hoping to find, because it gave the boundaries of the land. The Fishhook wasn't big at all as ranches go in Texas, only about fifty square miles, but it had been big enough to suit Abner.

I found a marriage license in the Bible, too, telling me that

Abner James Tillotson had married Martha Grace Hargity in San Marcos, Texas, on October 12, 1882. That put a name on the woman standing beside Abner in the photograph, I thought, although I supposed she could have been somebody else.

There was some paperwork registering the Fishhook brand with the state, some county tax records, and a few receipts that didn't mean anything to me. I'd found what I was looking for, but instead of putting the Bible away I turned a few more pages and came to the family record. A woman's hand had recorded the dates that Abner and Martha were born and the date of their marriage. On the page after that, in the *Births* section, in a man's much cruder script, was written *John Abbott Tillotson, b. September 17, 1883.*

The reason for the change in who had entered that information was in the *Deaths* section on the next page, where the same hand had printed with obvious effort: *Martha Grace Tillotson, d. September 18, 1883,* and *John Abbott Tillotson, d. September 18, 1883.*

"Well, hell, Abner," I said quietly. "I'm sorry, old son." I figured he had lived here by himself ever since.

I found one other thing of interest in the trunk, a coiled cartridge belt with an attached holster that held a long-barreled Remington revolver. It was a fine-looking gun and obviously well cared for. Abner must have taken it out and cleaned it pretty regular-like. I stood up and tried on the belt. It fit well enough, although Abner had been thicker through the middle than me and must have fastened the buckle in a different hole. The gun wasn't loaded, but there were a couple of boxes of cartridges in the trunk. They might be too old to fire properly, I thought, but I left them out when I replaced everything else from the trunk and put it away. The Remington's weight felt pretty good on my hip.

So I had a place to live, five horses, two mules, a couple of hundred head of stock, a rifle, and two pistols. I've held small fortunes in my hands on a number of occasions, but right then, as I walked outside and looked around my ranch, I felt pretty rich.

CHAPTER 5

It had been a while since I worked a spread like this, but I remembered what needed to be done. Abner had done a good job of keeping the place up, and that sure helped. By the time spring was about to roll around, I had fixed everything that needed fixing. It had been a pretty mild winter. That first morning, back before Christmastime, was probably the coldest it got. The cattle came through it pretty well and were in good shape.

The nearest town, about fifteen miles southeast, was a wide place in the road called Largo. Not much there, but it had a store, and I had hitched the mules to the buckboard and driven in a few times for supplies. The first time I did, the storekeeper, a man named Clyde Farnum, had looked out the front window for a long moment and then said, "Ain't that Abner Tillotson's buckboard?"

"It was," I said. "I bought it from him, along with everything else on the place."

"Did you now?" Farnum said. He was a small man with perpetual beard stubble and a wary merchant's look in his eyes.

"Yes, sir, lock, stock, and barrel." I put out my hand across the counter between us. "Jim Strickland's the name."

He hesitated, but not long enough to be insulting about it. Then he shook and told me his name.

"Hard to believe ol' Abner would sell out," he said. "He's lived on that spread for as far back as I can remember."

"He said his health was goin' south on him." I put a solemn look on my face. "To tell you the truth, Mr. Farnum, I don't think he had a lot of time left to him, and he knew it. I figure he wanted to be sure that his place was left in good hands, him having put so much work into it and all."

"How'd he come to sell it to you? I don't like bein' nosy, mind you, but I considered Abner a friend."

"So did a lot of people, I reckon. That's how he and I met, through some mutual friends back in San Marcos."

That was a shot in the dark, but I thought since Abner had gotten married in San Marcos, he might still know some folks there.

Farnum didn't seem to think that was unusual. He just nodded and said, "I used to see a letter for Abner come through here now and then with a San Marcos postmark on it. I'm the local postmaster, you know."

"Well, there you go," I said with an easy grin. I've found that folks tend to be a lot less suspicious of me when I grin at 'em. I guess I've just got a friendly, trustworthy face.

"Are you going to change the brand?" Farnum asked.

"No, sir, I don't believe I will. I'd be honored to run the same brand that Abner established for all these years." I thought that might help endear me to the locals, and again, make them less suspicious of me.

"That's a nice thing to do. What can I get you today?"

That was all it took. Farnum was a talkative sort and well-respected thereabouts, so after he accepted me I was a member of the community as far as other folks were concerned.

And I didn't even have to show him the bill of sale Abner had signed, although I was prepared to do so if need be.

Except when I went into town, I didn't see many people during those months. There was a road of sorts from the Fishhook to Largo, and somebody could have driven a car over it, I supposed, but nobody did. One day an itinerant preacher came by in a buggy and offered to save my soul in exchange for a meal. I gave him the meal but told him my soul was just fine.

"It's good that you're right with the Lord, son," he told me. "You just never know in this world. You just never know."

I couldn't argue with that. Life was a continual surprise. Sometimes I thought I was the never-knowingest son of a bitch on the face of the earth.

Another day I saw a rider coming over the hills to the north while he was still quite a ways off. I'm not as young as I used to be, but my eyes are still keen. I was outside working on the corral fence at the time. The Winchester leaned against the fence not far from where I was. But I put my hammer down anyway, went in the house, and buckled on that old gun belt of Abner's. I had tried some of that ammunition he had for the Remington, and it fired just fine. I went back to work but kept one eye on the rider.

He slowed his horse to a walk as he came up. As far as I could see, he wasn't armed. His horse looked plumb worn-out and so did he. Eighteen or twenty years old, I thought. The boy, not the horse, although I wouldn't have ventured a guess as to its age. He had the gauntness of long, weary trails about him.

It was a look I knew well.

He reined in and said, "Good day to you, sir," nice and polite-like.

"Hello, son," I said. "Your horse looks like he could do with some water." I nodded toward the well. "Help yourself."

"Thank you, sir. Is it all right if I have some for myself?"

"No."

He frowned in confusion, then started to look mad.

"I've got coffee in the pot in the house, and you're welcome to some," I went on. "I seen a lot colder, but it's still sort of a chilly day."

He relaxed then and said, "I'm obliged to you again. I'll tend to my horse first."

"That's what I'd expect."

Every instinct I had told me somebody was after him, probably the law. But it was none of my business and that's the way I wanted to keep it. He watered his horse, and I gave him some coffee and wrapped up some biscuits for him to take along with him when he left. I could tell by the awkward, grateful way he took the little bundle that he hadn't had anything to eat for a while but didn't want to wolf them down right in front of me.

He started to mount up, then paused and asked, "You wouldn't be looking to take on any riders, would you, sir?"

"No, son, I'm afraid I wouldn't." Whatever trouble was dogging his trail, I didn't want any part of it.

He didn't tell me his name and I didn't offer mine. He rode on, and I kept an eye on him until he was out of sight.

A week or so after that, three more riders approached the ranch, but they came from the south this time. Since they came from the opposite direction I figured they probably didn't have anything to do with the youngster. As they drew closer I saw they were Mexicans in well-worn vaquero clothes. I met them out in front of the house with the Remington on my hip and the Winchester in the crook of my left arm.

"Howdy," I called as they reined in. They were all in their twenties. One of them edged his mount slightly ahead of the others. He had a thick black mustache and the face of a hawk and looked like he should have been riding with Pancho Villa.

His voice was quiet, though, as he said, "Donde esta Señor Tillotson?"

I understood what he was asking, but I said, "Can you speak English, my friend?" I could get along in Spanish, but if he thought I spoke it fluently he might start going too fast for me to keep up.

"Sí, of course. Where is Señor Tillotson?"

"He sold the ranch to me a while back. Who are you?"

"Santiago Marquez," he answered without hesitation. He tipped his head toward the other two. "These are my cousins Javier and Fernando. We work for Señor Tillotson. Or I should say, we did. We came to see if he was ready for us to start preparing for the spring roundup."

Santiago was a well-spoken man and obviously intelligent. Apparently he accepted my story about buying the ranch from

Abner, but I had a hunch he didn't trust me completely. I wouldn't have been surprised if when he and his cousins rode out, they headed straight for Largo to ask around about me.

For that matter, I didn't trust him completely, either. All I had was his word that the three of them had worked for Abner. They might be as crooked as the Daughtrys were. If I was going to give this business of being an honest rancher a try, I wanted to go about it the right way.

So I said, "Let me study on that, Señor Marquez." What I really wanted to do was ask Clyde Farnum about him. "Can you ride back by here in, say, a week or so? I'm sorry to inconvenience you—"

He shook his head and said, "De nada. A week will be fine, Señor . . . ?"

"Strickland," I told him. "Jim Strickland."

He lifted his reins and nodded.

"We will see you in a week, señor."

Neither of the other two had said a word so far. But before Santiago could turn his horse to ride away, one of them spoke up, and sure enough, the words came out so fast I didn't know what he was saying. But Santiago pointed to the northeast and told me, "It looks like you have more company coming, señor. This is a popular place today."

Too popular, as far as I was concerned. I had come to value my privacy. I squinted into the distance and saw a buggy rolling toward the ranch houses. For a second I thought the preacher was back until I realized it was a different vehicle.

"Now who the blazes . . . ," I muttered.

"I can tell you that, Señor Strickland," Santiago said with a hint of a smile on his lips under that drooping mustache. "It appears that the sheriff is about to pay you a visit."

CHAPTER 6

I'd been living an honest, respectable life for several years now. It wasn't so much a matter of choice as it was of circumstances. And I had nothing to fear where my dealings with Abner Tillotson were concerned. Abner and I had struck an honest bargain, and we had both lived up to our ends of it . . . so to speak.

But old habits die hard, and just hearing the word "sheriff" made me look around for the nearest horse I could jump onto and light a shuck out of there. I tried to control that reaction, but I thought Santiago might've caught a hint of it. Like I said, he was smart and observant.

I kept my voice casual as I said, "The sheriff, eh? Wonder what he wants."

"I suspect we will find out, señor."

I thought maybe there was a trace of mockery in Santiago's words. He didn't act like he was leaving anymore, and the other vaqueros sat there stolidly on their horses, following their cousin's lead. They wanted to see what was going to happen. I couldn't blame them for being curious. I was wondering about that myself.

The sheriff's buggy rolled steadily closer. A fine matched pair of bay horses pulled it. Only one man rode on the seat. He wore a gray pinstriped suit, a black vest, and a white shirt buttoned up to the collar with no tie. A flat-crowned gray hat sat square on his head. Bushy side whiskers came down onto his jaw, flanking a rough-hewn face. Under a prominent nose that reminded me of a potato was a brown mustache. He wasn't what you'd call a handsome man.

He brought the buggy to a stop, gave the Mexicans a dismissive glance as if they didn't matter, and nodded to me.

"Good day, sir," he said. He pulled back his lapel a little so the sun reflected off the badge pinned to his vest. "I'm Sheriff Emil Lester."

"Pleased to make your acquaintance, Sheriff," I said with the usual friendly smile on my face. "Jim Strickland's my handle."

Sheriff Lester looked around at the house and the outbuildings.

"This is Abner Tillotson's ranch," he said.

"It was," I agreed easily enough. "I bought it from him."

"So I was told in Largo. I don't get up this way very often. Doings in the county seat, down on the railroad, usually keep me occupied."

"Sheriff, I'd be glad to tell you the whole story," I said, "but it'd please me if you'd light down and come inside so we can talk in the house."

He didn't respond to the offer. Instead he looked at the vaqueros again and said, "Marquez, did you and the Gallardo boys know Señor Tillotson had sold his ranch?"

"No, Sheriff," Santiago replied with a shake of his head. "Not until we rode up just a few minutes ago."

"Farnum and the other folks in Largo knew about it." Lester's voice had a challenging note to it, as if he didn't believe what Santiago had just told him.

Santiago shrugged and said, "We do not shop at Señor Farnum's store. When we go to Largo, we stop at the cantina, and when we leave the cantina, we go back to our rancho."

"Fine, fine." Lester tied the reins around the buggy's brake lever and started to climb down from the seat. "You boys can go on about your business now. You can come back later and talk to Señor Strickland about working for him . . . if he's still here."

That comment with its veiled threat nettled me a little, but I kept the smile on my face. Santiago lifted a hand slightly and said to me, "Adios, Señor Strickland." I got the feeling that he disliked Sheriff Lester more than he distrusted me.

"Adios, Santiago," I called to him. "You, too, Javier and Fernando."

They rode off at a good clip, dust kicking up from their horses' hooves.

Lester looked at me and said, "I suppose you can prove you bought the place from Tillotson?"

"I sure can. Come on in and I'll show you the bill of sale. Got coffee on the fire, too."

He grunted noncommittally. When he was climbing down from the buggy his coat had swung open enough for me to see the butt of a revolver in a cross-draw rig on his left side. I would have been willing to bet that I was faster than he was, but I didn't see any need to prove it unless I was forced to.

We went into the ranch house, and I hung my hat on one peg near the door and the Winchester on a couple of others close by. Since I was the only one living here I didn't use the cook shack but did all my cooking in the fireplace instead. I had the coffeepot sitting on the hearth now, staying warm. I gestured toward it and said, "Arbuckle's?"

"Thanks."

I got a couple of cups from a shelf and poured. As I handed Lester's cup to him, I said, "You know, Sheriff, you don't really sound much like a Texan."

"I'm from Iowa," he said. He didn't say what had brought him to Texas or how long he'd been here.

"I was born in Utah, myself." I never minded admitting that. A lot of people were born in Utah.

He hadn't said thanks for the coffee, and when he took a sip of it, he didn't say that it was good or anything else about it. Some folks are just brusque by nature, and a significant number of them seem to become lawmen. I think maybe that's because they just don't like to talk much, and they think they can get by with saying, "Hands up" or "You're under arrest" now and then.

He got right to the point, asking, "When did you buy this ranch from Abner Tillotson?"

"Back in December it was." When I had run into Abner and the Daughtry brothers that cold night, I hadn't been sure of the date, but I knew the month. Just as a guess I had put December 12th on the bill of sale, because I thought it was about two weeks until Christmas.

"You say you have proof of that?"

"Yes, sir, I sure do."

I went over to a little box I'd found and started using for important papers. It wouldn't do for anybody to know that I still had Abner's trunk and the old Bible in it. That would raise too many questions, because anybody would figure he'd take personal possessions like that with him if he'd sold the place. They weren't like the tools and the furniture and the livestock.

I took out the bill of sale and the deed, which Abner would have given to me if we'd concluded our transaction the normal way. I handed them to Sheriff Lester to look at to his heart's content.

He didn't seem too impressed. He said, "You should have gone to a lawyer and had a proper bill of sale drawn up and witnessed. This is worthless in a court of law."

"Well, sir, I suggested as much to Abner, but he was in a bit of a hurry. He said that would stand up just fine, because everybody around here knows his signature."

"Possibly," Lester said. "The sale should have been recorded with the county clerk, too."

"I just haven't had a chance yet to get down to the county seat and take care of that. I plan on doing it, though, as soon as I can."

"I wouldn't tarry if I was you." Lester handed the papers back to me. "Where can I find Mr. Tillotson, so I can check on all this with him?"

I shook my head and said, "I don't rightly know. He didn't say where he was going when he pulled out."

"Clyde Farnum says Tillotson was in poor health."

Actually, I had told Farnum that, but evidently the store-keeper had taken it as gospel, which was a good break for me. I said, "You know, I got the same feeling, but I didn't ask for details. I don't like to pry too much in a man's business."

Lester grunted. Prying was what he did for a living, I supposed.

"I'd feel better about this whole affair if I could talk to Tillotson," he said. "For all I know, you murdered him and just moved in on the place."

It wouldn't be natural for a man not to be a little offended at an accusation like that. So I huffed up a mite and said, "By God, Sheriff, I don't care for what you're insinuatin'."

"I'm not insinuating anything. I'm flat out saying it." He looked at me like he was daring me to prove otherwise, too.

"If you think I murdered Abner Tillotson, what you are is flat-out wrong. I wouldn't have harmed a hair on that old man's head."

"Good friends, were you?"

"No, but I liked him, and I wish we'd gotten to spend more time together. Now, I don't want to get too testy, Sheriff, but I've shown you the bill of sale and the deed. What more do you need to see?"

"What about if I take a look around the place and see if there's a grave a few months old?"

"Go ahead," I told him. "You won't find any, because there ain't none."

I was glad I'd changed my mind about putting up a marker for Abner, up yonder on the hill. I had decided it might be safer in the long run to let the grave go back to nature, and I didn't figure Abner would mind. To that end, I'd tamped the dirt down good, scattered some rocks around, and even transplanted a couple of cactuses over there, making it look like they'd been growing there all along. I didn't think the sheriff would spot anything different about the ground by now.

Some people might wonder why I didn't just tell the law everything that had happened to start with. I was in the right for once. Everything I'd done had been to bring the killers of an old man to justice and recover his stolen property.

The problem was that the bodies of the Daughtry brothers had me leery. I worried that some hotshot lawman might make me out to be a murderer. I was the only man alive who knew the truth of what had happened that night, and that right there would be enough to make a lot of badge-toters suspicious. Better to keep everything as simple as possible, I thought.

For a minute I thought the sheriff was going to take me up on my invitation to go ahead and search the place. Then he took another drink of coffee and set the cup on the table.

"All right," he said. "But I'm going to look into this, Strickland. If I come out here to talk to you again, you'd better be here."

"Sheriff, I'm not planning on going anywhere," I said honestly. I was taking to the ranching life better than I thought I might, and I figured I'd stay on until I got tired of it.

Lester gave me a curt nod and started to turn away. He stopped and said, "You know the Daughtry brothers?"

He probably hoped to throw me for a loop by asking it out of the blue that way, but I didn't let it faze me.

"Can't say as I do," I told him. "Do they live around here?"

"They did. Folks in Largo said they hadn't seen them for several months, so I drove up to their place before I came here."

I shook my head and said, "I don't even know where it is."

"About four miles northeast of here. Sorry little outfit on the edge of Fishhook range. I've had it in mind that the brothers— there were three of them—had been rustling some of Tillotson's stock."

"I haven't lost any cattle," I said, telling the truth again.

"I suppose not. The Daughtrys are gone. Looks like they abandoned the place. No horses, no cattle, and the shack was falling in. They'd left some personal things behind, but nothing to amount to anything."

It appeared that I owed a debt of gratitude to the buzzards, the coyotes, and the wolves. They had dragged off and disposed of the remains, probably scattering the bones across the prairie. A Daughtry skull might turn up sooner or later, but likely it would just remain an unsolved mystery.

I said, "No offense, Sheriff, but from the way you described them, it's good riddance to those fellas, wherever they went."

Lester nodded slowly and said, "I suspect most of the citizens in the county would agree with you, Strickland." This time he turned and went to the door, pausing only to say, "Thanks for the coffee."

That surprised me, but I had the presence of mind to say, "You're welcome. Come on back any time you're of a mind to."

He gave me a hard look.

"If I have a reason to be here, I will be."

With that he climbed up into the buggy and drove off. I wasn't sorry to see him go.

Even when I haven't done anything wrong, me and star packers just don't mix.

CHAPTER 7

Since Sheriff Lester had told me about the Daughtry place being abandoned, I didn't think it would be too suspicious for me to ride over there and take a look around. As the new owner of the Fishhook, I had a right to scout out the boundaries of my range, didn't I?

So I saddled up and headed in that direction a day or two later. I wanted to make sure there was nothing there the sheriff could trace back to me.

Of course, in the back of my mind was the thought that maybe he had baited a trap for me, and paying a visit to the place was exactly what he wanted me to do.

I had discovered that in life there's often a fine line between thinking too little and thinking too much, so I'd learned to trust my instincts. They said to head in that direction, so I did.

Sheriff Lester was right: the house looked like it had been abandoned. A gusty spring wind was blowing when I rode up. The door swung open on its leather hinges, one of which had partially rotted because of exposure to the weather, making the door hang crooked. The wind blew it back and forth, but one corner dragged in the dirt, and the motion worked that bad place in the leather even more. In another month or so it would come apart.

I thought about going inside to see if anything could be salvaged, but I didn't want to step in there. I was sure it stunk, and

I didn't want anything that had belonged to the Daughtrys. I'd never worn the buffalo coat when I went to town, and as soon as I was able to buy another sheepskin jacket at Farnum's store I burned the damned stinking thing.

I rode all around the shack, but I didn't see any bones anywhere. Satisfied, I turned and headed south toward the settlement. I needed a few things at the store.

As soon as I got there, I could tell that Farnum was excited about something and couldn't wait to tell me about it.

"Howdy, Jim," he said eagerly as he rested his hands on the counter at the rear of the store. We called each other by our first names by then. "You heard about what happened?"

"Well, I've heard about a lot of things that happened, Clyde," I told him. "Which thing in particular are you talkin' about?"

"The train holdup."

That got my attention right away. Robbing trains is a subject that holds a particular interest for me. And for once, a holdup was news to me. I said, "Tell me about it."

"It was over at Cougar Pass, early this mornin'. A gang of bandits stopped the westbound not long after dawn."

I'd heard of Cougar Pass, about seven miles east of the county seat. Since this part of the country was mostly flat, it wasn't really much of a pass, just an open spot between two little hills.

"How'd they do that?"

"Pried up a rail, then piled brush in front of the place and set it on fire. The engineer couldn't see that the rail was gone, so he tried to barrel on through the bonfire."

"Good Lord!" I said. "Did the whole train derail?" I hated to think about the devastation and likely loss of life if that was the case.

"No, just the engine and the coal car. The other cars buckled up some but didn't crash. That was a stroke of luck, they say. The whole thing could've gone over. Not so lucky for the engineer and the fireman, though. They were both killed."

I hated to hear that. Like I said before, even though I'd done some things in my earlier days I wasn't particularly proud of, I'd tried my best to see to it that nobody was killed or even seriously hurt.

"Once the train was stopped, the bandits came chargin' in and tried to bust into the express car," Farnum went on. "From what I hear, there was a big money shipment in there. Reckon the outlaws must've known about it somehow. The Wells Fargo guards were waitin' for 'em, though. There was a hell of a gun battle."

"How do you know all this?" I asked him. If the holdup happened that morning, then news of it had reached Largo mighty fast.

"Charley Davenport and his wife were down in the county seat last night. They took their old maid daughter to town to put her on an eastbound train. She's goin' to visit relatives in Dallas and find herself a husband. Then they stayed the night and came back today. Stopped by here on the way to their place and told me all about it. It was the talk of the town."

I had met Charley Davenport once, here at Farnum's. His spread was farther west. Seemed like a good sort, if a little close-mouthed. I had a hunch it was Mrs. Davenport who'd done most of the talking about the robbery.

"Anyway," Farnum went on, seeming a little put out that I'd interrupted him, "one of the guards was wounded in all the shootin', but two of the bandits were killed and the other four got away. The way I hear it, one of 'em was wounded."

"They didn't get the money?"

"Nary a penny. Those guards are heroes, if you ask me."

I hadn't asked him, and given my background, I had a hard time seeing it the same way he did. Of course, I didn't particularly admire the holdup men, either. To my way of thinking, what they'd done was crude and sloppy. They could have killed dozens of innocent people by derailing the locomotive. There are less destructive ways of stopping a train.

But a derailment was effective, I had to give them that. A train can't run if it's not on the rails. And a crash likely would have busted the express car open and might have even killed the guards, so they could have waltzed in and made off with that loot pretty easy. That's fine and dandy, if all you care about is the money.

"What happened after the robbers lit out?" I asked.

"The conductor shinnied up a telegraph pole and cut in on the wire," Farnum said. "He got help from the county seat. Sheriff Lester went chargin' out there with a posse, sent the wounded guard back to town, and took off after the bandits. That's the last Charley and his missus heard about it, so I don't know if they caught the varmints yet or not."

I didn't really care one way or the other, but at least the sheriff would be busy for a while chasing after outlaws and wouldn't have time to wonder about me and how I'd got hold of Abner Tillotson's ranch.

"The railroad's shut down," Farnum added. "They'll have to send a work train out, maybe all the way from San Antone. Wouldn't surprise me if they don't get the mess cleaned up until sometime tomorrow. Maybe even the next day."

"Well, I'm not plannin' on going anywhere, so that won't cause me any problems." I took the list I'd written out of my pocket. "I need a pound of coffee, some beans . . ."

I told him the rest of the supplies I needed, and he started gathering them up with a surly expression on his face. He would have rather gossiped some more about the train robbery than do any actual work.

I'd heard enough about it, though, and it had stirred up some uncomfortable memories for me. I don't plan on apologizing for anything I've done in the past, and I learned a long time ago that regrets don't change a damned thing. But I didn't need any reminders, either. I especially didn't cotton to the avid look on Farnum's face when he talked about the engineer and the fireman dying in the crash, or the way he eagerly described the shootout between the robbers and the Wells Fargo men.

The whole thing stuck with me stubbornly on the ride back to the Fishhook, and it didn't go away as I tended to the chores the rest of the day. When I laid down in the bed that night, sleep didn't come easy to me, like it usually does.

Those railroad tracks stretched across the plains some thirty miles from where I'd laid my head, I thought, and trains carrying plenty of passengers and loot rolled over them in both directions several times a day.

Not many people bothered to hold up trains anymore. Black Jack Ketchum had still been at it over in New Mexico a few years earlier, but the law had caught him and he'd wound up on a gallows.

Ol' Black Jack had come to an even grislier end than usual, though, because the hangman hadn't been very good at his job and when Black Jack dropped through the trap, the noose popped his head right off his shoulders. The body fell all the way to the ground, and Black Jack's head bounced off to one side. Lord have mercy, what a way to go. The crowd that had gathered to watch the hanging got more than they bargained for. I didn't feel sorry for 'em, the damned buzzards.

But remembering what had happened to Black Jack Ketchum just sort of ricocheted through my head. Mostly I was wondering how much trouble it would be to put together a big enough bunch to stop one of those trains the right way.

That brought me up against a stone wall in my thinking. The old bunch I'd used to run with was gone. Nearly all of them were dead. I was in Texas and one other fella was out in California, last I'd heard, livin' a law-abiding life, and the two gals who had been part of the gang didn't want anything to do with that life anymore. When I'd stopped in New York to visit with one of them, being the bearer of bad tidings that I was, she'd told me in no uncertain terms not to darken her doorstep ever again.

But enough of that. One thing you can't do in life is go back. You can turn and look at the past, you can even stick out your hand and try to touch it, but it's always going to be just beyond your reach.

I was finally about to doze off when I heard hoofbeats outside.

They were slow but not too steady, as if the horse would walk a few steps and then stop for a second before moving on again, the way it would do if it didn't have a rider. My first thought was that one of the horses had gotten out of the barn and was wandering around in the night.

But I didn't rightly see how that could have happened, because I knew those stalls were solid and secure. Abner had seen to that, and I had kept them in good repair.

So if it wasn't my horse, it had to belong to somebody else. Maybe it had wandered off from another ranch. Or maybe one of the Daughtrys' mounts had found its way back to this area. I didn't care for that thought. I'm not given to flights of fancy, but for a split second I wondered if maybe a Daughtry ghost had come looking for me, and I liked that idea even less.

"Hell's bells, you've gone loco, old son," I muttered to myself as I swung my legs out of bed and stuck my feet in my boots. Wearing the boots and a pair of long underwear, I picked up my rifle and went to the window to look out.

The horse had come to a stop between the house and the barn and looked lost. It wasn't riderless, though. A dark shape hunched forward in the saddle, leaning over the horse's neck. I knew a hurt man when I saw one, even in bad light.

The hope that the horse would move on and take its burden with it never crossed my mind. In those days, unless you were the sorriest no-account that there was—like the Daughtrys— when you saw somebody in trouble you tried to lend a hand if you could. So I grabbed my hat off the peg, stuck it on my head, and went outside in my long johns to find out what was wrong.

I wasn't careless about it, though. I took the Winchester with me.

Pausing on the little gallery in front of the house, I called, "Hola, amigo! Are you hurt?" In that part of the country there was a good chance the fella was a Mexican, so that's the way I greeted him.

He didn't say anything, but the horse turned its head toward the sound of my voice. I walked toward it, watching for any sign of a trap or an ambush.

The horse shied away from me. The man in the saddle swayed back and forth like he was about to fall off, and I realized that he might be unconscious. I knew a man could pass out and still manage to remain mounted. I'd done it myself a time or two.

I spoke softly to the horse, but it danced farther away and the rider swayed even more. I could tell he was about to lose his balance. Without thinking about what I was doing, I jumped forward to catch him as he pitched out of the saddle.

He was lucky I was there and lucky as well that his foot didn't catch in the stirrup, because the horse ran off toward the barn. I caught my mysterious visitor, staggering a little under his weight even though he was slender. Because I was still holding the rifle at the same time, hanging on to him was awkward. As carefully as I could, because I felt a sticky place on his shirt that had to be blood, I lowered him to the ground.

His hat fell off as I did so, and in the light from a half-moon that hung over the hills, I saw that his face was familiar. The last time I'd seen it was right here in front of the ranch house as I gave him those wrapped-up biscuits to keep him from starving.

The young fella I'd been convinced was on the dodge had come back to the Fishhook, and now he had at least one bullet hole in him.

CHAPTER 8

One good thing about living an active life is that not many things take you completely by surprise. No matter what happens, there's at least a chance that you've run into it before. For example, this wasn't the first time I'd had a wounded man land on my doorstep.

So this didn't exactly throw me for a loop. The first thing I did was straighten up and listen. Any time you've got a wounded man, there's a good chance somebody's chasing after him. I listened as hard as I could for the sound of rapid hoofbeats.

The night was quiet, though. Could be he'd given the slip to whoever shot him. But just in case somebody who wasn't friendly might show up in the near future, I decided I'd better get him into the house.

I leaned the Winchester against one of the posts holding up the thatched awning over the gallery. Then I bent and got my hands under the wounded man's arms. I lifted him, my back protesting some as I did so, and slung him over my left shoulder. I took him inside, balanced him precariously while I took the blanket from the bed and threw it on the sofa, and then lowered him onto it. He was out cold and never stirred or made a sound.

I fetched in the rifle, hung it on the wall, and lit the lamp. The glow from it told me that the young fella was still alive. His chest rose and fell in a shallow motion.

His horse was still out there and needed to be dealt with. I left him there on the sofa and went outside again. The horse was still skittish, but I'd had practice catching animals that didn't want to be caught. When I had hold of the reins I led the critter into the barn, put him in an empty stall, and took the saddle off him. It was just a well-worn old saddle, nothing really to distinguish it, so I stuck it in the tack room.

With that taken care of, I went back to the house, pausing on the gallery to listen again. The night was still quiet.

When I stepped inside, I found myself looking down the barrel of a gun.

My visitor had come to and rolled onto his side. He lacked the strength to get off the sofa, but he had been able to pull a small revolver from his pocket. I knew that must be where he'd gotten it, because it sure as hell wasn't one of my guns. As he pointed it at me his hand shook so much the barrel must have traveled a good six inches back and forth. That made me sort of nervous, because the hammer was cocked and all it would take to fire the blasted thing was a little pressure on the trigger.

"You don't want to shoot me, son," I told him. "I'm tryin' to help you. Why don't you put the gun down?"

"Wh . . . where . . . ?"

"This is the Fishhook Ranch. You stopped by here a while back, remember? You watered your horse and I gave you a cup of coffee and some biscuits. My name's Jim Strickland."

He was in too much pain to remember much of anything, I realized. He kept wobbling that gun at me and said, "Stay . . . stay back . . . I'll shoot . . ."

I was getting a little disgusted. You try to help somebody and they point a gun at you. That's just not civilized behavior.

I held out both hands and approached him slowly, saying, "Now just take it easy, take it easy, I'm a friend, I won't hurt you, son—"

I saw his eyes roll up in his head and knew he was about to pass out again. The gun sagged toward the floor. But as it did his finger tightened on the trigger and I had to make a wild jump to keep from getting a toe shot off as the revolver barked. I must have been a pretty funny sight, hopping around in boots, hat, and long underwear like that.

The slug smacked into the floorboards. A second later the gun slipped from his fingers and thudded to the floor. I kicked it and sent it sliding well out of reach.

Then I took hold of his arm and rolled him onto his back again. I wanted to get a look at that wound.

He had lost quite a bit of blood, but as soon as I peeled his shirt back I saw that the injury wasn't serious, even though it probably hurt like blazes. A bullet had plowed an inch-deep furrow along his rib cage. I worried that he might have a cracked or broken rib in there, but if that was the case it hadn't punctured a lung. He didn't have any bloody froth on his lips, and when I put my ear next to his mouth I could tell that his breathing was normal. I didn't hear any wheezing or whistling as I would have if he'd had a hole in one of his lungs.

I cut the blood-soaked shirt off him, then used a whiskey-soaked rag to swab the blood away from the wound. The kid groaned when the liquor bit into raw flesh but didn't wake up. The gash was still oozing crimson when I bandaged it, but I could tell it was going to stop soon.

With that done, I straightened up and thumbed my hat to the back of my head as I looked down at him. His cheeks were gaunt, and his dark hair was matted with sweat. I could tell that he'd been on the run for a while. I knew the look well. I had seen it gazing back at me from the mirror often enough.

"Kid," I said, "what in the hell am I gonna do with you?"

I couldn't stop thinking about what Clyde Farnum had told me about that attempted train robbery. It was thought that one of the outlaws had been wounded in the shootout with the Wells Fargo men, and now here was this youngster showing up with a bullet crease in his side. The two things didn't have to be connected, of course, but it made sense that they might be.

If that was true, the law was after him, and that was trouble I didn't need. Sheriff Emil Lester was already suspicious of me. If he found me harboring a wanted fugitive, he might decide I'd been part of the gang that tried to hold up the train. He might dig around enough in my background to discover that Jim Strickland wasn't my real name. He might even figure out the name I was best known by, and I sure didn't want that. I was doing my damnedest to put those days behind me.

So if I wanted to look out for my own best interests, helping this kid was a damned fool thing to do. I knew that . . . but I also knew that I wasn't going to turn my back on him. The Good Lord just hadn't made me that way.

Those thoughts were going through my head when I heard swift hoofbeats outside.

When you hear that sound at night, you know there's a good chance trouble has come to call. I whipped over to the table and blew out that light, knowing that I was too late. Whoever was out there would have seen the yellow glow in the windows already. But even so, there was no need for me to make things easier for 'em. Moving by feel in the darkness, because I already knew every inch of that house like I had lived there for ten years, I plucked the Winchester from its hooks on the wall near the door and waited.

The hoofbeats came to a stop. I couldn't hear much through the door, but I knew the horses had been run hard enough that they would be moving around restlessly out there, snorting and blowing.

A man called, "Hello, the house!"

The windows opened from the middle like shutters. I eased one of them back a little and asked, "What do you want?"

I halfway expected the riders to be a posse from the county seat, but the man who had spoken wasn't Sheriff Lester. He might be one of the deputies, though, I thought.

"We're lookin' for a friend of ours. He might've ridden in here a little while ago. Young fella, about twenty years old."

"If he's a friend of yours, you ought to know for sure how old he is," I said.

The man sounded impatient as he said, "Never mind about that. Have you seen any strangers tonight?"

"Not a one," I said, and I told myself that was an honest answer. I might not know the wounded man's name, but he wasn't a complete stranger. I had offered my hospitality to him before and he had accepted, so as far as I was concerned that meant we were acquainted.

"You haven't heard a horse go by?"

"Nope." That was true, too. None of the horses that had come up tonight had gone by. They were all still here.

"You wouldn't mind if we take a look around?"

"As a matter of fact, I would. I don't cotton to folks nosin' around my place at night."

My eyes had adjusted to the dark. From where I was, I could see two men on horseback. Judging by the sound of the hoof-beats I'd heard a few minutes earlier, at least one more man had ridden up with them. That meant he was unaccounted for, and I had a hunch he'd gone around to cover the back of the house. There was a window back there, but no door.

My last statement had drawn a few seconds of silence. Then the man who'd been doing the talking said, "Mister, I don't really care what you cotton to. If our pard's here, we're gonna find him, and you'd be wise not to try to stop us."

"Bein' wise is something that nobody's ever accused me of," I said. "I've got a Winchester pointed at you. Rattle your hocks out of here while you still can."

They weren't quite sure what to do. I was pretty good at sensing such things. If I was alone, they had me outnumbered. But they had no way of being sure I didn't have half a dozen well-armed men in here with me.

The fella decided to try to repair the damage. He said, "Look here, amigo, we got off on the wrong foot. We're not huntin' trouble. Our friend's hurt. We just want to help him, that's all. If he's here, we'll take him and go, and you won't have to see any of us ever again."

It was a tempting offer in a way, but I can count. Four men had gotten away from that holdup, and one of them was wounded. Now I had a wounded, unconscious man on my sofa and three men, more than likely, outside my house. Three men on the run from the law, I reminded myself. They might be desperate enough they wouldn't want to leave any witnesses behind to tell the sheriff that they'd been here or which way they went when they rode off. I knew there was a better than even chance if I opened that door, they'd shoot me down.

Besides which, some other thoughts were percolating around inside my brain. When the kid stopped by here before, he sure hadn't acted like he was part of a gang. Instead he had given the impression that he was on his own, without any friends or family within a hundred miles, at least.

So if my suspicions were right and he had fallen in with this bunch during the time since he'd been here, they likely weren't the good friends to him the spokesman was making them out to be. I didn't have any real reason not to trust them, other than what my gut was telling me, but that was enough.

"I told you, the fella you're looking for ain't here, and I'm not in the mood for company. So turn around and ride off."

They were just shadows in the dark to me. I couldn't see their faces. But I could tell from their attitudes they were torn about what to do. The air held a sense of menace that told me they wanted to yank out their guns and start blasting.

Then something tipped the scale. The third man hadn't gone around to the back after all. He was over at the barn. I heard his voice come from there as he yelled, "Hey, Steve, Randy's horse is in one of those stalls! The yellow bastard's here, all right."

The one called Steve ripped out a curse and told the man with him, "Scatter!" At the same time, both of them jerked guns from their holsters.

There was no point in waiting any longer. I stuck the barrel of that Winchester through the window and cut loose my wolf.

CHAPTER 9

The two men in front of the house were already moving, but I was pretty sure I winged one of them. He let out a yelp, and I saw him twist sideways in the saddle.

About then bullets smashed the window and sent glass flying, and I had to duck. I hoped none of the slugs whipping around the room hit the kid where he lay on the sofa, but there was nothing I could do about that now except try to end the fight as quickly as possible.

I rolled across the floor to the window on the other side of the door and came up on my knees. Instead of taking the time to open the window, I broke out the glass with my rifle barrel. One of the men was right in front of me, trying to get his horse back under control. The shooting had caused the animal to spook, and it was crowhopping around so that the rider had his hands full just staying in the saddle.

I solved that problem for him by blowing him off the horse's back.

He threw his arms in the air and screamed as he fell. As I shifted my aim and searched for the other men, I heard something smash through the rear window. I twisted around so that my back was against the wall. The man at the window opened fire, spraying bullets across the adobe wall above me as he triggered wildly. I went flat on my belly, staying low, and aimed just above his muzzle flashes, firing three shots of my own as fast as I could work the Winchester's lever. The man stopped shooting and disappeared from the window.

The door crashed open then, but the third man had sense enough not to just charge in blindly. Instead he threw something in ahead of him.

My eyes widened as I saw a stick of dynamite go bouncing across the floor with sparks flying from its burning fuse.

There was no time to think about what to do. I moved, diving toward the dynamite as it started to roll under the sofa where the wounded youngster still sprawled. I couldn't reach it in time with my hand, but I stuck out the Winchester and used the barrel to bat the red cylinder away from the sofa.

I'd like to claim credit for what happened next and say that it was because of my quick thinking and hair-trigger reflexes, but to tell you the truth it was just pure dumb luck. The dynamite went spinning back through the open door onto the gallery just as the spark on the fuse reached the blasting cap. It went off with a boom, blew the hell out of the awning, knocked down one of the posts, cracked the adobe wall, and left a big hole in the boards of the gallery. The thunderclap of the explosion deafened me for a minute or so as well.

I stayed there on the floor, trying to catch my breath while my hearing came back to me. My head swiveled from side to side. I couldn't hear anything, so I had to rely on my eyes to warn me if more trouble came my way.

It didn't, and when my ears started working again I heard the ugly sound of somebody gasping and gurgling for air they just couldn't get.

I climbed to my feet and felt my way over to the table where the lamp sat. I kept some matches there, and I lit one of them and held it above my head in my left hand while I pointed the Winchester in front of me with my right. If I fired the thing one-handed it might break my wrist, but I had to be able to see.

When I stepped outside, the flickering light from the match barely reached a dark shape spread out on the ground about ten feet from the gallery. I moved around the hole the dynamite had left and approached the figure.

The man lay on his back, his feet kicking feebly as he pawed at his neck with his hands. He was trying to get hold of a large, jagged splinter of wood that had lodged in his throat. The explosion must have sent it flying right at him. As I watched, he managed to pull it loose.

That was a mistake, although leaving the splinter in his throat wouldn't have done anything except postpone the inevitable. Blood poured from the wound, his feet scrabbled a frantic little dance in the dirt for a few seconds, and then he went limp. I knew he was dead, but I lowered the match close to his face anyway and saw the glassiness that was spreading over his eyes.

The match burned out. I went inside and used another one to light the lamp, and then I took it back out to check on the other two. They were dead as well, one in front of the house with half his face blown away and the other at the back window with a couple of bullet holes in his chest.

That just left the kid, and when I went inside again I was relieved to see that he was still alive. All that lead whistling around the room, and none of it had found him. He had to be leading a charmed life.

In a way I felt sorry for him. I knew the feeling of being untouchable, of believing that no matter how bad things got, somehow they were going to work out. I remembered thinking that I would always be able to dodge the worst trouble, that something—call it God or fate or just plain luck—would intervene at the last moment and turn aside whatever disaster was barreling down on me.

And for a lot of years, that was exactly the way things happened.

Until they didn't. And after that, nothing in my life was ever the same.

"Enjoy it while you can, kid," I told him, even though he couldn't hear me while he was unconscious. "It won't last. And in the meantime, you've left me a hell of a mess to clean up."

CHAPTER 10

I started by dragging the bodies into the barn and hoisting them onto the buckboard. The horses and mules didn't like the smell of all that freshly spilled blood, but there was nothing they could do about it except stomp around restlessly and whinny their complaints.

The horses the three men had ridden in on were gone, having run off after their owners were shot. I'd probably be able to find them in the morning, I thought. Once I had the bodies loaded on the buckboard, I threw a piece of canvas over them and tied it down good. That would keep varmints away from them.

That was really all I could do tonight. The damage to the house from the explosion would take several days to repair, maybe as much as a week. I went back inside, found the pistol the kid had pointed at me, unloaded it, and stowed it away in Abner's trunk where the kid couldn't find it if he woke up.

Then I took off my hat and boots, crawled back into bed, and went to sleep. Killing wore me out. I was glad I hadn't had to do it for all those years. But these three varmints hadn't given me any choice, and I was damned if I was going to lie awake tossing and turning over what I'd done.

When I woke up in the morning the kid was trying to stand up, but he was too weak from losing all that blood to make it. He couldn't even sit up. He slumped back on the sofa and let out a bitter curse before he knew I was awake. I'd been watching him with one hand on the Remington, which I'd slipped under my pillow the night before.

"Take it easy," I told him. His head jerked toward me, and his eyes were open so wide I could see white all around them. "You're not hurt that bad, but you're gonna need some rest while you're recuperatin'."

"Who . . . where . . ."

"Those are good questions," I said as I sat up. "Why don't you answer the first one? What's your name?"

The night before, I'd heard one of the men say that Randy's horse was in the barn, so I was curious to see if the kid would tell me the truth.

After a moment of lying there looking like he wanted to jump up and bolt out the door, he said quietly, "Randall."

"What'd you say?" I asked, even though I had heard him.

"Randall," he repeated, and his voice was stronger this time. "Randall McClellan."

"Pleased to meet you, Randy," I said. "I'm Jim Strickland. I introduced myself last night, but the shape you were in at the time, I sort of doubt that you recall it. This is my place."

"I know. I remember being here before. What I don't understand is how I got here now."

"Your horse brought you. I reckon you passed out from bein' shot, but your horse kept goin'. Lucky for you that he did, too. I got the feeling that the hombres who were lookin' for you weren't real happy with you. Not much tellin' what they might have done if they'd caught up to you out on the prairie."

"Tate!" he said. He started getting that wild-eyed look again. "Is Tate here?"

"I don't know," I said. "There are three dead men out in the barn, but I didn't ask their names before I killed them." I paused. "Seems like I remember that one of them was called Steve, though."

Randy leaned his head back and closed his eyes as a sigh came from him.

"Steve Tate," he said, opening his eyes again. "You say he's dead?"

"Dead as can be. So are the other two."

"Williams and Perkins," Randy said.

"Your partners in that train robbery?"

He jerked again. He was a jumpy cuss, even wounded like that.

"How did you—"

I held up a hand to stop him.

"You need some coffee and something to eat," I told him. "The sooner we get some food in you, the sooner you'll start getting over bein' shot like that."

I got out of bed, pulled on some clothes, and began rustling some breakfast for us. I hadn't forgotten about those three corpses out in the barn, but I wanted to get things squared away with Randy first.

When I had the coffee brewed and the bacon and flapjacks were ready, I helped him sit up on the sofa and set a tray with a cup and plate on it in his lap. After we had eaten, I would check that bandage on his side.

He was still shaky, but he was strong enough to hold his own coffee cup and feed himself. I sat at the table to eat. The room wasn't so big we had to yell at each other to be heard.

"You fellas were the ones who tried to hold up that train, right?" I asked him.

"It wasn't my idea," he said with a sullen look on his face. "Tate came up with the plan. He said we could make a fortune. I'd been drifting for a long time, ever since my folks died, and I thought if I could make some money, everything would finally be all right again."

"People tend to think that, all right," I said. "Most of the time, it don't work out that way, though."

"Yeah, I'm starting to realize that. I didn't know at first he planned to derail the train. When I found out I told him we shouldn't do it. I said we might kill a bunch of innocent people. You know what he did?"

I shook my head.

"He just laughed at me and said there aren't any innocent people, just them that have and them that don't. I was brand-new to the gang. I couldn't stop them."

"You could've ridden away," I pointed out.

"They would have killed me rather than risk me putting the law on their trail."

I thought about it for a moment and nodded.

"More than likely," I agreed.

He took another drink of the coffee to brace himself up some more, then went on, "When things didn't work out just like Tate hoped, he said we'd have to charge in and kill the express messengers. But it wasn't just clerks in the express car. There were armed guards in there, too, and they opened fire on us before we could even start shooting at them. I . . . I squeezed off a few rounds, then I couldn't take it anymore. I turned around and tried to get out of there. But Tate saw me, and he . . . he shot me himself. He was like a wild man, raving and cussing and shooting. I didn't think I'd get out of there alive, Mr. Strickland."

"You probably didn't miss being dead by much," I said. "Why were they trying to track you down? I would've thought they'd be puttin' as many miles between them and Cougar Pass as they could."

"I guess Tate didn't want me telling the law who they were. We wore bandannas over our faces, and everything was so mixed up because of the wreck and all the shooting I don't think anybody could have identified us later."

He was probably right about that, too, I thought.

"And I think Tate was loco," Randy added in a hushed voice. "I think he might've wanted to kill me just because I tried to run out on them. Williams and Perkins would have gone along with him on that. They were sort of scared of him."

"What you're tellin' me all makes sense," I said. "But I've got another question for you . . . do you still have your heart set on being a train robber?"

"I *never* set out to be a train robber," he said. "I told you, I just sort of fell in with those men, Mr. Strickland. I've done some things I'm not proud of. I've stolen to eat, stole money and food both. But I didn't want to kill anybody."

That was what I'd thought he would say, but I was glad to hear it anyway. I drank the last of my coffee and said, "All right, Randy, here's what we're gonna do. I'm gonna change that bandage on your side, and then I'm taking those three dead outlaws to Largo and sending word to Sheriff Emil Lester about them. I'm gonna tell the sheriff that they showed up here last night and tried to kill me and my new hired man so they could loot the place and steal some fresh horses."

"New hired man? You mean me?"

"That's right." I stood up. "You signed up to work for the Fishhook spread yesterday morning, you understand? So there's no way you could've been anywhere near Cougar Pass when that locomotive went off the rails." He started to say something, but I held up a hand to stop him. "Not only that, but you were wounded valiantly in the fight when we downed those owlhoots. As far as I'm concerned, you're a hero, and as soon as you can ride again, you've got a job here on the Fishhook for as long as you want it."

He stared at me, unable to speak. When he finally found his tongue again, he asked, "Why would you do that for me? You don't know me. You don't know anything about me."

"Well, hell, son," I told him with a grin, "I've been in some pretty desperate straits myself from time to time. I know what it feels like to not have any hope, and then somebody holds out a sliver of it. You grab on to it because there's nothin' else you can do, not if you're human. We're all weak now and again. That don't mean we don't deserve a second chance."

"I . . . I can't believe it."

"You'd better believe it, because it's the truth. There's only one thing you've got to do right now for me."

He got a wary look on his face again, and I didn't blame him a bit. It was probably going to be a long time before he trusted anybody completely again, if he ever did.

"What's that?" he asked.

"You've got to give me your word you won't do anything stupid while I'm gone, like trying to get on a horse and ride away from here. You've got to promise that you'll be here when I get back from town."

He didn't answer right away, even though we both knew he had plumb run out of options. I guess he still had enough pride he wanted to make it look like he was thinking about it.

Finally he nodded and said, "All right. I give you my word. I'll be here, Mr. Strickland."

I grinned at him again and told him, "Good. Finish your breakfast. You need to get your strength back as soon as you can. If you're gonna ride for the Fishhook brand, you're gonna earn your keep, son!"

CHAPTER 11

Blood had soaked through the canvas in places, so I drew quite a bit of attention when I drove the buckboard into Largo late that morning with one of my saddle horses tied to the back. Farnum's store was the center of the community, so that's where I headed. Several men and even a couple of women followed me, forming a small crowd around the back of the buckboard as I stopped in front of the store, next to a Model T Ford somebody had parked there. I always saw a few automobiles every time I came to town, but bad roads and isolation meant most people out here still used horses and wagons.

"What in tarnation do you have there, Mr. Strickland?" Tom Mulrooney asked me. He was a burly fella who owned the blacksmith shop.

"Is that . . . blood?" one of the women asked. I didn't know her name, but I recalled that she was a seamstress and ran the millinery shop. Her question managed to sound both horrifyng and interesting at the same time.

"Yes, ma'am," I told her as I hopped down from the seat. "You might want to step back. I'm afraid what's under here would offend those with delicate sensibilities."

"It's dead men, isn't it?" she asked.

"Yes, ma'am, it is."

I could tell she wanted me to peel back that canvas and let her have a look. So did most of the others. I saw the morbid curiosity in their eyes.

Maybe it's because of my own background, but it always bothered me the way any time an outlaw got killed, honest, respectable citizens would prop his bullet-riddled body up on a board and put it on display for folks to gawk at. Lawmen posed proudly and triumphantly with the corpse while photographs were made. Undertakers sometimes charged an admission fee just to gaze at the unlucky bastard. I'd even heard a story about how the body of a famous gunman had been stuffed and turned into an exhibit in a damned medicine show. I don't mind admitting the whole thing annoyed the hell out of me. Even an owlhoot ought to have a right to a little dignity once he'd crossed the divide. Being left for the coyotes was better than having your death turned into a spectacle.

I was trying to make my home here, though, so I held my tongue and didn't tell those good, churchgoing, God-fearing folks what no-account vultures they were acting like. Anyway, I guess they were just following human nature, which most of the time isn't much to be proud of, but you can't really help it, either. That's why they call it human nature.

Clyde Farnum came out on the porch of his store, drawn by the commotion in the street, and said, "Good Lord, Jim, what you got there?"

"Three dead outlaws, Clyde," I told him. "This is the rest of the gang that derailed the locomotive in Cougar Pass yesterday morning."

That caused even more of a stir. People really did want to get a look under that canvas then.

I went on, "I need somebody to take a ride down to the county seat and fetch back the sheriff, I guess. He's the one who ought to take charge of these bodies."

"No need for that," Farnum said. "The sheriff ain't there. He's right here in Largo." He pointed down the street to the settlement's only café. "He and the posse rode in a little while ago. They're down there gettin' something to eat before they start out on the trail again. Reckon now they won't have to."

I turned to ask if somebody in the crowd would be kind

enough to let the sheriff know I needed to see him. I didn't have to voice the request. A couple of men were already hustling in that direction, and I knew good and well what their destination was.

Sure enough, they went into the café, and less than a minute later Sheriff Lester came out in a hurry, followed by a couple of his deputies. He wasn't wearing a hat, and he had a napkin tucked into his collar. He realized the napkin was still there after he'd already started into the street. With a disgusted motion, he plucked it loose and tossed it to the ground behind him. I thought that was a mite rude. The café owner would have to retrieve that napkin.

The crowd around the buckboard had continued to grow while I was talking to Farnum. More than a dozen people stood around it now, waiting to see what was going to happen. They probably figured that with the sheriff on his way, there was a good chance they'd get a look at the bodies after all.

Folks got out of Lester's way. He came up to me, red-faced and glaring, and demanded, "Strickland, what the hell is all this?"

"Just what I imagine you've already been told, Sheriff." I nodded toward the canvas-covered cargo. "I've got the three outlaws who tried to hold up the train yesterday."

"How in blazes do you know that?"

"Heard 'em say as much before the shooting started," I replied. I had worked out my story on the way into town. "One of them let it slip while they were dickering with me, trying to get me to trade them some fresh horses. I've got a hunch they planned to kill me and my new hired man anyway, but once that business about the train robbery was out in the open, they didn't waste any time slappin' leather."

"They tried to kill you?" Lester snapped.

"Yep. Things got pretty hot there for a while. We fought them off and managed to bring down all three of 'em, but Randy took a bullet in the side."

"Who's Randy?"

"That new rider I hired. Randy McClellan."

I could tell the name didn't mean a blessed thing to Lester, and I was glad to see that. As long as the sheriff didn't know who he was, I had a chance of keeping any more trouble from dogging Randy's trail. And mine, too, of course. I was at least as worried about that as I was about Randy's welfare.

Lester gave me a curt nod and said, "Let's see 'em." A stir of anticipation went through the crowd.

I had known Lester would want to take a look at them, so I was ready. I jerked loose a couple of knots and threw the canvas back far enough to reveal the faces of the dead men. The one I'd shot in the chest didn't look too bad, but the fella who'd caught a couple of slugs in the face was ugly as hell, of course. The one whose throat had been ripped open by that flying splinter didn't look much better. Gasps of fascinated horror came from the women in the crowd. The men did a lot of muttering to each other.

"According to Wells Fargo, four outlaws got away after that train robbery," Lester said.

"That's what I heard," I said with a shrug. "But these hombres were the only ones who showed up at my ranch. Wasn't one of them wounded in the fight with the guards? He probably didn't make it and they left his body for the buzzards somewhere out there on the trail."

Lester grunted and said, "Yeah, you might be right about that." He jerked a hand at the bodies. "Cover them back up."

The crowd was probably disappointed, but I did what the sheriff told me. Lester went on, "There's no undertaker here in Largo. I'll have to take these bodies back to the county seat with me this afternoon. I'm commandeering your buckboard."

"I thought you might want to do that. That's why I brought along a horse to ride back to the ranch. You'll see to it the buckboard's returned to me, won't you, Sheriff?"

"Yes, yes," he said, visibly irritated. "You said that rider of yours was wounded? Why didn't you bring him with you if he needs medical attention?"

"He just got a bullet crease in his side," I explained. "I cleaned and bandaged it. That's all a sawbones would've done."

That wasn't strictly true. A doctor likely would've sewed up the wound, too. But I had drawn the edges tight together before I bound it up, and I was confident it would heal without stitches. If I saw that wasn't going to be the case, I could fetch Randy to the doc then.

Lester accepted that explanation. He said, "You'll have a reward coming for these men, Strickland. The railroad doesn't take kindly to being robbed."

I could have told him that I was all too aware of that, but instead I said, "I don't need any blood money. Randy and me were just trying to keep those varmints from ventilating us. I heard the engineer and the fireman were killed when the locomotive derailed?"

"That's right."

"See to it that the reward money goes to their families, Sheriff." I hadn't asked Randy about that, but it wasn't really his decision to make. "Can you do that?"

Lester regarded me with a suspicious stare for a long moment, but he finally nodded and said, "If that's the way you want it, sure. I'll see to it, Strickland."

"I'm obliged to you." Enough people had heard what the sheriff said that I figured he would keep his word. I went to the back of the buckboard and untied my horse. "Reckon I'll head on back out to the Fishhook now."

"Hold on," Lester ordered. "I didn't say I was through asking you questions yet."

"What else do you want to know, Sheriff? Those fellas tried to kill Randy and me, and we killed them instead. The whole thing's pretty doggone simple."

His eyes were still narrow with suspicion, but I had a strong hunch that was just habit with him. After a second he nodded again and said, "All right. I know where to find you if I need to talk to you again."

"Yes, sir, you sure do."

I swung up into the saddle and lifted a hand in farewell. The townspeople got out of my way as I turned the horse. I heard a lot of low-voiced chatter behind me. It wouldn't be long before the story spread and got bigger than it really was, I thought. Five hundred people would claim to have been in Largo the day I brought the bodies in, instead of the twenty-five or thirty who were really there. The number of corpses would grow from three men in a buckboard to a whole pile of dead outlaws in the back of a prairie schooner.

The truth was never as good as a legend, I thought as I rode away from Largo.

CHAPTER 12

Randy had kept his word to me. He was still there on the ranch when I rode in. He was dozing on the sofa, getting some of his strength back.

The wound in his side was still raw and sore-looking when I changed the bandage that evening after supper, but I didn't see any of the telltale red streaks running away from it that would have told me it was festering.

By the next morning the crease was starting to look a little better. I cleaned it with whiskey again, and he was strong enough to cuss some at the sting.

Any man who's been on the drift for a while starts to feel restless if he has to stay in one place for very long. After a couple more days I could tell that Randy was getting fiddle-footed again. He insisted that he was strong enough to get up and come to the supper table, and after we had eaten, I said, "Don't forget we had a deal. I kept the law from coming after you for that train robbery, and you agreed to stay here and work for me."

"I haven't said anything about leaving, have I?"

"You didn't need to," I told him. "I can see it in your eyes. And if you're bound and determined to do it, I won't stop you. But I can tell you right now, if you do you stand a good chance of coming to a bad end. The West ain't like it used to be. There's no place for a horseback desperado anymore. The real bandits drive automobiles and live in cities now."

"You sound like you're talking from experience."

"Never you mind about that. Just take some advice from somebody who's older and—"

I started to say "wiser," but then I remembered how I'd said that nobody ever accused me of that. It was true. So I went on, "Older, anyway. If you want to make something of yourself, this is the place to start."

"You sound like a preacher or a schoolteacher."

I grinned and said, "Son, if you knew how funny that was, you'd be laughin', too."

He didn't say anything for a few minutes, then, "I still don't know why you're doing this."

"Well, hell, I don't, either," I said. "But just because I don't know why I'm doin' something has never stopped me."

After a few more days, Randy insisted he was strong enough to go outside. He even offered to do a little light work around the place, but I wouldn't let him. The wound in his side had scabbed over and seemed to be healing just fine, but I didn't want him to break it open again. That might wind up wasting all my efforts so far.

Winter seemed like it was over, but officially the seasons hadn't changed yet, and I knew how unpredictable Texas weather could be. I saw proof of it over the next few days, as some of them were sunny and warm enough to make a man break a sweat if he did any work outside while others were overcast and cold, with a wind whipping down from the north that reminded me of the night I'd met Abner Tillotson.

On one of the warmer days, Randy and I were in the barn when we heard horses coming. He had pestered me so much I'd finally given him some harness to mend, and I was wrestling with a rock that one of my saddle mounts had picked up in a shoe. I was trying to coax the pesky devil out with my clasp knife when I first heard the hoofbeats. Randy looked up from his chore a second later and said, "Is that somebody—"

"Yeah," I said. I closed my knife and slipped it back in my pocket. "Stay in here."

I was wearing the holstered Remington. I never went anywhere without a gun. Several times I had caught Randy sneaking admiring glances at the revolver, and I didn't blame him. It was a fine weapon, especially in comparison with that little pocket pistol of his. Steve Tate had given it to him, he'd explained, because he didn't have a gun of any sort when he joined up with the outlaws.

I knew he worried that he might have hit somebody with those shots he fired during the train robbery, but I didn't think that was very likely. He had squeezed off a few rounds with the pistol while I was practicing with the Remington, and the thing was so wildly inaccurate beyond about ten feet that I didn't think he could be held accountable for any damage he'd done with it. Anytime anybody actually hit anything with that gun, it was just blind luck, as far as I was concerned.

So when he started to get up from the stool where he'd been sitting and reached in his pocket for the pistol, I shook my head and said again, "Stay here."

"What if you need help?"

"Then you can come a-runnin'," I told him, although I thought that was pretty unlikely.

I stepped out of the barn just as the three riders came to a stop in front of the house. Right away I recognized Santiago Marquez and his cousins Javier and Fernando Gallardo.

"Hola, amigos," I called to them. "Over here." I took my hat off and used my other arm to sleeve sweat off my forehead as they turned their horses and rode over to the barn.

"I see you are still here, Señor Strickland," Santiago said, and although his face was as grim and solemn as it had been before, I thought I saw a small twinkle of amusement in his dark eyes.

"What, you didn't think the sheriff was gonna drag me off to jail, did you, Santiago?"

"With Sheriff Lester it is hard to say what he might do. But I suppose you are right. He would not arrest the hero of Cougar Pass."

"Good Lord," I said. "Is that what folks are callin' me? Hell, I wasn't even there!"

"No, but you killed three of the outlaws who got away. You are a famous man, señor."

I didn't have any desire to be famous anymore. I had tried that, and while it had its good points, sure enough, in the end it hadn't meant a damned thing.

"Folks will forget all about me in a month's time," I said. "At least I hope they will. I'm just a simple, hard-workin' rancher, that's all."

"And that is why we are here. It has been a week. Do you want to hire us to help with the spring roundup?"

I'd been giving it some thought, and since it looked like I was going to stay on for a while, I would need some help with the spread. Santiago and his cousins knew the range, knew the stock, and knew what needed to be done. I nodded and said, "Yeah, I do. I need a foreman, too, and the job's yours if you want it, Santiago."

He frowned slightly, and considering his impassive nature I knew I'd surprised him.

"Señor Tillotson always served as his own foreman," he said.

"That's fine, but it's been a while since I've worked on a roundup. You and your cousins have your own ranch, right?"

"Sí, much smaller than this one."

"But keeping it running isn't that much different, I'll bet. You know what you're doin', and I trust you, Santiago."

"You barely know me," he pointed out.

I chuckled and said, "But I'm a good judge of character."

Santiago looked at Javier and Fernando. They both shrugged. He looked at me again and said, "All right, señor. We will not let you down."

"I don't expect you will. You won't have to do all the work yourself. I'll pitch in, and we'll have another hand, too." I turned my head and called into the barn, "Randy, come on out here."

He didn't come out right away, but after a few seconds went by he shuffled into sight. His right hand was in his jeans pocket, and I knew he was clutching that little pistol. I hoped he had sense enough to leave it where it was.

"Randy, come here," I said. "I want you to meet the fellas you'll be workin' with."

He was sort of washed out and didn't look too healthy, especially compared to the three vaqueros, who might have been hewn out of oak. The clothes he'd been wearing when he showed up were so soaked with blood that I hadn't been able to save them, so now Randy was wearing some of Abner's clothes, and they were pretty baggy on him. It occurred to me that Santiago might recognize the duds and get suspicious again, but jeans and work shirts are pretty common and I didn't see anything distinctive about the garments Randy had on.

"Fellas, this is Randy McClellan," I told the vaqueros.

"The one who helped you kill the outlaws," Santiago said. "The one who was wounded."

"That's right. Randy, meet Santiago Marquez and Javier and Fernando Gallardo." I paused. "No offense, but I don't reckon I know which of you is Javier and which is Fernando."

Even that didn't prompt them to say anything. Santiago pointed at one and said, "Javier," then pointed at the other and said, "Fernando." Seeing as how they were almost as alike as the proverbial two peas in a pod, I wasn't sure how much that was going to help.

Randy nodded and said, "Howdy." I was glad to see that he'd taken his hand out of his pocket, away from the gun.

"Santiago's my foreman. Once you're able to work again, you'll be taking your orders from him."

"I could work now. I can sit a saddle."

"Give it another week, and then we'll see," I told him. I looked at Santiago again and said, "What do we need to do to get ready for roundup?"

"You'll need a few more hombres. And a cook."

"Where do I find a cook?"

Santiago shrugged.

"I would look in the saloon in Largo. There are old cowboys who come there to pass the time of day. Some of them hire out to the ranches around here during roundup. And there are young cowboys looking for work as well. I would say you need . . . three more men."

I had a feeling that he knew perfectly well who would be willing to hire on and who would be good for the jobs. But he was leaving it to me, as a test to see what sort of crew I would put together. If that was the way he wanted it, fine. I had gotten together a pretty good bunch of fellas in the past when jobs needed to be done.

"All right, I'll go to Largo tomorrow and see who I can find. In the meantime—"

"We will start scouting your range to see where all the cattle are. Some of them like to hide in the hills to the south."

"That's what I was just about to say," I told him. "You'll be here bright and early in the morning?"

"Bright and early, Señor Strickland."

They rode off, and as Randy watched them go, he said, "I hope you know what you're doing, boss. Those fellas look like bandits to me."

"Trust me," I told him. "I know bandits when I see 'em."

CHAPTER 13

As it turned out, Randy, Santiago, and the Gallardo boys weren't the only newcomers to the Fishhook. That night, Randy and I were in the house when we heard a commotion out in the barn. I had just checked the wound in his side and was pleased to see that it was still healing just fine, as far as I could tell. One of the windows I had replaced after the shootout with Tate and the other outlaws was open to let in some night breezes, and it let in the racket all the horses were kicking up, too.

"Something's sure spooking those critters," I said as I stood up from the table. Randy started to get up, too, but I motioned him back into his chair. "No, sit down, I'll check it out. No need for you to come along."

"Damn it, Mr. Strickland," he said. "You don't let me do a thing around here."

"That's not true. You worked on mendin' that harness today."

He gave me a disgusted look that made it clear how he felt about that job. It's true, that was a chore usually reserved for the old, stove-up cowboys. That and cooking.

"All right, come on," I told him. "But if there's any shootin' to be done, let me handle it. When that popgun of yours goes off, the only safe place to be is behind you, and I ain't altogether certain of that."

"You plan on paying me wages?" he asked as I took the Winchester down from its pegs.

"What? Of course I do."

"Well, when I've got my first month's wages I'm going to Largo and buying a decent revolver."

"All right, fine. Until then, leave that gun you've got in your pocket."

I had replaced the boards in the gallery, too. I was a pretty fair carpenter, if I do say so myself. We walked over them and headed for the barn, where the horses were still carrying on. I heard horseshoes thudding against the sides of several stalls as they tried to kick their way out.

"Better be careful," Randy said. "There must be some sort of varmint in there."

"A wolf, maybe. Or a bear."

"I'm not sure there are any bears in this part of the country. More likely a coyote. Maybe a panther."

"You make fun of me sayin' there might be a bear, and then you start talkin' about panthers?" I said.

"There are panthers around here," he insisted. "At least I think so."

"Let's just go take a look—"

A deep, throaty growl from the open doors of the barn made us both stop right where we were. The shape that stalked out of the shadows in a slow, menacing glide was big and shaggy.

"Good Lord," Randy said quietly in an awed voice. "Maybe it is a bear after all."

"It don't move like a bear," I told him without taking my eyes off the critter. It had stopped, but I sensed that if it wanted to, it could move again in one hell of a hurry. "And it's too shaggy to be a panther," I went on. "Randy, I think . . . I think that's a dog."

"A wolf, maybe."

I studied the animal for a moment and shook my head.

"No, I don't think so. The ears ain't right. Look how they sort of flop over. That's a big dog."

"Maybe." He still didn't sound convinced.

"I'll prove it to you." I took a step toward the critter. "Here, boy," I said. "Come on, fella."

The damn thing charged me.

It was fast, all right, and I hesitated for just a second because I didn't want to shoot a dog. That gave it enough time to launch into a leap that sent it crashing into my chest. I went over backward and lost my grip on the Winchester when I hit the ground. The thing's hot, slobbery breath gusted against my face as its bared teeth poised just above my throat, ready to rip it out. After everything that had happened to me in my life, it would be a hell of a note if I died because I tried to call a dog.

It didn't tear into me, though, just kept me pinned there with a hundred pounds of furry beast on my chest while it snarled and drooled on me. Randy was yelling, and I worried that he might try to shoot the dog and hit me instead, so I shouted, "Hold your fire! By God, don't you shoot that gun, Randy!"

"But . . . but, Mr. Strickland, the dog—"

I stayed as still as I could as I told him, "The dog ain't done nothin' so far but knock me down. Fetch the lamp."

"But—"

"Fetch the damn lamp!"

Randy hurried back into the house and returned a moment later with the lamp. He held it high so the light from it washed over us.

I saw that I'd been right. The varmint wasn't a bear, a panther, or even a wolf. It was a dog. The shaggy brown hair that covered it couldn't hide how skinny he was, either. He looked half-starved, and I was surprised he hadn't tried to eat me for that reason alone. His muzzle had scars on it, as if he'd been in plenty of fights with other animals, and his big, floppy ears were sort of ragged in places like his opponents had gnawed on them.

"Take it easy, old son," I said as quietly and calmly as I could manage. "Nobody wants to hurt you."

"It's gonna kill you, Mr. Strickland—," Randy began.

"No, he's not," I said. "If that's what he wanted to do, he would have done it already. He's just scared . . . scared and hungry, from the looks of him. Set that lamp on the ground and go get a biscuit."

"What?"

"A biscuit!" I repeated, trying to keep the impatience I felt under control. "There were some left over at supper, remember? Go get one of 'em."

Randy must have figured out I wanted to distract the dog, because he did like I said and hurried into the house. When he came back, he had one of the biscuits in his hand.

"Now break off a piece and toss it over here next to us," I told him.

He fumbled with the biscuit. The dog kept his eyes on me, but I could tell he was interested in what Randy was doing. Maybe he could smell the biscuit. Maybe he was so hungry, he could just sense that food was close by.

Randy said, "Here you go, uh, doggy," and threw the piece of biscuit so hard it bounced off the dog's head instead of landing on the ground beside him. The dog jerked a little and snarled even louder. More slobber dripped from his muzzle onto my face.

"Not that hard," I told Randy through clenched teeth. I like to think I'm pretty cool-headed, but controlling the urge to panic and start flailing around was getting tough.

"Sorry, sorry," Randy said. He tried again, and this time the chunk of biscuit landed on the ground a couple of feet away from me and the dog.

That finally made the dog take his eyes off of me. He looked at the biscuit for a few seconds, then abruptly lunged for it. The slavering jaws snapped up the morsel.

"Throw another!" I yelled at Randy. "Closer to you this time!"

He did, and the dog got off of me entirely to go after it. I rolled the other way as fast as I could and came up in a crouch. I was ready to run, but I knew that wouldn't do any good. The dog could chase me down in a heartbeat if he wanted to.

Right now, all the varmint wanted to do was gobble down the pieces of biscuit, including the first one Randy had thrown. I said, "Give him the whole thing!"

Randy threw the rest of the biscuit on the ground and started to back off.

"You gonna get the rifle and shoot it now?" he asked.

"Shoot him? Why the hell would I want to shoot him?"

"Why . . . Because it's a wild beast, that's why!"

"Naw," I said. "He's just hungry, and he's had a hard life. That's all that's wrong with him."

"How do you know it's a he?"

That was a good question. I'd just started thinking of the dog as male, maybe because he was so big and ugly. Sort of like some human galoots I've known.

The dog had swallowed all the pieces of biscuit. I told Randy, "Go get him something else to eat."

"What should I get?"

"I don't care, just find something."

Muttering, he retreated toward the house, afraid to turn his own back on the dog. I held out a hand and said, "Easy there, big fella. Nobody's gonna hurt you here. You got my word on that."

He couldn't understand me, of course . . . but he gave me a long, wary, yet somehow hopeful look that almost made me think he did.

Randy came back with a ham from the butcher counter at Farnum's. As soon as the dog caught a whiff of it, he came at Randy like a runaway freight train. I yelled, "Throw it to him!"

Randy yelped and threw the ham up into the air. It never hit the ground. The dog went up and got it with a snap of those powerful jaws. He headed toward the barn with it, growling ferociously again.

"That's a waste of a good ham," Randy said.

"Maybe not," I told him. "Let's see what happens."

The dog trotted into the barn carrying the ham. He must have laid down right inside the door, because I could still hear him without any trouble as he started tearing into it, snarling all the time to warn any other creatures nearby to steer clear of him and to not even think about trying to take his treasure.

"Go on back inside," I said to Randy. "Take the lamp with you."

"What are you going to do?"

"Think I'll sit out on the gallery for a while," I drawled.

He thought I was loco, but he did like I said, picking up the lamp and going inside the house with it. I sat down in one of the ladderback chairs on the gallery and tipped it back against the wall to wait.

After a while the dog came out of the barn again. He had the ham bone in his mouth. He'd torn all the meat off it. Once he was out in the open, he stopped and eyed me suspiciously. I stayed where I was and called to him, "That's your bone. I won't take it away from you."

He padded toward the house, but he didn't come all the way up to the gallery. When he was still about ten feet away, he laid down and started gnawing on that bone, keeping an eye on me at the same time. He wasn't growling anymore. If I'd made a move toward him, he likely would have, but as long as I didn't threaten him, he was willing to tolerate me.

After half an hour, I let the chair ease back down on all four legs and stood up. The dog watched me but didn't growl or get up. I said, "I'm goin' on inside now. See you in the mornin' . . . Scar."

I don't know where the name came from. Those scars on his muzzle, maybe. But I knew it seemed to fit him, just like I knew he was male.

I also knew—or at least I hoped—that he would be there in the morning, too.

"Where's the dog?" Randy asked when I went inside.

"Out there," I said. "Keepin' an eye on the place for us."

"Looking for a way to get in so he can kill us in our sleep, you mean."

"We'll see," I said.

CHAPTER 14

Scar was still there in the morning, sleeping on the gallery. He raised his head and looked at me when I came outside, but he didn't run off. I nodded to him and said, "Howdy."

He laid his head back down on his paws but kept watching me.

Randy stuck his head out the door behind me.

"That beast really is still here," he said. "I thought for sure he'd run off during the night."

"Nope. And it's safe for you to come out. He won't bother you if you don't bother him."

"He's going to chew my leg off."

"Last night he might have," I said. "I don't think he's quite that hungry anymore."

Now that it was daylight and I could get a better look at him, I was able to confirm my impression that he was a boy dog, if you know what I mean. I could also tell how rough life had treated him. He had patches of bare hide where something had ripped out his hair and it hadn't grown back. His grizzled appearance made him look like an old dog, but I wasn't sure if it was the years or the hardships he'd endured that were responsible for that.

As I started toward the barn, I told Randy, "I'm riding to Largo this mornin' to see about hirin' a cook and some more hands, the way Santiago said. You and Scar can stay here and keep an eye on the place."

"You're leaving me here with that . . . that beast?"

"The two of you will get along just fine," I told him.

Randy looked sort of doubtful about that, and to tell the truth, so did Scar. But I had work to do, and the two of them would just have to learn to tolerate each other.

I saddled up one of the horses and headed for town. I hadn't been to Largo since taking in the bodies of the dead outlaws, so I hoped Sheriff Lester had brought my buckboard back by now. I didn't think of the buckboard as Abner's anymore, nor did I think of the Fishhook that way. The ranch was mine now. Hard as it was for me to believe, I was starting to put down roots.

It was still early enough when I got to town that I didn't figure I'd want to hire anybody I found in the saloon at that hour. I wouldn't be able to depend on somebody who had a thirst for rotgut at ten o'clock in the morning. So I went into the store instead. A big, fancy car was parked in front of the place, and when I went in I found Clyde Farnum talking to a fella in a city suit and hat.

"Howdy, Jim," Farnum said as he gave me a nod. "Can you believe it? I'm thinkin' about puttin' in one of those new-fangled gasoline pumps."

"The stuff that makes the automobiles go?" I asked with a frown.

"That's right. If I do, then folks hereabouts won't have to go all the way to the county seat to buy it."

The city man held out his hand to me and said, "I'm Morris Dobbs, sir. I represent Continental Oil."

I shook his hand because I was raised to be polite that way, but I didn't see where I had any business with this fella. I told him my name anyway and gave him a friendly nod.

"Oh, yeah, Jim, your buckboard's parked out back," Farnum said. "Couple of deputies brought it back a few days ago. I told 'em they ought to just take it on out to your ranch, but they said the sheriff told 'em to deliver it here. Said this is where they got it, and this is where they were bringin' it back."

"That's fine, Clyde," I assured him. "I'm obliged to you for lookin' after it."

"If you had a car, Mr. Strickland, you wouldn't need a buck-board," Morris Dobbs said.

I grinned and said, "I'm not sure a car would go everywhere I need to go. And if I had one I'd be a sure enough menace to society, because I've never been very good at piloting one of the blasted things."

"It just takes practice, that's all." He waved a hand toward the front of the building. "Did you see my Hupmobile out there?"

"Is that what you call it?"

"It's the latest model. I'll take you for a spin in it if you like. Even let you try your hand at driving it."

"No thanks," I told him. "A horse is plenty good enough for me."

He shook his head and said, "It's no use trying to fight the future, Mr. Strickland. Why, in a few more years, as the roads improve, you're going to see automobiles everywhere, even in ranching country like this. Trucks can carry goods where the railroads don't go, and do it much more cheaply and efficiently than horse-drawn wagons. Wouldn't you like to be able to stock your store that way, Mr. Farnum?"

Farnum scratched at his stubble and said, "Well, it does sound like it'd be a whole heap easier . . ."

I couldn't imagine anything taking the place of railroads when it came to carrying freight. If that day ever came, I'd be sad to see it. Railroads had played a big part in my life.

"You sound so proud of the things, Mr. Dobbs," I said, "if I didn't know better I'd say you made 'em."

He smiled and shook his head.

"No, but I sell the stuff they run on. The whole world is going to run on oil and gas one of these days, Mr. Strickland, you mark my words."

It's been my experience that when somebody tells you to mark their words, they're not really predicting. They're hoping. They hope that what they're saying will turn out to be right because they've got a lot riding on it.

Me, I didn't really spend a lot of time thinking about the future anymore. In the past I'd made plans and had hopes and dreams, and I had seen how all that panned out. Now I just sort of took things day to day and tried to find things to enjoy about each one of them.

"I'll leave you fellas to your business," I said. At different times in my life I'd tried to become a city slicker, and it never took. Being around one of them now sort of irritated me. I added, "I'll be back by later to pick up that wagon, Clyde. I suppose the team's down at Mulrooney's?" The blacksmith also had the only stable in town.

"Yep. See you, Jim."

"Good-bye, Mr. Strickland," Dobbs said. "Don't forget what I told you."

"Oh, I'm not likely to," I said. I wouldn't forget it, but I wouldn't put much stock in it, either.

Since it was still too early to go to the saloon, I stopped at the café instead and lingered for a couple of hours over several cups of coffee and a second breakfast. Anybody who's damned near starved to death in the past, like I have, knows that it's a good idea to take advantage of every opportunity to eat.

By the time I went into the saloon, it was almost noon. Late enough that the fellas along the bar wouldn't be necessarily hopeless drunks. Maybe.

I'd seen half a dozen horses tied up outside, and that was how many men were leaning on the hardwood bar that ran along the right-hand wall. They weren't all together, though. Four men stood at the nearer end of the bar, while the other two were down at the far end. In addition, two more men sat at one of the tables scattered to the left of the entrance. One of them had dealt himself a hand of solitaire, while the other was reading a newspaper and nursing a beer.

That was everybody in the room except for a sleepy-looking bartender with a soup-strainer mustache, an unruly thatch of brown hair, and big enough bags under his eyes to stuff a cat into.

The four men closest to me were sharing a bottle of rotgut, passing it back and forth to fill their glasses and then tossing back the drinks. From the loud, slurred sound of their voices, they had been at it for a while. I was pretty sure that wasn't their first bottle of the day.

They were young and dressed like cowboys and might have been good at the job for all I know. But they looked and sounded like troublemakers, too. That was something I knew pretty well. Hell, I'd been one for most of my life. If I was really going to try to become a respectable rancher, I didn't need a bunch of hell-raisers around me.

So I walked on past them toward the two men at the end of the bar.

They were young, too, but a lot quieter and more subdued than the other bunch. One was big, but round and soft-looking at the same time. He had a moon face under a tipped-back hat with a high, round crown. His partner was a short redhead with an innocent, freckled face. Neither of them looked like they had much experience with cows, but if they were willing to work, that shouldn't matter. Santiago knew what he was doing, and they could learn from him.

They glanced at me when I stepped up to the bar. I gave them a nod and a smile and said, "Howdy, fellas."

"How're you doin', mister?" the fat one asked. He reminded me of a big, friendly puppy.

"Why, just fine, son," I told him. "How about you?"

"All right, I guess," he answered with a shrug.

"Something wrong?" I asked. I could see worry lurking in his pale blue eyes.

"No, not really," he said. "It's just that, you see, me and my friend here, we're sort of low on funds."

"Well, shoot, I'd be glad to buy you a drink," I offered.

Without a second's hesitation, he shook his head.

"No, sir," he said. "We ain't beggars. We don't look for charity, and we don't take it."

"Buyin' a man a drink ain't what I call charity. It's just bein' friendly."

"Well, in that case . . ."

I signaled to the bartender, and when he ambled down to us I told him, "Bring these boys another round."

He filled up beer mugs and slid them across the hardwood. The two youngsters drank thirstily, but not like they were desperate for it.

"We're obliged to you, mister," the redhead said.

"We sure are," the fat one added. "My name's Bert, by the way. My pard's Vince."

"Glad to make your acquaintance," I told them. "I'm Jim Strickland." I waited a couple of seconds, then asked, "You fellas wouldn't happen to be lookin' for work, would you?"

I could tell by the way their eyes lit up that they were. I liked the way they looked even more eager for a job than they were for a drink, too.

Before either of them could answer me, though, one of the men at the other end of the bar called out, "If you're lookin' for men to ride for you, mister, you shouldn't be askin' those two. They're nothin' but wet-behind-the-ears calves! You should hire yourself some real men, like us."

I ignored him and said to Bert and Vince, "I need a couple of hombres who ain't afraid of a little hard work—"

"Didn't you hear me, mister?" the man at the end of the bar said. "I told you, those two are worthless. Nothin' but a couple of dime-novel cowboys!"

That brought raucous laughs from the hombre's companions. I kept my back toward them and held my temper, although it wasn't easy. I don't like being interrupted and interfered with.

Bert said, "It's true we could sure use jobs, Mr. Strickland, but I reckon that fella's right. We don't know much about cowboying. Fact of the matter is, we've, uh, never really been ranch hands."

"What have you done?"

"We worked at the train station in the county seat. Vince's pa got us the job. He works for the railroad."

"Well, what did you do there?"

With a note of bitterness in his voice, Vince said, "You're lookin' at a couple of broom-pushers, Mr. Strickland."

"Honest work's nothin' to be ashamed of," I said, hardly believing that I was hearing such words come out of my mouth. Lord, how times had changed! I went on, "But how come you're up here in Largo?"

Bert said, "We thought it was time to move on. We wanted to do somethin' different, somethin' exciting—"

A hand fell on my shoulder, and a harsh voice said, "I was talkin' to you, mister, and I don't like bein' ignored."

Old habits are hard to break, and a man who says he can control his instincts all the time is a liar. So when that liquored-up young hellion grabbed me, I didn't really think about it. I just did what came natural to me.

I turned around and busted him in the snoot.

CHAPTER 15

He probably wasn't expecting an older fella like me to move quite as fast as I did. The punch landed clean. Blood spurted and his nose flattened with a crunch under my knuckles. The impact, along with the pain that must have exploded through his head, sent him reeling back toward his friends. He stumbled and probably would have fallen if one of them hadn't grabbed him.

Panting, gasping, he stared at me with wide eyes for a second while he got his feet back under him, and then he howled, "Get that son of a bitch!"

The words weren't quite that clear because his nose was broken, after all, but his pards didn't have any trouble understanding them. They charged toward me, yelling curses, while the bartender yelled at all of us, telling us to take it outside.

That wasn't likely to happen.

Looking back on it now, throwing that punch was probably a dumb thing to do. I was outnumbered four to one. Of course, the four cowboys were drunk, which meant they might not be able to fight as well as if they'd been sober, but still, four to one was bad odds.

But suddenly it was four to three, as Bert and Vince stepped up beside me, and I have to admit, the possibility that they would might have been in the back of my head when I started the ruckus. I was going to be mighty interested to see how the two of them stood up to trouble. The fact that they were siding me when they barely knew me already told me something.

The fella I had hit led the charge. Blood from his busted nose smeared the lower half of his face. He swung a wild, roundhouse right at my head. I ducked underneath it and buried my left fist in his belly. That made him bend forward and put his chin in good position for the right uppercut I lifted from my knees. His head went back so far it looked like his neck might break. His knees unhinged.

But when he fell, that created an opening for one of his friends. The man lunged at me and hit me in the chest. The blow made me take a step back. He was fast and got a punch in to my face before I could block it. That knocked me into Bert, who grabbed me and kept me from falling.

Vince waded into the man who'd just hit me, his arms flailing like windmills. Most of the punches went wild, but a couple of them connected.

I slapped a hand on the bar and pushed off, freeing Bert from the job of holding me up. With the broken-nosed gent now lying senseless on the floor, that left the odds even. I started slugging away at another of the hombres. Vince was still mixed up with his opponent, and Bert got into the fracas, too.

Since I was busy with my own man, who proved to be a pretty capable brawler, I didn't really have time to see how they were doing. I caught a glimpse from time to time, though, and I could tell that what Vince lacked in fighting skill, he was trying to make up for with enthusiasm. He threw more punches in a shorter amount of time than anybody I'd ever seen, and even though most of them missed, sheer luck dictated that some of them were going to land.

Bert, on the other hand, was slow as mud, and when he did manage to hit the man he was fighting, his punches didn't seem to pack much power despite his size. He was taking a lot of punishment. That big hat of his had gone flying off his head because he kept getting hit in the face.

My hat was gone, too, knocked off when I took a fist to the jaw that made stars erupt behind my eyes. The man I was tangling with was broad-shouldered and had a long reach. He could stand off where I'd have a hard time hitting him and pound on me all day. That wasn't what you'd call a recipe for success.

So I feinted a left to his head, and while he was watching it I kicked him in the balls. It was a tactic I'd used before, and while it wasn't exactly fair, I've always felt that once you were in a fight, the point was to win it, not to impress folks with how honorable you are.

He screamed and grabbed at himself and collapsed, and I kicked him in the head on the way down just to be sure he wouldn't get up and start plaguing me again. That gave me a chance to check on my newfound allies and see how they were doing.

Vince seemed to be holding his own. He was battling a tall, lanky cowboy, but his short stature allowed him to bore in and pepper the fella's midsection with punches. Once he was in there, he could still reach his opponent's jaw despite the height difference.

Bert was pinned up against the bar, though, and the man he was fighting pounded him mercilessly. Whenever the fella sunk a fist in Bert's belly, Bert bent over and tried to cover up. That left his head open, and the man smacked him over the ear time after time. I was about to step in and give Bert a hand when something suddenly seemed to change in him.

He let out a roar like a maddened grizzly and shrugged off a couple of punches to the head as he drove forward and wrapped his arms around the fella. His weight and the unexpected charge forced the cowboy backward. The man tripped and went down, landing on his back with Bert crashing down on top of him. I heard a sharp crack, like a twig snapping, and knew Bert had just broken one of the man's ribs.

As the man began to writhe on the floor and make a high-pitched, agonized wailing sound, I reached down and got hold of Bert's shirt collar.

"Come on, mad dog," I told him. "Get off of him. He ain't interested in fightin' anymore."

I couldn't have lifted Bert like that if he hadn't cooperated, but he was willing to get to his feet. He looked worried and upset.

"I didn't mean to hurt him," he said. "I swear I didn't. I just lost my head."

"I wouldn't worry about that too much, old son, because he was sure as hell tryin' to hurt you."

Vince had battered his man into submission. The guy huddled against the bar, hanging there by an elbow as blood streamed down his face. Vince had gone after him like one of those fierce little Chihuahua dogs that seems to think it can lick a critter ten times its own weight. Sometimes, like here, that's just what happened.

I put a hand on Vince's shoulder as he backed away from his beaten opponent. Unlikely as it might have seemed, the three of us had taken the four of them.

"Now, about those jobs—," I began.

The roar of a shot interrupted me.

I was wearing the Remington. I had it unleathered by the time I turned, but there was nothing to shoot at. The loudmouthed cowboy who had started the trouble, the one whose nose I'd busted, was sitting on the floor, slumped back against a table as he clutched his upper right arm. Blood welled between his fingers. A gun lay on the floor beside him.

Over at the table where the two older men sat, the one who'd been reading the newspaper had put it aside. He had a Colt in his hand instead, with the butt resting on top of the table. A thread of smoke curled from the weapon's muzzle.

It was obvious to me what had happened. I nodded to him and said, "I'm obliged to you, mister."

In a gravelly voice, he drawled, "I never did cotton to back-shooters. Young Wild West there figured he'd plug you while you weren't lookin', since he couldn't beat you any other way." He lifted the gun, pulled the hammer back a little, and blew the rest of the smoke out of the cylinder.

I grinned. It was just the sort of dramatic flourish I might have done myself in that situation. I sensed a kindred spirit.

"Dadgum it, now you're just showin' off," his solitaire-playing compadre said. "Shootin' the fella was fine, but you don't have to make a production of it."

The wounded man let out a groan. I turned to the one man who was still on his feet—barely—and said, "You're gonna have a hard time draggin' your friends out of here, son, but I suspect they could all use some medical attention." The ventilated one and the one with the busted rib needed a doctor, that was for sure.

The bartender said, "Never mind about that. I don't want this trash cluttering up my place, so I'll go get some help. There are always a few men playing dominoes in the Oddfellows' hall above the drugstore." As he came out from behind the bar he pointed at the hombre who'd fired the shot. "I'm counting on you to keep an eye on the place for me until I get back, Enoch."

"You can count on me, Dick."

The bartender, who was evidently also the proprietor, hustled out. The smaller of the two old-timers, who had dealt himself another hand of solitaire sometime during the ruckus, kept playing. His companion stood up, pouched his iron, and came over to me and the two youngsters who wanted to be cowboys.

"Enoch Cole," he introduced himself as he stuck out a hand. "The bashful, card-playin' one yonder is Gabe Wolverton."

"I ain't bashful," Gabe said. "I just don't see any point in flappin' my gums all the time like some people."

I shook hands with Enoch and introduced myself. He was a good ten years older than me, maybe more. His hair under a black Stetson was mostly silver and white with a few black strands still in it. He was tall and skinny enough, he looked like he wouldn't weigh a hundred pounds soaking wet, although I was sure he actually did weigh more than that. He had a loose-jointed way of moving, and I could tell by looking at him that he was made of rawhide, whang leather, and steel. I'd seen men like him in my time—I'd ridden with more than one of them—but most of them were dead and gone now, just like the times that had bred them.

Gabe was about the same age, shorter and stockier, with a close-cropped white beard.

I waved a hand at the two youngsters and said, "This is Bert and Vince. Don't reckon I know their last handles yet, but I'll have to since they're fixin' to hire on to ride for the Fishhook spread."

"I'm Vince Porter," he said. "Bert's last name is Chadwick."

Enoch shook hands with them and said, "Pleased to meet you boys. So you're gonna ride for the Fishhook, are you?"

"Well," Bert said as he and Vince looked at each other, "I guess so. Do you really want to hire us, Mr. Strickland?"

"I wouldn't have asked you if I didn't mean it," I assured them.

"But we don't have any experience as cowboys," Vince said. "Like that loudmouth said, you'd be better off hiring him and his friends."

I made a disgusted sound.

"Not hardly. I need fellas who ain't afraid of a little hard work, fellas who can be depended on. You can both ride, can't you?"

They nodded.

"Know how to handle a lasso?"

Bert said, "Well . . . not really."

"You can learn. A man who keeps his eyes open and is willin' to try can learn just about anything."

"We'll do our best, if you want us," Vince promised.

"That's all I can ask." I paused. "You wouldn't happen to know anybody who can cook, do you?"

From the table where he was putting a red seven on a black eight, Gabe said, "I can cook."

I cocked an eyebrow and asked, "Is that so?"

"Been told my biscuits are edible and my stew ain't bad," he said without looking up from his cards.

Enoch nodded and added, "He's tellin' the truth."

I looked at him and asked, "You wouldn't happen to be a top hand, would you?"

"I know which end of a horse is which."

"And both of you happen to be out of work?"

"We drifted this way figurin' that the spreads hereabouts would be hirin' for spring roundup soon," Enoch said. "We've been grub-line riders for so long we don't really know anything else."

"Well . . . according to my foreman, I do need one more man . . ."

"Then you're lucky. You got everybody you need right here in one room."

That *was* a stroke of luck. So much of one it almost made me suspicious. But I'd come to the saloon to hire the rest of my crew, and here they were. Along with Randy, Santiago, and the Gallardo brothers, that gave me seven punchers and a biscuit-shooter. It seemed like enough to get the job done.

The bartender came back in then with several loafers from the Oddfellows' hall. They dragged out the losers from the recent brawl and left them on the saloon's front porch. There was no doctor in Largo, so they'd have to wait until they were able to ride before seeking medical attention, but at least they wouldn't be cluttering up the saloon anymore.

"If you fellas want to, you can ride on out to the Fishhook with me in a little while and move into the bunkhouse," I told my newly hired crew. "I've got one more errand to run, but I'll be ready to leave in fifteen or twenty minutes."

"We'll be ready to go," Enoch said. Bert and Vince nodded. Gabe put a black four on a red five and never looked up, but at least he didn't object.

I stepped out of the saloon onto the porch, and as I did a buggy rolled past in the street. Something about it was familiar. I'd had that feeling before, when Sheriff Lester drove up to the ranch in his buggy, but this time it really was that traveling preacher at the reins, I realized, the one who had stopped by the Fishhook several weeks earlier. I recognized his sober black suit and his dour expression.

This time he wasn't alone, though. Sitting beside him was a young woman with flaming red hair, and she was so pretty she damn near took my breath away. She looked back at me as the buggy went by, and I would have sworn she started to smile. I couldn't be sure, though, because then the buggy was past and I couldn't see her anymore.

A couple of the men who had dragged the cowboys out of the saloon still lingered on the porch. I said to them, "Who was that?" and pointed my chin at the buggy as it rolled on up the street.

"You mean Reverend Hatfield?" one of them asked. "He's fixin' to build a church here. It'll be Largo's first one. If we could get a school, too, this place would be well on its way to being a real town."

I didn't care a whit about Largo's civic status. I said, "What about the girl with him?"

"Her? She's his daughter, I've heard."

The other man chuckled and said, "If she is, she must take after her ma. You wouldn't think a peach that ripe could come from such a dried-up little prune as the preacher, would you?"

His words struck me as disrespectful, but I suppressed the urge to snap at him. Reverend Hatfield's daughter didn't need me to defend her honor.

I had to give in to my curiosity, though, one more time.

"Do you know her name?" I asked.

"Daisy, I think. Yeah, that's it. Daisy Hatfield."

It suited her, I thought, as I started toward Tom Mulrooney's blacksmith shop to claim my buckboard team and settle up with Tom for keeping them in his stable for a few days.

But from time to time as I went about my business, I paused and said softly to myself, "Daisy Hatfield." The name stuck with me, and so did the memory of red hair, green eyes, and the creamiest skin I'd ever seen in all my borned days.

CHAPTER 16

That reaction wore off, of course. I wasn't a young man prone to getting all moon-eyed over every pretty girl who crossed my path. The fact of the matter was, I was almost old enough to be Daisy Hatfield's pa myself. When you got right down to it, I *was* old enough to be her pa. So I told myself to be sensible, and I went on about my real business, which was to make the Fishhook into a decent spread where I could live out the rest of my days in peace.

We made quite a procession as we headed back out to the ranch, me driving the buckboard with my saddle horse tied on behind, with the two young men and the two old men following on horseback. I wasn't sure the bunkhouse was big enough for all of them. Randy would have to move out there, too. He'd been staying in the house while he recuperated, but if he was going to be one of the crew I couldn't show him any favoritism. I was the boss, so I'd have the house to myself.

Well, except maybe for Scar. He could sleep at the foot of my bed, like the hounds did with the old Vikings I'd read about in a book one time. I like to think that I would have made a pretty good Viking.

The trail from town to the ranch was pretty easy to follow, but I pointed out various landmarks along the way to be sure the fellas wouldn't get lost the next time they had to make the trip. When I showed them the two little hills that looked like a camel's hump, Enoch said, "Looks more like a lady's bosoms to me."

"You wish," Gabe muttered.

"As a matter of fact—"

"And over yonder on the other side of the trail," I said, "there's a tree that was struck by lightning sometime in the past. You can see the scar down its side where the fire went."

"Let's see you compare that to some part of a lady's anatomy," Gabe challenged his friend.

"Well, now that you mention it—," Enoch began.

I interrupted him again by saying, "Then there's that rock spire with the two boulders at the base, and before you go tellin' us what it looks like, I reckon we can all guess, Enoch."

"I've found that I can recall things better if I relate 'em to things I'm familiar with," he said.

Gabe snorted.

The whole conversation made the two youngsters turn pink, or maybe it was just the sun. Anyway, we pushed on, and by late afternoon we reached the Fishhook.

Scar came out barking and snarling to greet us. Enoch said, "Lord, if that ain't the ugliest dog I ever seen."

"He was here before you were," I reminded him.

"But an ugly dog's got character, I always say." That quick comeback made me smile. Enoch went on, "There's a fella at the door with a rifle."

"That's Randy," I told them. "Randy McClellan. He's been laid up with a bullet crease he got helpin' me fight some outlaws." I'd been telling that story long enough I was almost starting to believe it. "He's part of the crew, too. Foreman's a vaquero by the name of Santiago Marquez. He and his two cousins Javier and Fernando ride with us, too. They have their own little rancho, though, so you won't have to share the bunkhouse with them."

"Good," Gabe said. "It don't look big enough for the rest of us as it is."

"You might be a little crowded. I figure you'll work it out, though."

I waved Randy out of the house and introduced him to the rest of the bunch. There was a certain wariness among them.

That didn't surprise me. They didn't really know each other yet. They would have to ride together for a while before they became an actual crew.

"I reckon the cook shack's out back?" Gabe asked.

"Yep. The supplies are in the house because I've been doin' all the cooking in there, but you can move anything out there you want to."

Gabe nodded and said, "Might as well get started rustlin' some supper now, I suppose. You boys are gonna have to get used to my cookin' sooner or later."

He went off to have a look at the cook shack, and when he was gone I said to Enoch, "You did tell me he's a good cook, didn't you? What he said there at the end didn't sound too encouragin'."

"Don't worry," Enoch said. "You won't be disappointed."

"We could've had ham for supper," Randy put in, "but that wild beast got it."

"Randy and Scar don't get along too well," I explained.

That wasn't the case with Bert and Scar. The youngster's face lit up when he saw the dog, and I was about to warn him to be careful when I saw him approaching Scar. Then I realized that Scar wasn't growling and snarling like he usually did whenever anybody got too close to him. I held my breath a little as Bert reached out to scratch those ragged ears, but Scar not only tolerated it, he looked like he enjoyed it.

"Well, I'll swan," I said. "I thought ol' Bert might get his hand bit off."

"He's got a way with animals," Vince said. "They all seem to like him, even when they don't like anybody else."

Bert got down on one knee and loved all over Scar. I just shook my head in amazement and went on into the house.

Enoch turned out to be right about Gabe's skills in the cook shack. My biscuits weren't exactly hard as rocks, but Gabe's were a lot better. The stew he whipped up out of not much was pretty good, too.

After we'd eaten that evening, Gabe announced, "I'm takin'

the buckboard back down to town tomorrow so I can stock up on some real food instead of the scraps you got around here. It takes plenty of provisions to feed a handful of hungry cowboys. Might need to slaughter a steer for beef, too."

"I reckon I can spare it," I told him. "Do what you need to do."

He nodded, and I knew that part of the operation was in good hands.

I hoped the rest of it would turn out to be, too.

CHAPTER 17

For the next two weeks, I worked as hard—maybe harder—than I ever had in my life, and the long days in the saddle were constant reminders that I wasn't as young as I used to be. Even though I was the boss, Santiago pushed me as much as he did the rest of the crew. I didn't mind, but sometimes my sore muscles did.

Since Santiago and the Gallardos had been working for Abner Tillotson for several years, I knew they had to be good hands. Enoch proved to be one, too, and even though he was considerably older than me the work didn't seem to bother him. He went from dawn to dusk and seemed as fresh when he stopped as when he started.

Randy, Bert, and Vince were the ones who really suffered starting out. I told Santiago to take it easy on Randy as much as he could because of that wound, but Santiago said, "He'll finish healing better if he gets out and moves around. The sun and the air will be good for him."

I figured he knew what he was talking about, and sure enough Randy's pallor started to go away and he seemed stronger. It helped, too, that he was eating better once Gabe took over the cooking.

I heard Santiago muttering to himself in Spanish a few times when he tried to work with Bert and Vince. They didn't know what they were doing, but like I had told them, they kept their eyes open and gave every job an honest effort. Sure, they let some cows get away from them now and then, they couldn't handle a branding iron very well, and their throws with a lasso usually fell short or went way wide of the mark. But gradually they began to get better at those chores and the other things Santiago told them to do.

We hazed in the cattle from the east and west pastures first, since that was the easiest job. Then Santiago turned our attention to the rugged hills to the south, and we spent long days rounding up the stock that had strayed into the canyons and valleys and brush-choked draws. It was hot, difficult work chousing those critters out of their hidey-holes and driving them down to the bedground we'd established along the creek. Even before we finished doing that, Santiago split the crew in half, four men working on the roundup while the other four got started branding all the new calves.

Once, near the end of the two weeks, Santiago and I paused and sat our saddles while we watched Randy, Vince, and Bert struggling to herd a jag of balky cattle. Grim as ever, Santiago said, "A crew of experienced men would have done this job in half the time, Señor Strickland."

"Next time, those boys will be experienced men," I pointed out. "Well, less inexperienced, anyway."

Santiago shrugged and said, "That is one way to look at it, I suppose."

"Might as well," I told him. "What matters to me is that we're getting it done."

"Do you wish me to cut out a trail herd?"

I scratched my jaw and frowned in thought. I'd had a good deal of cash with me when I came across Abner on that cold night back in December, but most of it had gone to getting the ranch operating properly and keeping it that way during the time since then. I needed to fill out my poke a little, and since I'd decided not to do that the way I used to, I said, "Yeah, I guess we'd better drive some of them down to the county seat and sell them. You'll pick out the best ones for that?"

"Sí, señor. We can have the herd ready in another three or four days."

"All right, then," I told him with a grin. "Have at it, amigo."

Gabe came to me that night and said, "If you're gonna have a cattle drive, you gotta have a chuck wagon, too."

"We're just driving to the railroad at the county seat," I said. "That'll take, what, three days?"

"If you want to go without eatin' for three days, that's up to you, but I ain't sure the rest of the bunch will go along with that idea."

"We can use the mules as pack animals and just carry our supplies with us that way."

Gabe drew himself up to his full height, which wasn't all that much, and glared at me.

"That ain't the way it's done," he declared.

"Well, what about the buckboard? Can you turn the buckboard into a chuck wagon?"

"Not a proper one," he answered without missing a lick. "But I suppose it'd be better than nothin'."

"I ain't trying to make things harder on you, Gabe," I told him. "But the truth of the matter is, I'm not all that flush right now. I can't afford to buy a chuck wagon. But maybe next time."

"All right," he said with grudging agreement. "Just nobody better complain about what I'm feedin' 'em, that's all I got to say."

By the time Santiago and the rest of the boys got the trail herd ready to go, Gabe had hammered together some cabinets and attached them to the back of the buckboard. The provisions and all the pots and pans would go in them. He had found a Dutch oven stored in the house, as well, and loaded it up.

I asked Santiago, "How come Señor Tillotson didn't have his own chuck wagon? He must have driven herds to market before."

"Sí, but the cook he always hired had his own wagon."

"Well, why didn't you tell me that before? I could've hired that fella."

Santiago shook his head and said, "No, you could not, señor. He passed away last fall."

"Oh. Yeah, that would make it kind of hard to hire him, wouldn't it?"

"Señor Wolverton will do all right. He plans to take along tortillas and beans and cabrito, so my cousins and I will eat well."

"Where's he gettin' the goat meat?"

"From my madre and papa. They raise the goats."

"Nobody said anything to me about this. I'm not sure I can afford it."

He shook his head and said, "Not to worry. They will extend credit."

So I was going to be in the hole before we even started on the drive. I wasn't sure I liked that, but there didn't seem to be anything I could do about it.

The day came when we were ready to start the drive. We had two hundred head in the herd. I'd been under the impression that was how many cattle were on the ranch, period, but when we did the final tally the number was closer to four hundred. I was far from rich, and once I covered expenses, the money I made from this drive wouldn't amount to all that much. But it was a start, I told myself. I had come to being an honest man a mite late in life, but so far I sort of enjoyed it.

I had been on cattle drives before, of course, but it had been a good many years since my last one. The roundup had been necessary in more ways than one. It had gotten me in shape for the chore of prodding a couple of hundred unwilling cattle into walking thirty miles to their doom . . . although they didn't have any clue about that last part, of course.

Most of the time none of us do.

CHAPTER 18

The drive went well. It was three days of hard work and eating dust, but I expected that. And when we reached the county seat and drove the cows into the stock pens along the railroad tracks, I felt a real sense of accomplishment.

I also got my first look at the county seat. Largo could almost pass for the sort of cowtown I'd known in the old days, except for the presence of a few automobiles and the telephone wires coming into town.

The county seat was different, though. It was a real city, with paved streets, cars and trucks everywhere, and electric lights. I had seen such places before, of course. I'd been to Europe, as well as New York, not to mention Denver, San Francisco, Dallas, San Antonio, places like that. So I wasn't some yokel who'd never been to the big city.

Still, it had been a while since I'd been around so many reminders of what the rest of the world was turning into. This went far beyond Morris Dobbs of Continental Oil and his Hupmobile.

The offices of the cattle company were in a four-story brick building. I took Santiago with me and left the rest of the crew at a café near the stock pens. Santiago introduced me to the buyer Abner had always dealt with, and I explained that I was the new owner of the Fishhook. We struck a deal pretty quickly, with me glancing at Santiago every now and then and getting tiny nods that let me know the terms were all right, and then the fella had a clerk draw up the paperwork and write me a check.

When we came out of the building, I looked at the piece of paper in my hand. Santiago said, "I will show you the bank where Señor Tillotson had his account."

It occurred to me that Abner's account would still be there. Dying like he had, he'd never had a chance to close it out. If Santiago found out about that, he was bound to wonder why Abner hadn't taken his money with him when he left.

"That's all right, I can take care of this part," I told him. "You go on back to the café and let the others know about the sale."

I thought I saw a flicker of something in Santiago's eyes, like maybe he thought I didn't trust him. He didn't fully trust me, though, because he said, "You would not cash the check and then, how would you say it, take off for the tall and uncut, would you, Señor Strickland?"

"Santiago!" I said, taking on like I was mortally offended. "You think I'd run out on you boys while I still owe you wages?"

"If a man is going to run away, that would be the time to do it," he said.

I shook my head and said, "I thought you knew me better than that. I owe you fellas more than wages. You're all my friends. I couldn't hope to make a go of the Fishhook without your help. I'd never run out on you."

"My apologies, Señor Strickland," he murmured.

"Just to prove that you don't have anything to worry about, you come on with me to the bank after all."

He shook his head.

"It will not be necessary. If we are going to work together, we should trust each other, no?"

"Well . . . you've got a point there. Just tell me where the bank is, and I'll take care of the rest."

"The First National, three blocks down this street on the left."

"All right. I'll see you back at the café in just a little while . . . *with* the money I owe you."

He nodded and said, "Sí."

I didn't figure shaming him like that would work, and sure enough it didn't. He trailed me to the bank, thinking that I didn't see him. But when it comes to skulking around, I had a lot more experience than he did and knew what to look for. At least he didn't come inside with me, though, and that was really all I was after. I was able to open a new account, deposit some of the money and get what I needed in cash, and never once mention Abner Tillotson's name.

When I got to the café I found all eight members of the crew sitting in a round booth at the back of the room. They made space for me. I took the envelope of cash out of my pocket and handed out the wages. As Santiago took his and muttered, "Gracias, señor," he had the decency to look a mite crestfallen. From here on out he would trust me.

"Well, the roundup's done, boys," I said with a certain amount of satisfaction. "What do you plan to do now?"

I admit, when I looked around that table at them, an idea tickled the back of my brain. There were things I could do with eight good hombres. Enoch and Gabe still had plenty of bark on 'em, despite their age, and I would have been willing to bet they had smelled some powdersmoke in their time. They were old enough they might have ridden some lonely trails, back before the turn of the century. Santiago and the Gallardo brothers were tough as nails, too, although they'd never given me any reason to think they might have strayed across the line laid down by the law. I knew Randy had been on the other side of that line, although by his own admission he hadn't been very good at it. That was only because he'd fallen in with some fools who didn't know what they were doing.

That just left Bert and Vince. The idea of making owlhoots out of them put a smile on my face. Some chores were too big even for me.

But six good men—seven counting me—there were jobs we could pull off, I thought. Money to be made without much risk, the sort of money that would make what I'd just been paid for those cows seem like chicken feed. And maybe even more important, it would be fun. Just like the old days, a band of boon compadres, a life full of deviltry and reckless excitement, the sort of things that had been like air and water to me for so long, the necessities of life . . .

I let those thoughts prance around in my brain for a minute or two, then put them aside. Those days were gone, I told myself. They weren't coming again. All I had to do to prove that was to step outside and see all the signs of progress and civilization around me.

Some things, once they were gone, you could never get them back. I just had to accept that.

They hadn't answered my question. Finally, Randy said, "We, uh, we sort of thought we'd keep on working for you, Mr. Strickland."

That took me by surprise. I said, "All of you?"

"Not my cousins and I," Santiago said. "We have our own rancho to look after. But any time you need extra hands, we will be glad to pitch in and help."

Enoch said, "The rest of us thought we might stick around, though. If that's all right with you, Jim."

I didn't know what to make of that. I said, "I hired you fellas to work the roundup. I might be able to keep a couple of you on to help around the ranch. It's a little big for one man to keep up with. Randy was hired first, so I reckon he's got first claim on one of the jobs."

"I'll take it," he said without hesitation. I knew he didn't have any family or anywhere else to go.

"And Gabe and me will work cheap," Enoch said. "Hell, at our age, a place to sleep and some grub is almost enough. We don't need much else. Ain't that right, Gabe?"

"I'm a little tired of driftin'," Gabe admitted. "Besides, if you have to go back to eatin' your own cookin', you're liable to starve to death."

I didn't think my cooking was that bad, but maybe he had a point. I might be able to stretch the ranch's income to cover all three hands.

But that left Bert and Vince, and Bert was giving me a look like a lost soul.

"We really don't want to go back to pushing brooms at the depot, Mr. Strickland," he said.

"Maybe you could find something better," I suggested. "You said Vince's pa works for the railroad."

"Yeah, but he's just a brakeman," Vince said. "He called in the only favor he had to get us those jobs the first time. He wouldn't be able to help us again."

"Well . . . well, dadgum it . . ."

That's always been my problem. I'm just too blasted soft-hearted. I couldn't bring myself to throw any of them to the wolves.

So I said, "All right. The five of you can all come back to the ranch with me. I warn you, though. There may be some lean times ahead of us."

"That's all right, Mr. Strickland," Bert said with a relieved grin. "We'll all work together to make the Fishhook the best spread west of San Antonio!"

How could you argue with optimism like that? I said, "Damn right we will, Bert."

"You know," Randy said, "I heard there's gonna be a dance in Largo tomorrow night. We all ought to go, to celebrate a successful roundup and cattle drive."

"Yeah," Bert agreed. "That sounds like a good idea. What do you think, Mr. Strickland?"

I looked around the table at them again and thought about how crazy my speculations of a few minutes earlier had been. Three green kids, two old-timers, and a trio of vaqueros . . .

Not exactly what you'd call a Wild Bunch.

But they were my friends, so I nodded and said, "Sure. We'll go to the dance."

CHAPTER 19

The three youngsters talked about the dance all the way back to the ranch. We didn't get there until well after dark. Enoch and Gabe and I weren't quite so enthusiastic about it. Dances are for young men. But I planned to go anyway because I knew I'd enjoy the music and the good fellowship. I might even take a turn or two around the floor with a gal in my arms, if there were any there who struck my fancy and would be willing to dance with a disreputable old cuss like me.

About three-fourths of the way back to the Fishhook, Santiago and his cousins bid the rest of us farewell when we reached a trail that angled off to the west. Their ranch lay in that direction, Santiago told me.

Before they left, Bert asked them, "Will you fellas be at the dance tomorrow night?"

"The dances in Largo are not for the likes of us, amigo," Santiago told him. "We have our own fiestas and dances."

"Oh. Well, I reckon that makes sense," Bert said, although he sounded like it really didn't. He was young and innocent enough that he hadn't learned yet about all the things in the world that don't make sense but just are, anyway.

When we reached the ranch, Scar came out of the barn to meet us. I had worried about leaving him there at the ranch alone, but there was water in the creek and he could find plenty of jackrabbits around there, as well. He barked, but he didn't growl this time. He even wagged his tail a time or two, like he was glad to see us.

The next day the fellas were almost too excited about the dance to tend to their chores, but with Santiago gone, Enoch sort of took over the role of foreman and made sure that all the essential jobs got done. Around mid-afternoon, though, he told them they ought to start getting ready for the dance.

"I reckon it'll take a while for scoundrels like you to make yourselves presentable enough to be around civilized folks," he said.

Randy, Bert, and Vince didn't waste any time. They headed for the creek to wash off all the trail dust from the past week.

I cleaned up as well. Washed, shaved, slicked down my hair, splashed some bay rum on my face. I remembered that photograph my pards and I had had made in Fort Worth more than a dozen years earlier. That day I'd been freshly barbered, dressed in a fancy suit, and had a derby hat on my head. I was a real dandy, let me tell you.

I couldn't make myself look that spiffy for the dance because I didn't have any duds like that anymore, but I put on my best jeans and a clean white shirt with pearl snaps instead of buttons. I brushed my hat to get all the dust off it and polished up my boots. I thought I looked presentable enough. When I asked Scar for his opinion, though, he just looked at me. The lesson being, never ask a dog for fashion advice, I suppose.

When it came time to leave, I was a little surprised to see that Enoch and Gabe had cleaned up, too. I said, "I thought you fellas weren't goin'."

"We never said that," Enoch insisted. "Just that dances are more for the young folks than for old pelicans like us. We like listenin' to the music, though."

"Speak for yourself," Gabe said. "If there are any comely widow women there, I intend to dance with 'em."

The sun was still well up in the sky when we mounted up for the ride. We would get to Largo about dusk, I thought, and that was when the dance was supposed to get underway.

Randy, Bert, and Vince chattered the whole time we were riding. For the first few days when they started working together, Randy had been a little standoffish from the other two, probably because Bert and Vince had been friends for a long time. Gradually, though, and mostly because Bert was so naturally friendly, Randy had been drawn into their circle, so now they were a trio instead of a duo.

I followed behind with Enoch and Gabe, who weren't near as talkative. That had something to do with their ages. The old-time Westerners didn't believe in flapping their gums without a good reason. They considered such behavior a waste of time and energy. The tight-lipped cowboy you see in the moving pictures, there was a lot of truth to that character, not just Hollywood hokum.

As we got closer to town, I saw columns of dust rising here and there, all of them converging on Largo. I knew they came from wagons and groups of riders, all of them bound for town. A dance like this would draw nearly every able-bodied person for miles around. The population of Largo tonight would be four or five times what it usually was, maybe even more.

I even spotted a couple of Model A and Model T automobiles bouncing and jouncing over the rough ground when we were nearly to town.

The dance was being held in the schoolhouse. When we arrived, the open area around the big, whitewashed building was already full of parked wagons and automobiles. Dozens of saddle horses were tied to anything sturdy enough to hold them. Kids ran here and there among the wagons, shouting and laughing, while men shook hands and women hugged each other. Ranch families might see their friends only a few times each year, so they took advantage of those opportunities to visit.

"It's a big crowd," Randy said while we were dismounting. I heard a slight edge of nervousness in his voice and knew what he was thinking. He hadn't forgotten that he'd taken part in that attempted train robbery, and even though the likelihood of him being recognized was very small, I could tell he was still worried about it.

I clapped a hand on his shoulder and said quietly, "Nothing wrong with big crowds. They're easier to blend into."

He gave me a narrow-eyed look.

"You sound like you're speaking from experience, Mr. Strickland."

"Just common sense," I said. "You don't have anything to worry about, son, except maybe finding some pretty gals to dance with you."

We joined the people who were streaming inside. The school's benches, chairs, and desks had all been shoved over to the wall or carried outside to make room for folks to move around. Streamers and paper lanterns were hung here and there for decoration. Crates had been brought in and placed at the front of the room so the musicians could stand on them. A table with a punch bowl and cups on it sat to one side. On the other side of the room was another table, this one loaded down with pies and cakes that would be raffled off later.

"Think I'll go have a look at them pies," Enoch drawled. "I might buy a chance on one of 'em. I got a hankerin' for a good apple pie."

"Nothin' wrong with the pies I make," Gabe said.

"No man can bake a pie as good as a woman."

Gabe snorted and said, "That's just plumb loco! I'll stack my pies up against any you'll find here."

"Why didn't you bake one and bring it with you, then?"

"Because I didn't think of it, that's why! Anyway, there wouldn't have been time."

"Yeah, sure," Enoch said. The two of them went off sniping at each other.

Two men with guitars, one with a fiddle, and one with a big bass fiddle carried their instruments to the front of the room near the crates and started tuning up. That wasn't enough to make all the folks in the room hush, but they would once the men actually began to play.

I looked around the room and saw a number of girls and young women congregating along the wall where the table with the punch bowl sat. They cast sly looks at every man who came through the door.

I nudged Randy with an elbow and said to him and Bert and Vince, "Looks like there's the bunch of fillies you'll have to choose from tonight."

"Not me," Bert said with a nervous swallow. "I, uh, I don't actually . . . dance."

"He's got two left feet," Vince said, "and that's being generous. They're more like two leftover feet, but I don't know what they were left over from."

"Now don't be like that," I told him. "I'm sure Bert can dance just fine."

Bert shook his head and said, "No, Vince is right, Mr. Strickland. I don't dare try to dance. If I did, it might cause a real calamity."

"Oh, I doubt that. You just need to seize your chances, Bert, and devil take the hindmost." I laughed. "Besides, life'd be mighty boring without a few calamities now and then."

I wasn't sure he'd take my advice, but at least he seemed to be thinking about it.

I heard my name being called—the name I was using in those days, anyway—and looked around to see Clyde Farnum waving to me. When I went over to him, he said, "I thought maybe you and your hands would come in for the dance, Jim."

"Are you still gettin' that gasoline pump for the store, Clyde?" I asked him.

"The Continental Oil Company is gonna put it in next week," he replied, beaming with pride. "It'll be the only one in the northern half of the county."

"Well, I wish you luck with it, even though I don't think I'll be drivin' an automobile and needin' to buy gasoline anytime soon."

"You never know. You might decide to up and join the twentieth century one of these days."

"Only when they make me," I said.

Not long after that, one of the guitar players got up on a crate and hollered for everybody's attention. When the room had quieted down, he said in a loud voice, "Welcome to the dance, folks. We hope all of you enjoy yourselves, and just as a reminder, there's a hat on the floor up here, so if any of you want to throw a nickel or a dime in it, me and the boys will appreciate it. Now, everybody on your best behavior—that means no fightin', no spittin', and no drinkin' in the schoolhouse—and here we go!"

The other three musicians had climbed up on their crates while he was talking, and when he finished they broke into a lively tune that he joined in on with his guitar, his fingers moving so fast they were almost a blur as he wielded that pick. Men and women paired off and started whirling around the floor, and those who weren't dancing drew off to the sides to give them room and clapped along with the music.

I had enjoyed my trips to Largo in the past, I suppose, but now for the first time, I really felt like part of the community as I stood there clapping and enjoying the sight of all those people dancing. Randy and Vince had found partners, but Bert stood alone near the punch bowl, watching. Maybe he would come around later, I told myself. Sometimes it just takes a while for a fella to work up his courage, especially when he's doing something as scary as asking a girl to dance.

I really wasn't paying attention to anything except what was going on out on the dance floor, so I didn't notice right away when someone came up beside me. In the old days I never would have let anyone get that close to me without being aware of it, but I wasn't expecting trouble at a dance.

And it wasn't trouble I got, either, at least not the kind that had plagued me off and on for most of my life. But maybe it was another kind.

The redheaded, green-eyed, milky-skinned kind of trouble.

CHAPTER 20

"It looks like they're having a lot of fun, doesn't it?"

The clear, almost musical voice made me look over quickly. Daisy Hatfield stood beside me, lightly clapping her hands together in time with the music. Her lips were curved in a smile as she watched the dancers. She wasn't looking at me, but I felt the unexpected power of her presence anyway.

"Uh, yeah, I reckon," I said. That was me, slick as calf slobber. I was way too old to have a pretty girl affect me that much, but there you go. Some things you don't get over completely no matter how old you are.

"Why aren't you dancing, Mr. Strickland?" she asked.

"I'll get around to it before the night's over, I expect. For now I'm enjoyin' watching these other folks have fun."

"It's more fun if you get right in there and do it yourself."

When she said that she turned her head and looked at me, and damned if that preacher's daughter didn't look downright sinful.

It took me a second to realize that she knew my name. That meant she must have asked somebody about me. Since that was the case, I thought turnabout was fair play. I said, "I'm surprised to see you here, Miss Hatfield. I figured your father didn't hold with dancing. Most preachers don't."

"Most Baptist preachers don't," she said. "My father is a Methodist."

"Ah. A sprinkler, not a dunker."

"That's right. But . . . well, to tell the truth, he doesn't know I'm here. He probably wouldn't approve. But if he devotes any thought to the matter at all, he probably thinks I'm in my room at the boardinghouse, studying the Bible."

"That sounds like fun, too, I suppose."

"Not nearly as much as dancing. Would you think I was being terribly forward if I asked you to dance, Mr. Strickland?"

"Not at all," I told her. "But wouldn't you rather dance with somebody closer to your own age?"

"You don't look all that much older than me."

I couldn't help but laugh.

"Darlin', you just don't know," I said without thinking. But if being called darlin' bothered her, I sure couldn't tell it.

She took my arm and said, "If you're not too old to get around the floor, that's all I care about. Come on."

One thing I've learned over the years is that if a pretty girl asks you to do something you want to do anyway, you'd be a damned fool not to oblige her. So we walked out on the dance floor, and I put my arm around her waist and took hold of her other hand, and off we went.

It wasn't like we were snuggled up together or anything. We kept a respectable distance between us at all times. But I was touching her enough to feel the supple warmth of her body, and as we looked in each other's eyes I sensed the current flowing between us. There's no fool like an old fool, the saying goes, and maybe that's what I was, but as I danced with Daisy Hatfield I forgot about the difference in our ages. She was a woman and I was a man, and I was mighty glad of it.

The song ended. I didn't notice at first, or maybe I just didn't want to notice. I didn't want to let go of Daisy, that's for sure. But I had to when she stepped back to applaud. I hoped those musicians wouldn't waste any time before launching into another tune.

Before they did, a man I didn't know stepped up to Daisy and asked, "May I have this dance, miss?"

"I'm sorry," she told him. "I've already promised it to Mr. Strickland here."

He glanced at me and frowned, like he wanted to ask her why she was dancing with somebody like me. He didn't do it, though, and I was glad because I might have taken offense if he had. Instead he shrugged and said, "Maybe the next one."

"I'm afraid not," she said. "You see, all my dances tonight are promised to Mr. Strickland."

A bow scraped on fiddle strings before the young man could say anything, and I told him, "Sorry, son, you'll have to excuse us now. We've got some dancin' to do."

As we started up again, Daisy said, "I'm sorry if I spoke out of turn, Mr. Strickland. I certainly understand if you don't want to dance every dance with me tonight. I wouldn't dream of monopolizing your time."

"Don't you worry about that," I told her.

"I just . . . well, it sounds bad, especially since Father's going to build a church here and I'll be seeing these people all the time, but I just don't feel any real connection with most of them. Do you know what I mean? They live their lives and there's no . . . no color, no adventure. But I look at you and I see something totally different. I see a man who's been places and done things."

That was true enough, I thought. They hadn't all been good places or good things, but except for a few short stretches here and there, my life had been pretty well packed. Not with regrets, either.

But that wasn't the sort of man I was trying to be now. I said, "I wouldn't dream of arguin' with you, Miss Hatfield, but you've got me wrong. I'm just a rancher, plain and simple."

She looked at me and slowly shook her head.

"No," she said, "I don't think there's anything plain and simple about you, Mr. Strickland."

"You know . . . if we're going to be dancing together all evenin', maybe you'd better call me Jim."

"I'd like that, but only if you call me Daisy."

"Then I reckon we've got a deal . . . Daisy."

I didn't really expect her to dance every dance with me. She'd get tired of me, probably sooner rather than later. But for the time being I planned to enjoy whirling around that dance floor with such a pretty gal in my arms that all the other fellas were shooting envious glances my way.

The musicians played four or five more songs before calling a halt. The one who did the talking said, "We'll be back in a spell, folks. Why don't y'all get some punch and take a gander at those pies and cakes the ladies'll be rafflin' off in a little while? Remember, all the proceeds will go to building a church here in Largo."

I looked at Daisy in surprise.

"This dance is to fund the church?" I asked her.

"That's right," she said.

"But your pa's not here."

"No. He'll take the money, but that doesn't mean he cares to associate himself with the way it's being raised."

That seemed more than a little hypocritical to me. But I didn't have much room to talk, seeing as how I was passing myself off as an honest, respectable cattleman. That's what I was trying to become, you understand, but it sure wasn't what I'd been in the past.

While I was dancing with Daisy I hadn't really paid any attention to the fellas who'd come to town with me, except for catching a glimpse now and then of Randy or Vince twirling around with one of the local girls. I looked around and saw the two of them now, eyeing the baked goods along with Enoch and Gabe. I didn't see Bert anywhere, though.

But I didn't worry about him. He was around somewhere. Instead I said to Daisy, "Can I fetch you some punch?"

"That would be very nice, thank you," she said with a smile.

I went over to the table and waited for my turn. If some of my old pards could see me now, I thought. There was one of them in particular, my closest friend for a lot of years, who would hooraw me mercilessly if he had seen me fixin' to fetch punch for a gal at a small-town dance. But he was gone, I reminded myself, and no matter how much I missed him sometimes, time keeps rolling along and things change.

I was just reaching for a cup when a young fella behind me said excitedly to a friend, "You better forget about the punch and come with me. There's gonna be trouble outside. Jed Flannery's got a guy cornered and is threatenin' to hand him a beatin'. But if you ask me, Flannery's tryin' to goad him into a real fight. A gunfight."

The friend asked, "Who's Flannery after now?"

"One of those guys who used to work at the train station down in the county seat. I think his name is Chadwick or something like that. If he draws against Flannery we can find out for sure when we read his name in the obituaries!"

CHAPTER 21

It took a second, but only that, for what the man had said to penetrate my brain. When it did, my eyes widened with shock. He had to be talking about Bert. I didn't know who Jed Flannery was, but Bert didn't need to be getting in a gunfight with anybody. I didn't think Bert even owned a gun. He sure hadn't brought one with him to the dance.

But that wouldn't stop this fella Flannery, who probably had friends with him. One of them would be glad to loan Bert a gun. I had seen that little trick pulled many times in the past, and it always put a burr under my saddle. Men who had no business matching their draw against someone else's were practically forced into it, and they nearly always wound up dead.

The man I'd overheard had said the trouble was outside. I wheeled away from the table and headed for the door as fast as my legs would carry me without running. The room was crowded, and I had to rein in the urge to knock some of the people out of my way. I weaved around them instead, hoping that the delay wouldn't prove fatal to Bert.

I wasn't the only one headed for the door. Quite a few young men were going in that direction as well. Word of the impending fight must have spread through the schoolhouse. Fistfights were common at dances like this. They were sort of an added attraction, I guess you could say. But gunfights were rare, especially since the turn of the century. This was supposed to be a new, modern, more enlightened era.

But some men still craved the smell of powdersmoke. I supposed they always would.

There was a momentary bottleneck at the door because of the men trying to get outside in time to see the action. I wasn't going to wait any longer, because I heard yelling outside and knew things had to be coming to a head. I shouldered a couple of men aside. They cursed and started to turn toward me, but the expression on my face made them step back instead and let me past.

Light spilled through the schoolhouse's open door and spread over the ground in front of the building. A couple of cottonwoods stood off to one side, giving shade to the area where the kids played when they had recess. Now a couple dozen men crowded under those trees, forming a rough half-circle. Bert was in that circle, with his back pressed up against one of the trees as if he'd retreated that far and couldn't go any farther.

I guessed that the man who stood in front of him, cussing and haranguing him, was Jed Flannery. Three other men were with him, standing back a little to let Flannery run the show.

He spit vile names at Bert, the sort of things that no man with any pride could take. Bert looked scared, no doubt about that, but a red flush of anger was spreading slowly over his face as well. Even as mild-mannered as he was, he would strike back soon if this kept up.

I recognized a couple of the other men with Flannery. One of them had his right arm in a sling. He was the drunken loudmouth from the saloon who Enoch had shot when he tried to plug me in the back. One of his buddies from that fight was with him. I didn't know the third man, but I figured he had to be part of Flannery's bunch, too.

I'd never seen Jed Flannery before, but I knew the type. He was just handsome enough that gals would like him, and he knew it well enough that the knowledge put an arrogant smirk on his face. He wore a holstered gun, which set him apart from the other men at the dance. Most of them weren't armed. I wasn't, although my Winchester was in the saddle boot on my horse.

It was easy enough to figure out what had happened. The

man Enoch had wounded knew there was a good chance the Fishhook crew would be here at the dance tonight. So he had shown up looking for revenge, bringing with him a friend of his who fancied himself a gunman. This fella Flannery had jumped on the first one of us to cross their path, who happened to be Bert.

No lawman was going to step in and put a stop to this, I thought. Largo had a constable, but Clyde Farnum had told me that he didn't amount to much. Sheriff Lester or one of his deputies came up this way every so often, but I hadn't seen any of them here tonight. It would have been just a fluke if one of them was on hand.

That left it up to Bert's friends to keep him from getting hurt. Which in this case meant me. I was about to step forward, raise my voice, and tell Flannery to leave Bert alone when a quiet voice spoke beside me.

"You ain't in this alone, boss."

I looked over and saw that Enoch had followed me out of the schoolhouse. He wasn't by himself, either. Gabe was with him, and right behind the two of them were Vince and Randy, both looking scared but determined.

"I'm the one who plugged that varmint," Enoch went on. "His fight's with me, not the rest of y'all."

"I don't imagine he sees it that way," I said. "I think they've got it in for all of us. So we'll just meet 'em all at once."

"I like the sound of that," Gabe said. "Come on."

His hands were clenched into fists as he moved into the crowd surrounding Bert and his tormentors. Enoch was on one side of him, I was on the other, and Vince and Randy were right behind us. People got out of our way as we strode forward.

Just before we reached the open area under the trees, I heard the unmistakable sound of a fist hitting flesh. Biting back a curse, I shoved ahead and emerged from the crowd in time to see Flannery draw back his arm to strike another blow. The two able-bodied men with him had hold of Bert, each of them holding an arm. The wounded hombre stood to the side, watching with an eager expression on his cruel features.

"If I can't make you fight like a man," Flannery was saying, "I'll whip you like a dog."

"I'd say that you remind me of a dog, all right," I spoke up, "but I like dogs, and that'd be insulting 'em. I reckon I'd rather compare you to a skunk."

My voice rang loud and clear as I said that, and the hubbub from the crowd died down immediately. They realized that a challenge had been thrown out, a challenge that was likely to be answered with violence, maybe even gunplay. I got the sense that everybody was holding their breath, waiting to see what was going to happen.

Slowly, Flannery lowered his arm and turned to look at me. He was older than I thought at first, probably close to forty. For a gunman to live to that age meant that he was smart, quick on the draw, or more likely both. A dangerous man, to be sure. But I had dealt myself in as soon as I opened my mouth, and there was nothing to do now but play out the hand.

"Did you say something to me, mister?" Flannery asked with a sneer.

"I did." I glanced past him and saw blood on Bert's mouth where Flannery had hit him. Fury welled up inside me.

I've always been the sort to live and let live, at least I like to think so, but sometimes when I see something unjust, a black tide of hate washes through me. That's what happened then, and I didn't even think about the fact that Flannery had a gun on his hip and I didn't as I went on, "I said that you're not good enough to be called a dog. You're a lowdown skunk and you're stinking up the place. Now let go of that boy and take your stench on out of here so decent folks can go back to havin' a good time."

I've been accused of being fond of the sound of my own voice, and I suppose there's some truth to that charge. But at that moment I wasn't really thinking about such things. I was just good and mad.

From the corner of my eye I saw Bert swallow hard. Flannery's smirk just got more arrogant as he said, "You talk mighty big. You figure on backing up what your big mouth says, mister?"

"He'll back it up," Enoch said, "and he won't have to do it alone, neither."

"That's right," Gabe added. Randy and Vince didn't say anything, but I could sense they were right there with me.

The man in the sling said, "That one, the tall, skinny bastard, he's the one who shot me when I wasn't lookin', Jed. Watch out for him."

"Nobody's shootin' tonight," Enoch said. He held his hands out at his side. "I ain't packin' an iron. Came to town to dance, not shoot."

"That was your mistake, old man," Flannery said.

I saw the little shift in his muscles and the tiny flick of his eyes. When you put yourself in tight spots on purpose, year after year, you learn to pick up those warning signs or else you don't survive. I knew Flannery was about to make his move as soon as he did.

So I made mine first.

I reached out with my left hand, caught hold of his shirt, and jerked him toward me. My right fist came up at the same time and cracked against his jaw, slewing his head around. He was fumbling at his gun, trying to get it out but not having much luck because he was stunned by my punch. I didn't give him time to recover. I got hold of his shirt with both hands, and as his head came back around toward me, I lowered my head and butted him in the face. A hard shove sent him staggering into one of the men who'd been holding Bert. Their feet got tangled up and both of them went down.

I bent over and plucked Flannery's gun from its holster. The crowd started to back off hurriedly. They had come out here to watch a fracas, but even the ones who had thought there might be gunplay were having second thoughts now about being this close when the bullets started to fly.

The man with the wounded arm was still on his feet, as was the other fella who'd been holding Bert while Flannery punched him. Neither of them looked like they wanted any part of this anymore, but I grabbed the one in the sling before he could crawfish out of there.

"You started all this, just like you started that trouble in the saloon," I said as I rammed the gun muzzle under his chin. "You brought your gunslingin' friend here hopin' somebody would die tonight, didn't you?"

He couldn't respond, of course. With that gun at his throat he couldn't talk or move his head.

"Well, somebody might," I went on. "All I'd have to do is pull this trigger. And I'm thinkin' mighty serious-like about it, too. If I let you go tonight, you'll just slink off and sull up somewhere like a possum until you've built up enough courage to come after me and my friends again. Seems to me the simplest thing to do would be to just go ahead and kill you right here and now and put an end to it. I know I'm sick of seein' your ugly face."

He looked like he wanted to talk, so I pulled the gun away a little.

"You got something to say?" I demanded.

"I . . . I'm sorry," he blubbered. I smelled a sharp stink coming from him and knew he was so scared he'd pissed his britches. "I w-won't ever bother you again, Mr. Strickland, I swear it!"

"So you know my name, do you? You been askin' around about me?"

"N-no, sir. I swear—"

I interrupted him by saying, "I don't want to listen to your damn promises. So I'll make you one. Here's what I'm gonna do. If I ever see you again, I'll kill you. No talking. I'll just kill you. If I see Flannery or any of your other friends, I'll kill them. And then I'll come find you. You know what I'll do then?"

"K-kill me?"

"That's right." I gave him a push and kept the gun pointed at him as he stumbled back a step. "Now get out of here, all of you."

From the ground, Flannery said, "I won't forget—"

I let him look down the barrel of the gun as I said, "You'd better. You'd better forget everything that happened here tonight, mister, otherwise you won't live much longer."

Flannery didn't say anything else, but he glared at me with snake-eyed hate as he climbed to his feet. The crowd had backed off so far now that the four men had plenty of room to walk away. I didn't lower the gun until they had swung up into their saddles and galloped off into the night.

"Mr. Strickland, you . . . you saved my life," Bert said.

That blackness was still roiling around inside me like a storm cloud, but I put a smile on my face and said, "Naw, they just wanted to push you around a little. I reckon the only ones they really wanted to kill were me and Enoch."

"They'd have had trouble doin' that," Enoch said. I noticed for the first time that he had a two-shot derringer in his hand.

"I thought you said you weren't armed."

"I stretched the truth a mite," he said as he tucked the derringer away at the small of his back, where his shirt covered it.

Vince took out his bandanna and handed it to Bert as he said, "Your mouth's bleeding, pard. Are you all right?"

"Yeah, I . . . I'm fine." Bert dabbed at the blood. "Let's just go on back inside."

"How'd they come to corner you out here?" Randy asked as the three of them started toward the schoolhouse.

"I just stepped out for some fresh air," Bert said. "It's a little warm in there."

He was right about that. A big crowd moving around fast gave off a lot of heat.

Enoch, Gabe, and I fell in behind the three of them. I still had the gun I had taken from Flannery in my hand. I tucked it behind my belt for the time being as I asked them, "How'd the two of you know there was trouble out here?"

"Saw you movin' fast toward the door," Enoch said. "We figured there had to be a good reason for it and came along to see what it was."

"Well, I'm glad you did."

Enoch chuckled and said, "I don't know why. Looked to me like you didn't need any help."

"But if I had needed it, you were there."

"We ride for the brand," Gabe said. "When a Fishhook man needs help, we'll be there."

It was good to see that some things about the West hadn't changed, even in a new century.

As we came up to the door, though, Enoch and Gabe suddenly shied away from me. I asked in surprise, "Where are you fellas goin'?"

"Somebody's waitin' for you," Enoch said.

He was right. Daisy Hatfield stood there just outside the door, and I couldn't tell from the look on her face whether she was appalled by what I'd done . . . or if it had stirred her emotions in some other way. She wore an intense expression, though.

"I thought you boys claimed to ride for the brand and stand by a pard in times of trouble," I said in a weak voice.

"Well, yeah," Gabe said, "but not where angry females are involved!"

CHAPTER 22

The crowd outside the schoolhouse had been mostly men, but some women had come out to watch the trouble, too, and it appeared that Daisy was one of them. As I came up to her, I said, "I'm sorry you had to see that, Miss Hatfield—"

"I'm not," she interrupted. "And I thought you were going to call me Daisy."

"Yeah, I reckon I forgot. But about that little ruckus—"

"I think it was thrilling the way you stood up for your friend. More people in this world need to stand up for what's right. That's the only way to keep the bad men from taking over."

"I can't argue with that," I said, even though in years past I had been what most of the people at the dance would consider a bad man.

"I should say not. Do you think those men are really gone, Jim?"

I glanced in the direction Jed Flannery and the other three men had disappeared when they rode off, and I said, "I sure hope so. I'd hate for anything else to interfere with our dancin'."

A smile lit up her face.

"Me, too," she said as she linked arms with me. "Come on. I think they're going to start playing again soon."

"I never got that punch for you."

"It can wait until next time," she said.

So it did. The musicians started up again, and we swung into a waltz. Daisy danced a little closer to me this time, although there was still nothing improper about it.

We danced until the next break. Daisy had to fend off several men who tried to cut in. She did it politely but firmly, and eventually they all gave up. She was insistent enough about having all the dances with me that I felt compelled to remind her of the difference in our ages.

"I really think you should be enjoyin' the company of fellas who ain't old enough to be your daddy," I told her.

"You're not that old," she said.

"You're wrong about that. I was born in 1867."

"You're not even fifty years old yet. My father is fifty-five. And he looks and acts older than that. You look and act like a man fifteen years younger than you really are, Jim."

"Even if I was fifteen years younger, I'd still be too old for you," I said.

She just laughed.

"You don't know much about women, do you?"

That sort of surprised me. I thought I was pretty well-versed in the ways of the fairer sex. I said, "I know plenty—"

"Women mature much faster than men. I feel like I've been grown up for decades now. That's why women prefer older men. Intelligent women do, anyway."

I didn't know what to say to that. So I didn't say anything. I just kept dancing with her. I'd made my feelings clear to her, I had warned her, if you will, so whatever happened from here on out, my conscience would be clear.

That's what I told myself, anyway. I wasn't sure if I believed it or not.

During one of the breaks during the evening, when I finally got around to fetching those cups of punch for Daisy and me, Randy, Vince, and Bert came over to the table where the punch bowl sat. Randy and Vince slapped Bert on the back, and Randy said, "You need to tell Bert how proud you are of him, Mr. Strickland. He's been dancing with some of the prettiest girls here."

"Well, is that right?" I said with a grin. "See how easy it is once you get over bein' scared, Bert?"

His mouth was a little swollen from the punch Flannery had landed on him, but that wasn't enough to keep a smile off of it. He said, "I never actually got over bein' scared, Mr. Strickland. But girls keep coming up to me wanting to dance. I don't understand it."

"He's too much of a gentleman to let them down, though, so he goes ahead and dances with 'em," Randy said.

Vince said, "Those gals heard that he was in a fight with Jed Flannery outside. That's all it took."

"Ah," I said. I put a hand on his shoulder. "Girls love a bad boy, Bert. You'd do well to remember that."

"I suppose so, sir," he said. "Nobody ever thought of me as a bad boy before!"

And they didn't have any reason to now, I thought, but I kept that to myself. Bert hadn't really done anything except get backed up against a tree and have his mouth walloped, but the girls at the dance didn't know that. All they knew was that he'd been mixed up in a fracas with a dangerous gunman. That was enough to make Bert intriguing to them. More power to him, as far as I was concerned.

I took the punch back to Daisy. She suggested that we go outside to drink it.

"I don't know if you'd want to do that," I said. "There are fellas out there passin' around flasks and chewin' tobacco. It's not really any place for a lady."

"I've seen plenty of unladylike behavior in my time," she said. "You forget, Jim, that a minister is sort of like a doctor. People usually don't show up on his doorstep unless they're in some sort of trouble and need help. Before my mother passed away she always tried to shield me from that part of my father's calling, and so does he to a certain extent, but I've still witnessed plenty of human misery."

"I'm not sure sippin' whiskey and chewin' Red Man qualifies

as human misery," I said, "but it is a mite warm in here. Some fresh air would be nice."

We carried our cups out of the schoolhouse and ambled over to the trees where the confrontation with Jed Flannery had happened earlier. Daisy sort of eased into the shadows, and I followed her. We stood there sipping punch while a night breeze stirred the branches over our heads. At that time of year those branches had started to put on leaves, and they seemed to whisper as they brushed against each other.

After a while it seemed like I ought to say something. Maybe I really am in love with the sound of my own voice. I began, "Other than that little scrape, it's been a fine evening—"

"Jim," Daisy said, "shut up."

She was in my arms before I could stop her . . . not that I would have tried very hard if I'd had advance warning. She must have been able to see pretty well in the dark, because her mouth came to mine like a shot. She tasted sweet from the punch, but that wasn't the only reason. Her kiss would have been sweet all by itself.

I was glad my cup was almost empty, because it slipped out of my fingers and fell to the ground. I put my arms around her waist and held her against me tight enough I could feel her heart beating fast. She slid her arms around my neck and held on to me like she planned on never letting me go.

Finally her lips moved away from mine, and the part of my brain that was still working forced me to say in a quiet, serious voice, "Daisy, this just isn't right—"

"Oh, hush up," she said. "I may be a preacher's daughter, but when it comes to things like this, women know a lot more about what's right and wrong than men do."

I wasn't so sure about that. A gal can get caught up in her emotions just like a fella can. Maybe they're more sensible overall, but they make plenty of mistakes, especially about who they fall in love with.

Still, Daisy obviously wasn't in the mood for a debate, and it wasn't like we were doing anything that improper, just a little sparkin' under a tree. So I kissed her again, and what with one thing and another we didn't go back inside the schoolhouse until we heard the fiddle player scraping his bow across the strings as another number started up.

The dance lasted pretty late, especially in a place where folks generally went to bed with the chickens. When it finally broke up, there were a lot of farewells shouted between the departing families. Boys and girls who had fallen in love that night held hands until the last possible second. Men who'd passed around the flask a little too much stumbled on their way. Automobiles started up with pops and rumbles as men worked the hand cranks on the front of them.

I walked out of the building with Daisy, and as we stepped out under the stars I said, "I hope to see you again the next time I come to town, Miss Hatfield."

"I hope so as well, Mr. Strickland," she said. "Do you know when that will be?"

"No, I don't," I admitted. "I've got a ranch to run, and I expect it'll take up most of my time. But my cook has to come to town for supplies now and then, and I might just come with him when he does."

"That would be nice. My father and I are staying at the boardinghouse, if you'd care to call on us."

I wasn't sure how the Reverend Franklin Hatfield would feel about his daughter having a suitor who was twice her age. I wasn't even sure how *I* felt about it. The idea still made guilty feelings stir around inside me. Daisy had a mind of her own, though, and she was determined. She had decided she wasn't going to dance with anybody but me tonight, and by Godfrey, that's the way it had turned out.

"We'll see," I said. "Your father's liable to need help gettin' that church built. I might make a donation."

"We all do the Lord's work in our own way, Mr. Strickland," she said, prim and proper as she could be.

But all I could think about as I looked at her was how sweet her mouth had tasted.

Later, as we were on our way to the ranch, Enoch eased his horse up alongside mine and said, "You spent a lot of time tonight with that preacher's gal, Jim."

"I did," I admitted.

Behind us, Gabe dozed in the saddle, clearly having mastered the old cowhand's art of sleeping and riding at the same time. Straggling behind him came the three youngsters. From time to time one of them let out a moan. They seemed to be taking turns. They had snuck outside too many times for a nip, and they would pay for that in the morning. A man can never welsh on the debt he owes to a bellyful of hooch.

"You sure it's a good idea gettin' mixed up with a girl as young as that one?" Enoch asked after a moment.

"I'm not mixed up with her. I just danced with her."

"And went outside with her. I ain't askin' what you did out there."

"And I ain't tellin'," I said. "But don't worry about it, Enoch. I didn't sully the young lady's honor, and I don't intend to."

"Good. I'd have a hard time ridin' for a man who'd take advantage of a girl."

That was an old-time Westerner for you. I had a hunch Enoch had burned plenty of powder in his time. Might have killed more men than some gunfighters who were a lot more notorious, and I was pretty sure he'd heard the owl hoot plenty of times. Don't ask me how I know, I just did. Like recognizes like, I guess you could say. But when it came to females, he was as stiff-necked and moral as Reverend Hatfield, maybe even more so.

"I won't let things get out of hand, Enoch," I promised. Hell, I didn't think it was a good idea for me to get mixed up with Daisy any more than he did. I'd figure out a way to divert her onto some other, more suitable path, I told myself.

But as things turned out, I didn't have much time to worry about that, because a few days later Sheriff Emil Lester came back to the Fishhook, and nothing was the same after that.

CHAPTER 23

The first time Sheriff Lester visited the ranch after I took it over, he drove up in a buggy. This time he came in an automobile, and we heard it coming before he even drove into sight. The thing rattled and belched and growled like some sort of monster crawling over the plains. I had seen and heard enough of the things to have a pretty good idea what it was, but anybody who hadn't might've been a little worried.

I saved my worrying until the car got close enough for me to recognize the man I saw through the glass window that stuck up in the front of it. The sheriff sat there sawing wildly back and forth with the wheel, making the automobile jerk from side to side. I had a hunch he hadn't driven much.

Gabe and I were the only ones at the house just then. Enoch and the boys were out helping the cattle drift back to the high pastures where they would graze for the summer. Randy, Vince, and Bert had been hungover and miserable the day after the dance, just as I expected them to be, but a day's hard work had driven most of the miseries out of them. They were almost back to normal now.

I thought about the dance when I saw the sheriff coming, and I wondered if the trouble with Jed Flannery and the other men was what had brought Lester out here. It didn't seem to me that I had done anything wrong by coming to Bert's aid, but come to think of it, I *had* threatened to kill four men. Sheriffs don't take kindly to such things, especially twentieth-century sheriffs like Lester. Maybe Flannery or one of the others had sworn out a complaint against me, embellishing the facts so that the story sounded like I was in the wrong.

There was only one way to find out, so I waited patiently on the gallery, where I'd been working on my saddle. Gabe came around the corner of the house from the cook shack and asked, "What's that god-awful racket? Sounds like a dragon from a story-book a-snortin' and a-bellerin'."

I pointed and said, "It's an automobile." Then I grinned. "You read storybooks, Gabe?"

He let out a snort of his own and ignored the question.

"I think I'd rather it was a dragon. I don't cotton to those con-traptions. There's such a thing as too much progress, if you ask me. Why, I remember hearin' about how they drove that Golden Spike and finished up the transcontinental railroad. I said it right then, I said to myself, this here is the beginnin' of the end of the frontier the way God intended it to be."

Seeing as how Gabe would have been all of ten or twelve years old when they drove the Golden Spike, I didn't think it was likely he'd had such profound, philosophical thoughts at the time. But if he wanted to remember it that way, it was no busi-ness of mine.

As the automobile carrying Sheriff Lester approached, I stood up, walked out in front of the house, and waited for him with my hands tucked in my hip pockets and my hat resting on the back of my head.

The car shook and rumbled to a stop, then belched a couple more times. Despite the dust that coated it, the black paint still had a new-looking sheen. Sheriff Lester climbed out, took his hat off, and used it to swat at his clothes.

"By God, that thing kicks up more dust than a whole herd of horses!" he said in a mixture of exasperation and disgust.

"Why'd you buy it then?" I asked.

"I didn't. The county bought it for me. The commissioners said it was time to bring law enforcement in the county up to date. If you ask me, they just wanted to be able to brag that the sheriff's department has an automobile." The sheriff brushed off his hat, too, and clapped it back on his head. "I've got business with one of your riders, Strickland."

That surprised me. As far as I knew, none of the hands had gotten into any trouble. Unless Flannery was claiming that Bert started the fight at the dance, which seemed pretty far-fetched to me. But if that was the case, I figured we could round up enough witnesses who would tell the sheriff the truth about what really happened. It would be an annoyance but nothing more.

Or maybe Randy's past had caught up to him after all, I thought. That was actually a pretty worrisome possibility. I was going to play my cards pretty close to the vest until I found out more about what Lester wanted.

"They're all out on the range," I told him. "Who is it you want to see?"

"Vince Porter. He does ride for you, doesn't he?"

"Yeah." That was another surprise. Vince was a little scrappier than Bert, but only because Bert was so gentle he'd never hurt anybody unless he was backed into it, like a cornered animal. "What do you want with Vince?"

"That's between him and me," Lester said. "Where can I find him?"

"Well, I don't know exactly. I reckon we can locate him, though. The boys are out movin' some stock to their summer graze."

"Point me in the right direction."

"Now hold on," I said. "You're not thinkin' about drivin' out there in that thing, are you?"

"Why not?"

"For one thing, the range may be too rugged for it, and for another, even if you can get there in it, the blamed noisy thing is liable to scare some beef right off my cows. How about I saddle up a couple of horses for us, and we both ride out to find Vince?"

"Thank God," Lester said, and he sounded like he meant it. "I was hoping you'd offer something like that, Strickland. I've got to drive that car all the way back to the county seat, and I'm not sure my butt can stand up to any extra miles in it!"

That declaration made me like Lester a little more. I was still pretty leery about his reasons for wanting to talk to Vince, though. If the boy was in trouble, I wanted to be there when Lester spilled the story, so I could lend Vince a hand if I needed to. I'd tackle the sheriff if I had to in order to give Vince a head start.

It didn't take long to slap saddles on a couple of horses. We rode along the creek and then turned south toward the hills. I gave some thought to leading Lester on a wild goose chase, but I decided to play it straight and take him to Vince. Finding out what was going on struck me as being more important than delaying the sheriff.

The thin haze of dust I saw rising between us and the hills gave me something to aim for. Within half an hour we came in sight of a good-size bunch of cows drifting along with Enoch and the three young punchers behind them.

Lester hadn't said much during the trip out here. I had tried a time or two to find out what he wanted with Vince, going about it subtle-like, you know, but the sheriff hadn't bit on any of the bait I threw out. Now he asked, "Which one is Porter?"

"That one there, with the red hair," I said, pointing at Vince. Since subtlety hadn't done any good, I asked Lester point blank, "Have you come out here to arrest him, Sheriff?"

"Arrest him?" Lester said, sounding genuinely surprised. "Why would I do that?"

"You tell me. As far as I know, the young fella hasn't done anything wrong."

"Well, as far as I know, he hasn't, either. If you must know, I came out here to deliver some news to him. Bad news. I could have sent a deputy, you know, but I thought it was important enough to take care of it myself."

"I sure don't like the sound of that."

"You're about to like it even less," Lester said as he heeled his horse into a faster gait. As I pulled my horse alongside his, he added, "But you're not the one it's meant for, so just back off and let me do my job, Strickland."

I didn't back off—I stayed right beside him as we rode up to the crew—but I didn't say anything else, either.

Not surprisingly, Enoch was the first one to know we were coming. It was hard to put anything past that old gun-wolf. He wheeled his horse around to face us, and his right hand moved closer to the butt of his holstered revolver. I held up my hand, hoping Enoch would understand I was telling him this was a peaceful visit.

If the sheriff noticed Enoch's reaction, he didn't give any sign of it. He kept riding as the three younger punchers reined in and turned their mounts as well. Lester and I came to a stop about ten feet from the little group of riders.

"Howdy, boss," Enoch drawled. "Looks like you brought us some company."

"The sheriff's got something to say to Vince," I said.

Vince looked shocked. He said, "To me? I haven't done anything wrong, Sheriff, I swear. At least, not that I know of."

"I know that, son," Lester said. His usually gruff tone suddenly had some sympathy in it, and even if he hadn't told me that he had bad news for Vince, that would have warned me something unpleasant was coming. Lester went on, "You'd better brace yourself. There was an accident in the railyard this morning. Your father was killed."

Lester hadn't tried to soften the blow. With terrible news like that, there was really no point in it. No matter how he put it, what he had to say was going to hit Vince like a pile-driver punch in the gut.

Vince sucked in his breath, but for a second that was his only reaction. He just stared at the sheriff like Lester had grown horns and started spouting a foreign language or something. He'd heard the words, but they didn't mean anything to him. He couldn't wrap his brain around them.

But then his understanding of what the sheriff had said

started to sink in. I could see it happening in the widening of Vince's eyes and the slackening of his jaw. He started breathing harder as he shook his head.

"No," he said. "No, it ain't possible. My dad's fine."

"I'm sorry," Lester said. "He isn't."

Randy and Bert actually looked more shocked than Vince did. Enoch was the great stone face, as usual, but I saw the sympathy in his eyes.

Vince leaned forward in his saddle and asked, "What happened?"

"You can get all the details later in town—," Lester began.

"No!" Vince breathed harder. "I want to know now! Tell me, Sheriff. Tell me or I won't ever believe it."

Lester's gaze narrowed as he regarded Vince for a couple of seconds. Then he nodded curtly and said, "All right. I reckon you've got a right to know. They were moving some freight cars around in the yard this morning when your father got pinned between a couple of them. He never had a chance. It was quick, though. That's what they told me, and I believe it."

Vince shook his head.

"He worked for the railroad for years. He wouldn't have been careless enough to get caught between two moving cars like that. He knew his way around the yard too well for that to happen."

"Like I told you, it was an accident," Lester said. "The cars weren't supposed to be moving. An engine bumped one of them and knocked it into the other one."

"Then it was the engineer's fault!"

"No," Lester said. "He tried to stop short of the freight car. The brakes went out and he couldn't. Nobody's to blame for it. It was just a tragic accident, and I'm sorry for your loss, Vince."

Tears started to trickle from Vince's eyes, cutting trails in the dust on his face. He said, "My ma . . . ?"

"She's all right. The railroad sent word to her right away. Some of her friends are with her, wives of the other railroad men . . ."

Lester's voice trailed off. There was really nothing else for him to say.

I felt sorry for Vince. Losing your pa is bad enough. Losing him in such a stupid, senseless way just makes it even worse. I wished there was something I could do to help him, but time was the only thing that was going to help Vince now.

"I'll take you back to town with me," Lester said after a minute or so. "You'll want to go to your mother."

Vince just nodded silently, like he didn't trust himself to talk. But then he looked at me and said, "I've got work to do."

"No, son," I told him with a shake of my head. "You go with Sheriff Lester. We'll finish up here and then head for town later ourselves."

"You can't—"

"This crew sticks together, through good and bad alike," I said. "We'll see you later. You go on now."

He looked like he wanted to argue some more, but my voice was firm enough he knew it wouldn't do any good. Besides, when you've suffered a really bad shock like that, there's a part of you that just wants to be told what to do for a while, so you won't have to think too much. I knew that because I'd gone through it myself. Not exactly the same thing, but close enough.

Looking pale and shaken, Vince rode off with Sheriff Lester. Once they were gone, Enoch said, "That's a damned shame. Vince is a good kid. He shouldn't have to lose his pa like that."

"I don't know what he's going to do," Bert said. "He'll have to support his ma now."

And what I was able to pay him for punching cows wasn't hardly enough to do that, I thought. I wouldn't blame him if he left the Fishhook to find another job.

That was a worry for the future, though. Right now Vince just had to get through the next few days, and I knew they were going to be bad ones for him.

CHAPTER 24

We pushed the cattle on into the hills, then headed back to the ranch headquarters to clean up. There was no air of impending celebration this time, like there had been before the dance. We were all quiet and solemn.

When we got there we found that Gabe already knew what had happened. Lester had told him when the sheriff returned there with Vince. The two of them had started off toward the county seat in Lester's automobile.

It was evening by the time we reached town, the sun having set while we were riding in. We didn't know where Vince's parents lived, but I figured they could tell us at the train station, so that's where we headed first. The ticket agent gave us directions to the house, which was a neat little white frame structure on a side street. A cottonwood stood next to it, and there was a little flower bed in front of the porch with a few green sprouts in it. In those hot, dry West Texas summers it would be a real battle getting any flowers to grow, but I supposed Vince's mother was the stubborn sort who gave it a try.

Several cars and buggies were parked on the edge of the street in front of the house. All the windows were lit up. We left our horses in the alley next to the house and went up the steps onto the porch, holding our hats. Some of the windows were open, and I heard a low buzz of conversation coming from inside as I knocked on the door.

The man who answered it was a stranger. He wore a sober dark suit and had a bald head and a white walrus mustache. He said, "Yes?"

"We're friends of Vince's," I said. "I own the Fishhook spread, where he works."

"So you're Jim Strickland," he said. "I've heard Vince's folks speak of you." He held out a hand and introduced himself. "John Hamilton. I'm a friend of the family." As I shook with him, he added, "Come on in."

He took us into a crowded parlor. The air was thick with grief and bay rum and perfume from all the visitors. Vince sat in an armchair that had been pulled over next to the end of a sofa. A slender, middle-aged woman with graying brown hair sat on that sofa, occasionally dabbing at her eyes with the lacy handkerchief she held. From time to time she reached over and squeezed Vince's arm. His face looked like it had been carved out of granite, and he didn't respond to the comforting touch of the woman I took to be his mother.

John Hamilton introduced me to some of the other people in the room, but I don't remember their names. I introduced Enoch, Gabe, and Randy. Bert seemed to know just about everybody already, which wasn't surprising considering that he and Vince had been best friends for a long time. Bert's folks were there, I think. I don't do too well with mourning. Things all sort of run together on me.

Eventually, though, I found myself shaking the hand of Vince's mother and saying, "I sure am sorry for your loss, ma'am. You have my deepest sympathy."

"Thank you, Mr. Strickland," she said. "I'm glad to know that my son has such good friends to stand with him at this time of trouble."

"Yes, ma'am. Anything we can do to help, don't you hesitate to call on us."

The other fellas shook her hand as well, Enoch and Gabe with the grave gallantry that men of their generation could summon up, Randy somewhat more awkwardly. Bert leaned over and gave her a hug, saying, "I'm so sorry, Mrs. Porter. I . . . I can't hardly believe that Mr. Porter is gone."

That made her dab at her eyes again. She said, "None of us can, Bert. It's all just so shocking and terrible."

I wanted to ask Vince how he was doing, but it didn't seem like the right time. Anyway, what could his answer be? Of course he wasn't doing any good.

The five of us drew off into a corner to stand together. Gabe muttered quietly enough that only we heard him, "Maybe we better leave. We done paid our respects. Ain't nothin' else we can do here."

He was right about that. I figured we'd spend the night in town and stay for the funeral if it was going to be the next day. I looked around for John Hamilton, the man who'd let us in, and when I spotted him across the room I said, "I'll go ask Mr. Hamilton if they know yet when the service will be."

I was making my way through the crowd when the room got quiet and folks started to shuffle aside from three men who had just come in. I didn't recognize any of them. They were all middle-aged, one tall and spare, the other two paunchy. The two paunchy ones wore suits that probably cost more than what most of the other men in the room earned in a year.

They went up to Mrs. Porter and Vince. The tall one shook hands with Vince, then took Mrs. Porter's right hand in both of his and said, "I just want you to know how sorry I am about this, Helen. If there was any way to bring Bob back, I would. I surely would."

"Thank you, Mr. Rutledge," she said. She seemed a little cooler and more reserved now, but her voice was sincere enough.

Rutledge let go of her hand and half-turned to gesture at the two men with him.

"This is Mr. Kennedy and Mr. Milton," he said. "They're exec-utives with the railroad."

The one called Kennedy took his hat off, revealing slicked-down black hair. He looked like he ought to be tending bar somewhere, not running a railroad. He said, "You and your son have our condolences, ma'am. Your husband was a fine railroad man."

I had a feeling Kennedy hadn't known Bob Porter or anything about what sort of railroad man Porter was. He was just there to express the line's sympathy. The other man, Milton, was more of the same, only with thinning fair hair.

I didn't like either of them. I knew their sort just by looking at them. Snake-oil salesmen, I thought.

Vince's mother was polite to them, though, even gracious. That was the way women were raised back then. They did most of their crying behind closed doors. In public they stayed as cool and unflappable as they could.

I eased on over beside John Hamilton and asked quietly, "Who's that fella Rutledge?"

"Stationmaster here in town," Hamilton said with a frown. "Kennedy's the railroad's regional superintendent, and Milton's his assistant."

His voice was curt. I said, "You sound like you don't like them very much."

"I'm a railroader, too. Chet Rutledge isn't a bad sort for a stationmaster, I suppose. He has to do what they tell him. Kennedy and Milton just sit in their fancy offices and try to figure out new ways to make things harder for the men who actually make sure the trains run on time, the freight gets loaded, and the passengers are taken care of. They squeeze every nickel, every drop of sweat and blood out of us, every chance they get."

I had known there was a good reason my instincts had told me I didn't like those two.

After mulling over what Hamilton had told me for a few seconds, I said, "When the sheriff brought the bad news out to the ranch and told Vince, he said something about the brakes on the engine giving out before it bumped that car?"

"That's what happened, all right," Hamilton replied, his frown deepening, "but you won't find anybody who'll admit it now. When talk about a brake failure started going around the yard, Rutledge clamped down on that right away. Clamped down hard. If you ask Pete Abercrombie, the man who was in that en-

gine, what happened, he'll tell you he hit the throttle by accident." Hamilton made a disgusted sound in his throat. "As if
Abercrombie would ever do that! He's been around engines,
man and boy, for more than thirty years!"

"Everybody makes mistakes sometimes," I said.

"Maybe so, but this wasn't one of those times. It was brake failure, all right, and I can tell you why it happened. Kennedy and
Milton push those engines too hard, just like they do the people
who work for them! The engines need to be brought into the
roundhouse a couple of times a year to have the brakes worked
over and everything else checked out, but that takes them out of
service and the line won't allow that as long as they're running."

"Sounds to me like you're sayin' the line's to blame for what
happened to Vince's dad."

"That's exactly what I'm saying." Hamilton sighed. "But I'm
the only one who'll still admit that. Rutledge shut everybody up
until he could wire Kennedy in San Antonio and find out what
to do. Kennedy gave him his orders over the telegraph and then
came out here as fast as he could to make sure they were carried
out. Anybody who wants to hang on to his job with the railroad
had best toe the company line on this. That's why Pete Abercrombie's taking all the blame now. It'll hurt his reputation as
an engineer, of course, but at least he'll still have a job." Hamilton shrugged. "All that happened after Sheriff Lester set off to
carry the bad news to the boy, I reckon. That's why he said what
he did about the brakes. He didn't know what was going on here
in town."

"What about now? Won't Lester know something happened
when he hears folks sayin' there was no brake failure?"

"How's he going to know any better? He's the sheriff, not a
railroader. Abercrombie was right there. Lester will take his word
for it, especially when everybody else who was in the yard backs
him up."

I studied Hamilton's rugged face for a moment and said,
"You're telling the truth, though. Aren't you worried about
losin' your job?"

"I would be if I gave a damn." A humorless smile curved his

mouth under that walrus mustache. "Doc says I've got some-thing wrong in my gut. All I know is it hurts like hell most of the time. I'll be dead in six months, he says. So what can the railroad do to me?"

"Sorry," I murmured.

Hamilton shook his head.

"Save your sympathy for the widow and Vince. I'm an old bachelor. Nobody'll be left behind to mourn me, and that's the way I like it. Whatever mark I make on the world, I'll make it while I'm here, and once I'm gone I won't give a good god-damn."

That was a pretty good way to look at it, I thought. I said, "You figure on stirrin' up trouble for the line over the way they're lyin' about what happened?"

He hesitated for a long moment before sighing and shaking his head.

"No, and I'll tell you why. Helen Porter's got some money coming from Bob's pension, and there's a good chance the line will give her even more than that, just to keep things looking good. Me raising a big stink would just slow things down and maybe even put all that in jeopardy. I won't risk that. Money won't bring Bob back, but neither will causing a fuss. Besides, I'd be just one lone voice crying out in the wilderness, as they say. Wouldn't do a damned bit of good."

"Probably not," I said, although that black tide started creep-ing up inside me as I looked across the room at the trio from the railroad. I'd seen plenty of slick bastards like that in my time, and they always got my hackles up. I forced the anger back down and went on, "I came over here to ask you if you know when Mr. Porter's funeral will be?"

"Two o'clock tomorrow afternoon at the Baptist church," Hamilton said. He was starting to look a little worried now. "You're not going to tell anybody what I said about . . . well, about the accident, are you, Mr. Strickland?"

I knew he was just worried about Mrs. Porter getting what was coming to her, so I smiled and shook my head. Hamilton wasn't scared of the railroad. No man who could face his own end as calmly as Hamilton appeared to be facing his could be considered a coward.

"No point in me saying anything," I told him. "I'm no railroad man, and I was thirty miles away when it happened, to boot. I don't know anything for a fact."

He nodded and said, "I'm obliged to you. I don't know what made me run off at the mouth that way."

"Folks say I'm easy to talk to."

He just grunted.

When I rejoined the rest of my bunch, Enoch said, "You and that fella palavered for a long time, considerin' that you just went to ask him when the funeral was."

"And I found out, too," I said. "Two o'clock tomorrow."

"You plan on us stayin' in town for it?"

"That's right." I was sure Chet Rutledge would show up for the service, since he'd been Porter's local boss. But I hoped that Kennedy and Milton would have the decency to stay away now that they'd paid their respects to the widow.

If I had to look at their faces again while everybody was mourning the loss of a man who'd died because of their penny-pinching, I wasn't sure what I would do.

But there was a good chance it wouldn't be pretty.

CHAPTER 25

One of the things I hate most is a funeral. The music, the preaching, the praying, the crying . . . all of it gives me the fantods and always has. And no man gets to be the age I am without going to a hell of a lot of them.

Bob Porter's funeral was no different. The Baptist church was almost full. Vince, wearing the same suit he'd had on the night before, sat up front with his mother, of course. Me and the rest of the fellas from the Fishhook stayed in the back, on the last pew, in fact.

Because getting pinned between those two freight cars had mashed Porter so bad, the casket was closed and nobody had to go through the ritual of walking by slowly and gazing at the dearly departed, which always struck me as just downright morbid. I don't know about you, but I don't want somebody's last memory of me to be what I looked like when I was dead. That old pard of mine, the one I'd ridden with for so many years and loved like a brother, the last time I'd seen him he was full of bullets and had bled out his life in a dirt-floored shack. There have been many times I wished I'd died with him that day.

Fate has its own plans for all of us, though, and you'd be wasting time to argue with them.

But sometimes you can sort of nudge fate into doing right by folks. That thought weighed heavy on my mind that day at Bob Porter's funeral.

When it was over we all walked out into the cemetery behind the church for the graveside service, which was even worse than the goings-on inside. The preacher finally wrapped that up, and folks started to leave. The gravediggers stood under the shade of a scrawny tree, leaning on their shovels and waiting until everybody was gone to start filling up the hole.

Vince came over to me and said, "I'll be coming back to the ranch with you and the rest of the fellas, if that's all right with you, Mr. Strickland."

That took me by surprise. I said, "Are you sure you want to do that, Vince? I figured you'd probably stay here in town so you could help your ma . . ."

"Mr. Rutledge offered me a job as a baggage handler," he said. "Told me I might be able to work my way up to ticket clerk one of these days. But I don't want to work for the railroad, Mr. Strickland. I'm a cowboy now. That's my job."

Vince had been cowboying for a couple of months, which was hardly long enough for him to decide that ought to be his lifelong profession, but I supposed I could understand why he didn't want to be around that railyard all the time.

"I don't mind you comin' back to the ranch," I told him, "but I'm not sure it's a good idea for you to leave your mother alone at a time like this."

"I already talked to her about it. She says it's fine. She has plenty of friends here in town who'll help her out any time she needs it. And she'll be getting the money from my dad's pension pretty soon. Whatever wages you pay me, I'll send 'em to her. I don't need any money."

"Are you sure about this, son?"

He nodded and said, "Certain sure, Mr. Strickland. As soon as I get out of this monkey suit and back into my regular duds, I'll ride on back with you and the boys, if that's all right."

I put a hand on his shoulder and nodded.

"Of course it's all right," I told him. "We'll be darned glad to have you back."

Despite what I said, I was worried about the youngster. He

hadn't cried any during the service, as far as I could tell, maybe hadn't cried since Sheriff Lester came out to the ranch to break the news to him. Some fellas are like that. They wrap everything up so tight inside 'em that nothing can get out, good or bad. And if that control ever slips, even a little, they're liable to fly apart like a balloon blown too full of air.

It might be a good idea for me and the rest of the crew to keep an eye on Vince for a while, I told myself.

We got back to the ranch late that night, and everybody was up early the next morning, going about their work. In fact, I drove the whole bunch of us pretty hard for the next few days, myself included. Staying busy was the best thing in the world for Vince right then, I figured, and not only that, it was getting a lot of work done around the place.

Four or five days had gone by when John Hamilton showed up. Scar's barking warned me that something was wrong. I stepped out of the barn where Enoch and I had been doing some horseshoeing and I shaded my eyes with a hand as I peered toward a buggy rolling toward the buildings from the direction of Largo.

At first I thought Sheriff Lester must've traded in that automobile the county bought for him and had gone back to a more familiar mode of transportation, and then I wondered for a second if it might be Reverend Hatfield and his daughter. The idea of seeing Daisy again made my pulse jump a little.

Then I realized the buggy wasn't either of those. When it came closer I recognized Hamilton's big white mustache.

"That's the fella you talked to for so long at Vince's mama's house, ain't it?" Enoch asked.

"Yeah. Wonder what he wants."

Hamilton brought the buggy to a halt in front of the barn and climbed down. His face was gray, and it wasn't just from the dust his two horses had kicked up.

"Howdy, Mr. Hamilton," I greeted him. "What brings you out here?"

"I need to talk to the boy," he said.

"You mean Vince?"

"That's right."

I said, "Last time somebody showed up and wanted to talk to Vince, they weren't deliverin' good news."

"Neither am I," Hamilton said. He winced and caught hold of the buggy to steady himself.

"Are you all right?" I asked him.

"Aw, this damned gut rot of mine is acting up. That six months the doc gave me might've been optimistic." He shook his head. "But that's not why I'm here. Something's happened that Vince needs to know about."

"Something happened to his ma?" I sure hoped that wasn't the case. The boy didn't need to lose both of his folks so close together.

"No, she's all right . . . physically."

I slipped my hands in my hip pockets and said, "You'd better go ahead and tell me what this is about, Mr. Hamilton."

"I'm not sure it's really any of your business," he said with a stubborn frown.

Enoch said, "That redheaded sprout's our friend, mister. I reckon that makes it our business."

Hamilton thought about it for a second and then shrugged. He said, "I don't suppose it really makes any difference. Vince would tell Bert, and Bert Chadwick never kept a secret in his life. That boy's face reads just like a book."

"You were about to tell us what happened," I reminded him.

"Yeah. Chet Rutledge came to see Helen Porter yesterday morning. He'd had word from the regional office in San Antonio about Bob's pension."

"They're fixin' to pay it?" I asked, but I already had a feeling that wasn't going to be Hamilton's answer.

"Hell, no," Hamilton said. He looked like he'd just bitten into the sourest persimmon ever grown. "According to Kennedy and Milton, Bob borrowed on what he had coming and never paid it back. There's nothing left. They're not going to pay her one thin dime." His voice shook with anger. "It's a damned lie. Bob

Porter wasn't a borrowing man. They faked up some paper and made it look like he signed it, but it's a lie."

A heavy silence lay there between us for a few seconds before I said, "The railroad's not givin' her anything?"

"Not a thing."

"Not even something for them bein' at fault for his death?"

"But they weren't at fault, according to the official report. It was an accident."

That sour taste was in my mouth now. I didn't like it, not one bit.

"As soon as I found out about it," Hamilton went on, "I hitched up my buggy and came to tell Vince. Made it to Largo yesterday afternoon and spent the night there last night. Figured the boy had a right to know."

"Yeah, he does," I agreed. I turned to Enoch. "Can you ride out on the range, find Vince and the other boys, and tell 'em to come on back in?"

"Sure. You want me to let Vince know what's happened?"

"No, I'll tell him." I looked at Hamilton. "Unless you'd rather."

He shook his head and said, "I don't suppose it really matters who tells him, as long as he knows. I'd just as soon get back home. I've never had any fanciful notions about dying with my boots on. I'd rather be in my own bed."

"You're welcome to spend the night here if you want," I offered.

"No, thanks. I'll be going."

"Mr. Hamilton," I said. He paused as he started to turn away. "I need to ask you one more question."

"All right."

"Are you absolutely sure there's no truth to what Kennedy and Milton are claiming about the money coming to Mrs. Porter? They'd really do that? Cheat a widow woman out of what's got to be a piddlin' amount to the likes of them?"

He looked me in the eye and said, "I swear on what's left of my life, Strickland, that's what they're doing."

I smiled and said, "All right, then." I put out my hand and shook his. "Thank you for makin' the trip out here. It couldn't have been easy for you."

"Not much in life is easy. But as long as we're here, there are things that have to be done."

"Yes, sir, there sure are," I agreed.

I had thought time was the only thing that would help Vince get over what had happened to his pa, but I knew now that I'd been wrong about that.

Vengeance might help, too.

CHAPTER 26

If anything, Vince took the news of the dirty trick Kennedy and Milton were pulling even worse than he had when Sheriff Lester told him his father had been killed. He ranted and cussed and raged around the room, nothing at all like the soft-spoken kid he usually was.

I had called everybody into the house before I told Vince what it was about. Like Hamilton had said, Vince didn't have any secrets from Bert, and Bert didn't have any secrets from anybody. Besides, with what I had in mind, they all had to know about it sooner or later.

After a while, Vince stopped carrying on. He just looked at me and said, "Why?"

"You mean, why would Kennedy and Milton do such a rotten thing?"

"Yeah. It's not even their money. It's the railroad's money! And the railroad would never miss it."

"Some fellas are like that," I said with a shrug. "They're just naturally greedy, and it slops over into their jobs. You can bet that Kennedy and Milton are rakin' off plenty for themselves. They want to make as much money as they can for the railroad so they'll stay in position to do that."

"Well, it's not right."

"No, son, it sure ain't. That's why—"

Scar started barking again, interrupting me. I was a mite annoyed, but I figured I'd better see what had him so worked up. When I went to the door and looked out, I saw three riders coming toward the ranch house. The easy way they sat their saddles and the wide-brimmed, high-crowned sombreros they wore told me who they were.

"Santiago and his cousins are here," I said. I wasn't sure why they had shown up today. We hadn't seen them since the round-up and the drive into town.

They were all as solemn as usual when they came in. Santiago nodded a greeting to us, then said, "Vince, we have heard what happened. We are very sorry, amigo."

"You mean you know about my dad getting killed?" Vince asked.

Santiago nodded.

"Sí, and about the evil thing being done by the men he worked for."

"How'd you know about that?" I asked. "John Hamilton just came up from the county seat and told us about it today."

"Yes, but Señor Hamilton spent last night in Largo, and he was so angry by what the railroad is doing that he spoke to people about it. We rode to Largo this morning, and while we were there we heard the talk. Many people are angry at the railroad."

"It's not really the railroad," Bert said. "It's Mr. Kennedy and Mr. Milton."

"Same thing as far as most folks are concerned," Enoch said.

The debate about that could go 'round and 'round, and it didn't interest me. Making things right for Vince and his ma was all I cared about just then. I said, "I'm glad you and your cousins are here, Santiago. Saves me the trouble of havin' to ride over to your rancho and talk to you. I planned to ask you to be part of this, too."

"Part of what, Señor Strickland?" he asked, but I could tell from the way his eyes narrowed that he might have a suspicion already about what I was thinking.

"We've got to do something about this," I said. "Too many times, folks see something wrong, and they just shake their heads and cluck their tongues and say ain't that a shame, but there's nothin' they can do. Well, I'm not put together that way. When the Good Lord made me, he didn't put in the part that stands aside and does nothin'."

"Are we gettin' to an answer to Santiago's question pretty soon?" Enoch drawled.

That made me laugh, despite the seriousness of the situation. I said, "Yeah, we are. Vince and his ma have money comin' from the railroad, and if the railroad won't give it to 'em, that just leaves us with one thing to do." I looked around at all eight of them. "We take it."

As they looked at me the seconds ticked by and stretched out into a minute. Finally, as if the others had been waiting for him to speak up, Vince said, "What do you mean, 'take it,' Mr. Strickland?"

Enoch said, "When a fella talks about takin' something away from the railroad, it usually means a holdup."

"That's right," I said. "If Kennedy and Milton don't want to do the right thing, we'll just do it for 'em."

"But we're not outlaws!" Bert said. "We wouldn't have any idea how to go about robbing a train."

Enoch looked at me, and I saw the amusement twinkling in his eyes. Maybe he knew who I really was right then and maybe he didn't, but he had an idea this wasn't the first time I'd been involved in something on the wrong side of the law.

"We'll figure it out," I said. "But nobody has to be mixed up in this if they don't want to. If any of you want to steer clear of it, nobody will think any less of you."

"I'm glad you said that, Mr. Strickland," Randy spoke up, "because I don't want any part of it."

That didn't surprise me. Randy had actually held up a train before, and he'd gotten shot for his trouble, by his own partner, to boot. So I'd halfway expected him to feel that way.

"That's fine," I told him. "Anybody else?"

"Gabe and me are in," Enoch said. "No offense, Jim, but ranch work ain't near as excitin' as robbin' trains."

Gabe said, "Speak for yourself, you ol' stringbean. Maybe I don't want to do somethin' that'll get the law after me."

"Didn't mean to speak out of turn," Enoch said. "Are you in, Gabe?"

"Durned tootin'," Gabe said. "Just wanted to make up my own mind, that's all."

Santiago said, "My cousins and I, we wish to be part of this effort as well, Señor Strickland."

"Is that right?" I asked Javier and Fernando.

They both nodded solemnly.

I looked at Santiago and said, "They *can* talk, can't they?"

"Get a bottle of mescal in them and you cannot shut them up," he replied with a little twitch at one corner of his mouth. I knew that was what passed for a grin with him.

I turned to Vince and Bert.

"That leaves you two fellas."

"No, it doesn't," Vince said. "Nobody's going out and holding up a train on my account. You'll all just get yourselves killed, and I won't have it. I went to my dad's funeral. That's enough for a while."

"Nobody's gonna get killed," I said. "As long as we're careful and figure out everything beforehand, we'll be fine. And you and your ma will get what's comin' to you, Vince."

He gave a stubborn shake of his head and insisted, "It's too dangerous."

"Why don't you let us work out a plan first, and then you can see if you still feel that way?" I suggested. "It won't hurt anything for some of us to take a ride down to Cougar Pass and have a look around."

"That's where you plan on hittin' the train?" Enoch asked.

"I don't know yet. It's a startin' point, though. We'll have to look around and see if we can find a better place."

Vince said, "Aren't any of you listening? I said no. I won't let you do this."

I smiled at him and said, "No offense, son, but I don't reckon it's up to you. If we want to hold up a train, we will, and if we want to hand over the loot to you and your ma, we'll do that, too."

"I won't take it! And when I tell her where you got it, neither will she!" Vince threw his hands in the air in frustration. "You're all crazy!"

He turned and paced over to the window. As he stood there with his back to us, staring through the glass, I saw his shoulders trembling just a little. I knew the emotions that had to be raging inside him. Sure, he wanted vengeance on the men who'd cheated him and his mother, and this was one way to get it. A successful robbery would reflect badly on Kennedy and Milton, over and above the money. But at the same time, Vince didn't want to see any of his friends get hurt or killed. He had a point when he said that he'd already grieved enough.

Bert spoke up for the first time since I'd revealed what I wanted to do. He said, "I think we should do what Mr. Strickland says."

Vince turned to frown at him.

"You want to be a train robber?" he said. "An outlaw? You?"

"Well, why not? The railroad's done wrong by you and your mother, Vince. You should've gotten that pension money and more besides." Bert paused, then went on, "Besides, there's something you don't know."

That brought Vince away from the window. He said, "What? What is there I don't know about this whole thing, Bert?"

"You don't know what Mr. Rutledge has been saying about your pa."

Vince looked like he'd been slapped. He couldn't get any words out for a few seconds. Then his face hardened and he asked in an equally hard voice, "What's Rutledge been saying?"

Now Bert looked like he wished he hadn't even brought it up, but he swallowed and said, "It was when he talked to me in town. He said I could come back to work as a baggage handler, too. He thought maybe if I took the job, so would you, and he wanted to do something to help you out, even though . . . even though it was really your dad's own fault, what happened to him."

Vince's eyes widened in anger and surprise.

"How in the hell does he figure that? Pete Abercrombie hit the throttle when he shouldn't have."

I kept my mouth shut. Vince had heard the story the railroad was spreading about Abercrombie and evidently accepted the idea that the initial talk about the brakes failing was just a mistake made in the confusion of the moment. John Hamilton was right: if the deception fooled somebody as close to the situation as Vince, it would fool everybody else.

The truth was my hole card, if I needed it.

Bert looked mighty uncomfortable as he said, "Mr. Rutledge told me that wasn't really what happened. He claims your dad had time to get out of the way of that freight car, but he'd been drinking and didn't see it because of that."

Vince's freckled face turned almost as red as his hair.

"Rutledge said my dad was drunk?" he demanded.

Bert swallowed again and nodded.

Kennedy and Milton must have ordered Rutledge to start spreading that rumor, I thought. It wasn't enough they had covered up the railroad's responsibility for those brakes failing. Now they were going to blacken Bob Porter's name by having Rutledge whisper about him being drunk when he was killed. It was as dirty a business as I'd ever heard of, and for a moment it made me want to forget all about robbing one of the railroad's trains.

What I wanted to do instead was to walk into the offices of Kennedy and Milton in San Antonio and gun down those black-hearted sons of bitches.

The problem with that idea was that while I'd killed in the past when I had to, I wasn't a murderer. Never had been, and I knew I wasn't going to turn into one now.

No, if I was going to help Vince strike back against Kennedy and Milton, it would have to be in a different way, a way I knew as well as my own name.

Vince was so mad he wasn't able to talk for a minute or so. When he could, he choked out, "It's a damned lie. I saw my dad drink a beer every now and then, but he wasn't a drunk. He never would have gone to work drunk. He was too dedicated to his job." His voice took on a bitter edge. "Too dedicated to the railroad. And now the men who run it are turning their backs on him."

"I didn't want to tell you, Vince," Bert said. "But that's why I've got to go along with Mr. Strickland on this. If there's some way we can make them pay, we've got to do it."

Vince nodded slowly. He said, "I think you're right." He looked at me. "If you've got a plan, sir, I won't try to stop you. And I'm in, all the way."

I clapped him on the shoulder and said, "Glad to hear it, son. I don't have a plan yet, but I will. I can promise you that."

Randy said, "I'm sorry, Vince. I still can't go along with it."

"That's all right, Randy," Vince said. The rage had faded from his face, but a cold determination had replaced it. "I don't blame you a bit. Anyway, Mr. Strickland's going to need somebody to stay here and keep an eye on the ranch. Isn't that right, sir?"

"It sure is," I agreed. "To tell you the truth, Randy, I'll feel better about things knowin' that somebody's here."

"All right, then. I guess I can wish you luck in good conscience. You're all my friends, after all."

"And I expect we'll need all the luck we can get," I told him.

CHAPTER 27

When I got a firsthand look at Cougar Pass, I realized just how dumb Steve Tate had been. It was a terrible place for a holdup. Derailing the train had really been the only way to stop it in that location. Tate was just lucky—if you could consider a fella who had long since been turned into coyote and buzzard droppings lucky—that the resulting death and destruction hadn't been even worse.

It was a good thing for Randy that he hadn't stayed mixed up with Tate. Even if that holdup had been successful, the damn fool would have gotten them all killed sooner or later, including Randy.

I looked at the flats stretching off to the west, toward the county seat, and asked Vince and Bert, "Is the country like this all the way on into town?"

"Pretty much," Vince replied.

I turned my horse and said, "We've got to go back the other way, then. There's nothing in this direction that'll work."

I'd brought the two youngsters and Enoch with me to scout out the lay of the land. Randy and Gabe were holding down the fort back at the ranch. Santiago and his cousins had gone back to their little spread but would rejoin us later.

We followed the tracks through the pass, such as it was, and headed east. In the distance I could see a series of shallow ridges, and even they looked a lot more promising than the area where Tate's gang had hit the train.

After a while I heard a rumble in the distance and pulled my horse to the left, away from the tracks. The other three followed suit. Bert asked, "Where are we going?"

"Train's comin'," Enoch said. "We don't want any of the passengers to remember seein' us nosin' around out here."

"Those trains go by pretty fast," Vince said. "They wouldn't be able to recognize us, would they?"

"Probably not," I said, "but there's no point in takin' chances. If you're about to tackle a chore that's risky to start with, you don't want to do anything that might increase the odds against you even more."

Bert said, "You two, uh, sound like you might've done something like this before." He seemed a little nervous as he glanced back and forth between me and Enoch.

I gave him a disarming grin and said, "Naw, it's just common sense, that's all."

"Yeah," Enoch said dryly. "Common sense."

We were a couple of hundred yards north of the tracks when the westbound train rumbled past with smoke and cinders spewing from the diamond-shaped stack on the big Baldwin locomotive. If any of the passengers spotted us through the windows, they would think we were just some punchers who had stopped to idly watch the train go by.

When the caboose was dwindling down the tracks to the west, I hitched my horse into motion again. We returned to the railroad and continued scouting.

A couple of miles further on we came to a place where the track had been laid in a narrow cut through one of those ridges, leaving banks of rock and red clay on both sides. Those banks were about fifteen feet tall, which made them a couple of feet taller than the top of a freight car.

The cut was maybe fifty yards long. I cocked my head to the side as I studied it. Enoch smiled and said, "I reckon I know what you're thinkin', Jim."

"Well, I don't," Vince said.

I pointed to the banks and said, "A man could jump from up there onto the top of a boxcar as it passed by."

"Sure he could," Bert said. "If he was loco!"

"No, you'd have to be careful, but you could do it."

Bert shook his head.

"Not me," he said. "I'd fall and break my neck, as sure as anything."

"He would," Vince agreed. "But I might be able to do it."

"Neither one of you is gonna do it," I said. "That'll be my job. Once I'm on the train, I can go over the cars and the coal tender up to the engine. Then I'll make the engineer stop where the rest of you boys are waitin' for us. After that it's just a matter of getting the fella in the express car to open up."

"What if the engineer won't stop?" Bert asked.

"Most of the time when a man's lookin' down the barrel of a gun, he don't think about anything except keepin' the fella on the other end of that gun happy."

"I don't want any railroaders killed," Vince said. "My dad was a railroad man, and he had a lot of friends on this line. He wouldn't want any of them to be hurt."

"I know that. Nobody's gonna get hurt. Not bad, anyway. I might have to clout a fella over the head or something like that to make him see reason."

"As long as nobody's killed," Vince insisted.

I nodded and said, "You've got my word on that."

I would do my best to keep that promise, too. I took pride in the fact that nobody had ever been killed in the robberies I'd pulled as a younger man.

We spent the rest of the day looking around the area, familiarizing ourselves with all the details of the terrain. There was a wash nearby where the rest of the bunch could wait out of sight with the horses while I stopped the train. I also explored both banks of the cut until I found just the right spot to make my jump.

While I was doing that, Enoch asked me, "Are you sure you're still spry enough to do this, Jim?"

"Of course I am," I answered without hesitation. "You're not volunteerin' to do it, are you? Hell, I'm at least ten years younger than you are. You've never told me how old you really are."

"No, I ain't volunteerin'. And my age is my own business. But I was thinkin' maybe Santiago ought to handle this part of the chore. I'll bet he'd be willin'."

"It don't matter if he's willin' or not," I said. "This is my job. I've got experience at it."

"What if you miss?"

"Then the train won't stop, and the rest of you boys can turn around and go home. We'll have tried to settle the score with the railroad, and that'll have to be good enough."

"Well, I know how stubborn you are," Enoch said with a shrug. "I don't reckon it'll do any good to argue with you."

"Nary a bit," I told him.

Santiago and the Gallardo brothers met us at the ranch that evening when we got back from our little expedition. All of us sat around the table to go over the plan, except for Randy. He was out in the bunkhouse. I trusted him, but if things went wrong and the sheriff ever questioned him, I wanted him to be able to say that he didn't know what the rest of us were doing. That would be stretching the truth a little, but at least he wouldn't know any of the details.

"Vince, you and Bert are gonna stay in the wash with the horses," I started off by saying.

"We're only doing this because of what happened to my father. I ought to run the same risks as the rest of you."

"Somebody's got to be responsible for those horses," I told him. "If they got loose and ran off, we'd be in a mighty bad fix. Not only that, but the two of you worked at the station in town, which means there's a better chance the members of that train crew might recognize you, even with your hats pulled down and bandannas over your faces. If we get in a tight spot and need help, you'll be close by. Otherwise, you stay out of sight."

"He's right that they might be able to tell who we are, Vince," Bert said.

"All right, all right," Vince said. "I guess we can do it that way."

I went on, "Once I've got the train stopped, Gabe, you'll come to the engine and climb into the cab. It'll be your job to keep an eye on the engineer and fireman and make sure they don't cause any trouble."

Gabe nodded and said, "I can do that."

"Santiago, you and your cousins will be responsible for the passenger cars. Just keep everybody quiet and settled down while Enoch and I deal with the express car."

"Do we take their valuables?" Santiago asked.

I looked at Vince, who shook his head. I was willing to let him make that decision. I said, "No, we're not going to rob the passengers. We're only taking what we find in the express car, because the railroad will have to make those losses good, and it's the railroad we're trying to hurt. Now, let's talk about the schedule. You two worked for the railroad. You ought to know when the trains run."

"There are two westbound and two eastbound every day," Vince said. "Does it matter?"

"The terrain's better if we hit a westbound."

Vince nodded.

"In that case, there's one that comes through about two o'clock in the afternoon and another about midnight."

I shook my head and said, "I'm not makin' that jump in the dark. I've got to see what I'm jumpin' on."

"So we're going to hold up the train in broad daylight?" Bert asked.

I chuckled.

"Wouldn't be the first holdup that's ever been pulled in broad daylight," I said, remembering a few eventful occasions in the past.

"Well, it'll be the first one one for me and Vince. But you seem to know what you're doing, Mr. Strickland. You're the boss."

"That's right, I am. And that brings up an important point." I looked around the table at them to reinforce what I was about to say. "Once things start poppin', I'm in charge out there. I give an order, you do what I tell you, without any hesitation, without any questions. Got that?"

They all nodded, and Santiago said, "Sí, señor."

"All right. We'll wait a couple of days, just to let the plan per-
colate in our minds. If any of you think of anything else we need
to talk about, anything that might go wrong we need to figure
out ahead of time, you come to me right away and tell me about
it. You'll all be riskin' your lives, or at least your freedom, so
don't hesitate to speak up."

Once again they all nodded in understanding, and then Bert
said, "You know, this sounds like one of those old-time train robberies people used to read about in dime novels or the *Police
Gazette*. You know, like something that Jesse James would do. Or
Butch Cassidy."

"Jesse James is dead," I said without thinking. It wasn't until
later, as I recalled the speculative look Enoch gave me when I
said that, that I thought about how somebody might take it.

But it was too late to worry about such things. In two more
days, we would be ready to make our move.

CHAPTER 28

I lay stretched out beside a greasewood bush on top of the ridge, with the edge of the bank about four feet in front of me. The sun was high in the brassy sky above me, and even though the season hadn't turned to summer yet, that big blazing ball packed plenty of heat. I wouldn't have wanted to lay out here all day.

Luckily, I didn't have to. The train was coming. I could already hear its faint rumble in the distance.

In the two days just past, we had gone over the plan more than a dozen times, talking it through until everybody knew exactly where he was supposed to be and what he was supposed to do. Enoch and Gabe were cool as they could be about the whole thing, making me more convinced than ever that they had done things like this before. I knew they were convinced that the same was true about me.

Santiago, Javier, and Fernando were pretty calm, too. I doubted if they had ever robbed a train before, but they might have driven some wet cattle across from Mexico. I hadn't asked Santiago how they had stocked their ranch, and he hadn't told me. For all I knew they had rustled some of Abner Tillotson's beeves, although I sort of doubted that.

That left Vince and Bert, and those two were nervous as cats but trying to control it. I was confident that once everything got started they would be all right, but there was no way of knowing that until the time came.

Randy was back at the Fishhook. If anybody showed up looking for me or any of the others, he would tell them that we were out on the range and that he didn't know exactly where to find us. Of course, if somebody wanted to search the whole spread they could do it, but I doubted if anybody would go to that much trouble. Besides, I wasn't expecting visitors.

The rails down in the cut began to hum. I could hear the sound even on top of the bank. The hum grew louder, and so did the rumble of the locomotive.

I kept my head down. I didn't think the engineer was likely to spot me on the other side of the greasewood bush, but I wore brown trousers and a tan shirt to help me blend into the ground. A low-crowned brown hat lay beside me.

The ground vibrated under me as the train entered the cut. It was easy to tell when the engine passed my position because of the terrible racket and the shaking. The clattering of the wheels on the rails was almost deafening.

I counted off a couple of beats before I lifted my head. The engine and the coal tender were past me. The first of a long string of boxcars rattled by. Behind the boxcars were three passenger cars, then the express car, and finally the caboose.

I came up on hands and knees, grabbed the hat, jammed it on my head, and tightened the chin strap. Then I pulled up the gray bandanna I wore so that it covered the lower half of my face and made sure the knot was tight on it, too.

There were still half a dozen boxcars to go when I surged to my feet. The blood pounding in my head sounded almost as loud as the train. It had been a long time since I'd done something like this. Too damned long, I told myself.

There are certain things in life that each man is cut out for, and they're different for everyone.

This was one of the things I'd been born to do.

Timing my jump, I waited for the next gap between cars to roll past below and in front of me. I took a deep breath as it did so, then launched into a short running jump that took me off the edge of the bank and sent me flying out over the cut. Once I was in midair, the top of the boxcar suddenly looked a lot narrower than it ought to. For a bad split-second I thought I had jumped too hard and was going to overshoot the car and fall into the deadly gap between it and the cutbank.

I didn't, of course. An instant later my feet hit smack-dab in the middle of the boxcar roof.

I twisted my body as I fell to my knees so that I would stay roughly in the center of the roof. I let myself go all the way to my belly and spread my arms. For a moment I just laid there stretched out on top of the boxcar, letting the rhythm of its rocking motion seep up into my body. When I climbed to my feet, I had adjusted to that motion and it didn't throw me off balance.

A quick slap of my hand against my right hip told me the Remington was still in its holster. The strap I'd rigged on it had kept the gun in place. I left the strap fastened for the moment since I still had some more jumping to do.

With their flatter roofs, boxcars were easier to move around on than passenger cars, although I'd done that, too, in the past. I trotted toward the front of this one and built up some speed so it wasn't too difficult to jump from it to the next car in line. When I landed on it I didn't go to my knees or even crouch, just kept moving instead.

They say that once you learn how to ride a bicycle, you never forget. I guess that robbing trains is something like that, because it all came back to me in a hurry. I didn't waste any time getting to the front of the train. On a long straight stretch like this, still well out of town, the brakies wouldn't have any reason to climb up where they could spot me, but you never knew when the engineer or fireman might take it into his head to look around.

The trickiest part was when I got to the coal tender and had to climb down the grab bars on the front of the first boxcar and swing over to the little ledge that ran along the outside of the tender. The engine and the boxcars were out of the cut by then, although the passenger cars, express car, and caboose were still rolling along between the banks.

I held my breath while I made the switch to the tender. The

ledge was only about six inches wide, but that was enough. I reached up, grasped the top of the side wall, and started edging toward the front. I wanted to get to the engine cab before we passed the wash where the rest of the bunch was waiting, but I supposed if I didn't, it wouldn't matter too much. They could catch up to us.

When I reached the front of the tender, it was easy enough to swing around the corner and step into the cab. Just as I did that, the fireman was about to reach through the door with his shovel and dig it into the coal. Instead, when he saw me he reacted fast, not even stopping to gape at me for a second before he swung the shovel at my head.

I ducked and let it go over me. While I was crouched like that, I flicked the strap off the Remington with my thumb and drew the long-barreled revolver. The fireman was going to try for me again with the backswing, but he froze when he saw me angling the gun up toward him.

"Drop it!" I ordered, shouting over the noise of the engine.

That was the first warning the engineer had that his cab had been invaded. His head jerked around toward me. I was far enough away from both of them that I could cover them at the same time.

Disgustedly, the fireman threw his shovel to the floor with a clatter and glared at me.

"You can't be robbing this train!" he said. "People don't rob trains anymore!"

I had to smile under the bandanna.

"You're wrong about that, old son," I told him. "That's exactly what I'm doin'." I nodded to the engineer and went on, "Go ahead and stop the train."

"I won't do it!" he said. In fact, he lunged for the throttle to make it go faster.

I fired from the hip, sending the bullet between them. It smashed one of the gauges. That was a lucky break, because I'd intended to bust up all the gauges anyway before we rode off. That was one I wouldn't have to break with my gun butt.

The shot made the engineer jerk his hand away from the throttle. I said, "I think you were reachin' for the brake."

He sighed. I could see the reaction, even though I couldn't hear it. He took hold of the brake and hauled back on it.

With a shriek of metal against metal, the train began to slow. I could see the wash now, coming up fast. The train shuddered and lurched and came to a halt less than a hundred yards past it.

The rest of the boys had already started running out of the wash. I heard the sharp crack of a shot from somewhere back along the train. Conductors were usually armed. I figured the one belonging to this train had spotted the fellas and realized what was going on.

Return fire came from the tall scarecrow I knew was Enoch. I hoped he was aiming high or low, so the promise I'd made to Vince about nobody being killed wouldn't be broken. But I couldn't blame Enoch for defending his own life and the lives of his friends.

"This is crazy!" the engineer said. "We're not carrying anything special."

"That's all right," I told him. "Bound to be something worthwhile in the express car."

But what if there wasn't, I suddenly asked myself. What if we'd risked our lives for nothing?

It was too late to call it off now. I motioned with the Remington's barrel and said, "Both of you get down on the floor. Move!"

They did what I told them, stretching out face down with their arms over their heads. They couldn't move very fast from that position.

The shooting from the rear of the train had stopped. I leaned out from the cab and glanced in that direction. Gabe was hurrying toward me, huffing and blowing. I hoped his ticker wouldn't give out on him.

I couldn't see Enoch or any of the vaqueros. They were probably inside the train already.

Gabe climbed into the cab and stood there for a second, bent over with his hands braced on his thighs. I asked him, "Are you all right?"

"Sure," he said between puffs. "Just been a while . . . since I done anything like this."

I waited until he had caught his breath and drawn his gun. Then I nodded to him and swung down from the cab.

Enoch had the conductor and a couple of brakemen out of the caboose and was prodding them forward along the tracks. He stopped next to the express car and waited for me to join them. When I got there I saw that the conductor had his bloody right hand cradled against the chest of his blue uniform jacket. Looked like Enoch had blown a hole through it.

"Before you say anything," Enoch spoke up, "he ventilated his own hand. Reckon he ain't used to handlin' a gun."

"Well, why would I be?" the conductor asked in an aggravated tone. "Nobody robs trains these days. This isn't the Wild West anymore!"

"That's where you're wrong, amigo," I told him. "The Wild West never dies. It just goes to sleep for a while."

He glared at me and didn't make any reply to that. I went to the door of the express car and hammered on it with the butt of my gun.

"Open up in there!" I yelled. "We got the conductor and the brakemen out here, and if you don't open that door I'll start shootin' 'em in about a minute!"

I didn't really plan to shoot anybody, but sometimes that threat worked. Sometimes you had to tell the express messenger you were fixing to blow the door off the car with dynamite. I've also threatened to run the car off the tracks into a ravine so that it'll bust open with the messenger still inside it. One time I actually had to dynamite the door. It made a mess, though, and I didn't want to do that again. Besides, I didn't have any dynamite.

The conductor sighed and shouted, "Open up, Carl! Looks like the Wild Bunch rides again!"

That made me give him a sharp look, but he didn't seem to mean anything by it. He was just disgusted and mad and hurting from that wounded hand. He probably thought he was being a little sarcastic.

From inside the express car, a muffled voice said, "But Mr. Newby—"

"Just do what I told you," the conductor said. "I'll take the responsibility for it."

A few more seconds went by, and then I heard the door being unfastened inside. It rolled back, revealing a young man awkwardly holding a rifle. I didn't give him a chance to figure out where to point it. I reached up, grabbed the barrel, and hauled the rifle out of the car, bringing the messenger with it. He let out a startled cry on his way to thudding down on the gravel at the edge of the tracks.

"Son, you're lucky I'm not in a killin' mood today," I told him as I handed the rifle to Enoch, who took it with his left hand while keeping everybody covered with the gun in his right.

The messenger was almost crying as he lay there on the ground. He said, "You don't understand. I'll lose my job over this!"

"Settle down," the conductor chided him. "There's nothing all that valuable in there."

Some instinct told me he was wrong. I hunkered on my heels next to the messenger and let the Remington's muzzle rest against his cheek.

"I've got a hunch Mr. Newby here doesn't know what he's talking about, Carl," I said. "Is there somethin' in the safe he don't know about?"

Before the young man could answer, Newby puffed up and glowered and said, "There damned well better not be. Nobody ships anything on my train without telling me!"

"Carl." I tapped his cheek with the gun barrel. "What's in there?"

He burst out, "The payroll for one of the mines across the border down in Mexico! It's more'n eight thousand dollars!"

Newby started cussing a blue streak. I grinned, took the gun away, and patted Carl's cheek with my left hand instead.

"That's a good boy," I said. "Now climb back in there and open the safe."

"I . . . I . . ."

"Don't bother tellin' me you can't. I know you can."

He didn't have it in him to be stubborn, not with that gun so close to his face. He got to his feet, and we climbed into the express car.

Banks, mining companies, rich ranchers, anybody who has to ship a lot of money, they tried all sort of things to get the loot safely to where it was going. Sometimes they put on a bunch of extra guards. Sometimes they used decoy shipments. Sometimes they tried to slip it in and out without anybody knowing except a small handful of people.

It appeared that was the case here. Pure luck had led us to stop this train today, when it was carrying a decent payoff.

I had just jumped down from the express car with a pair of canvas money pouches slung over my shoulder when that luck seemed to run out, though. I heard a familiar popping and rattling and looked toward town to see an automobile racing alongside the tracks toward us. To me, one of those contraptions looked pretty much like another, but from the way this one weaved back and forth, I had a pretty good hunch that Sheriff Emil Lester was at the wheel.

The next second, somebody leaned out to the side from the passenger seat and powdersmoke spurted as the varmint started shooting at us.

CHAPTER 29

The sharp cracks told me the passenger was firing a rifle at us, probably a Winchester. That automobile wasn't a very stable place to shoot from, though, especially with Sheriff Lester at the wheel. Sand kicked in the air a good twenty yards from the railroad tracks as a bullet struck there.

I had planned to disable the engine or at least do enough damage to the controls that all they'd be able to do was limp on into the county seat. That was out of the question now. We had to git.

"Go!" I barked at Enoch, then I ran alongside the passenger cars firing my gun in the air to get the attention of Santiago and his cousins. "Come on!" I bellowed at them.

Gabe stuck his head out from the cab. I waved the hand with the gun in it to let him know to leave the engineer and fireman there and rattle his hocks.

The vaqueros appeared on the rear platforms of the cars and leaped to the ground. We all took off in a straggling line toward the wash. I hung back a little, waiting for Gabe to catch up. When he did, I grabbed hold of his arm to help him along.

We could only hope that nobody got hit and the sheriff wasn't able to cut us off from the wash. It would have been all right with me if that blasted car blew a tire or busted an axle as it careened along. I had no idea what had brought Lester out here, but right now it didn't matter. The important thing was reaching the horses first. Once we were mounted we could take off along the wash and I was pretty sure the sheriff would never be able to catch us.

Vince and Bert must have been keeping a pretty close eye on things from the wash. Without warning, they charged out of it on horseback, each of them leading three of the other horses. They galloped out to meet us.

Lester was close, though. That damn car of his was fast. And his deputy, because that's who the passenger had to be, was a pretty good shot. The rifle bullets were whistling too close for comfort around us now as Vince and Bert reached us with the horses and we started trying to climb into the saddles.

A more distant rifle shot sounded. The sheriff's automobile slewed even more violently to one side. With a yell, the deputy went flying out the open door on his side. He lost his Winchester as he hit the ground.

More shots cracked, and a loud hissing sounded as steam boiled out from the front of the car. Somebody up on the ridge was shooting at Lester's vehicle, I realized, and doing a damned fine job of it, too. The automobile shuddered to a halt.

By that time I was in the saddle, and a quick glance told me the others were, too. I waved a hand toward the wash, not wanting to yell because Lester had heard my voice too often and might recognize it. The others were watching me, though, and followed orders. We all galloped at an angle away from the railroad tracks.

I looked back and saw Lester hopping around beside the car. He was so furious he couldn't stand still, I thought. He pointed a handgun at us and squeezed off a few rounds, but we were already out of effective range. He probably knew it, too. He was just blowing off steam—like his automobile—by shooting at us.

I didn't know for sure who had been up on the ridge helping us out, but I had a pretty good idea. Sure enough, when we emerged from the wash a little later I spotted a rider on a familiar horse galloping on a course that would intersect ours. I pointed him out, and we veered toward him to meet him quicker.

By now we had all pulled our bandanna masks down. The hombre who had come to our aid wasn't wearing one. When we came up to him and reined in, Bert exclaimed, "Randy!"

That's who it was, all right: Randy McClellan. With anxious fear on his face, he looked at each of us in turn.

"Nobody's hurt?" he asked.

"Nope," I said. "And you deserve some of the credit for that, son, stoppin' the sheriff in his tracks the way you did."

"I thought you weren't going to be part of this," Vince said.

Randy made a face and shrugged. He said, "That's what I thought, too, but the longer I sat there at the ranch the more it bothered me that I hadn't come with you. We're all supposed to be partners. That's what riding for the brand is all about, isn't it?"

"All for one and one for all," Bert said. "Like in a book I read once."

"Anyway," Randy went on, "when I couldn't stand it anymore I decided to come after you and keep an eye on you, just in case you needed help."

"I'm glad you did," I said. "But how'd you know where to find us? We didn't let you in on the details of the plan."

"Oh, I eavesdropped outside the window a couple of times when you were all talking," he said. "It wasn't hard."

I stared at him for a second, then burst out laughing.

"I didn't think you were that sneaky," I told him. "Good thing for us you were, though. We might've gotten away from Sheriff Lester anyway, but when you pitched in like that, you made sure of it."

Enoch said, "How'd that lawman know to come racin' out there from town?"

"I don't know. Maybe we can figure that out later. Right now let's just get back to the ranch before somebody happens to come along lookin' for us and wonders where we all are."

We set off for the Fishhook again, not galloping now but keeping the horses moving at a ground-eating lope. I kept an eye on our back trail, watching for any signs of pursuit. I didn't think Lester would get that automobile going again without some major repair work on it, and I didn't think he'd be able to get his hands on horses for him and his deputy without going back to the county seat first, but in this business it never hurts to expect the unexpected. Big surprises can be fatal.

I didn't see anyone following us, and that was the way I liked it.

As we rode along, Enoch asked me, "You really didn't know about that payroll bein' in the express car, did you, Jim?"

"Payroll?" Gabe echoed before I could say anything. "What's this about a payroll?"

"Eight grand that was bound for a mine below the border," Enoch said. "The conductor didn't even know it was on board. But I reckon you did, Jim."

"You reckon wrong," I told him. I could have let them think I was a lot smarter than I really was, or at least a lot more well-informed, but I wanted to play it straight with them. "You've got to have some luck in this business, and that's what this was."

Enoch shrugged. I could tell he didn't really believe me, but there was nothing I could do about that. I had told the truth.

"Eight thousand dollars?" Bert said, sounding like that was such a vast sum he couldn't even comprehend it. "Really?"

"Well, I haven't counted it yet," I said as I patted a hand against one of the money pouches I'd slung over the saddle. "But that's how much the express messenger claimed there was, and once he'd admitted it was there, I don't see why he'd have had any reason to lie about the amount."

"Eight thousand," Vince said. "That's . . ." He paused to do the ciphering in his head. "Almost nine hundred dollars for each of us!"

"No, amigo," Santiago said. "My cousins and I, we plan to take only half of the share coming to us. The other half goes to your madre."

"You can't do that," Vince protested. "It's not fair to you, after all the risks you ran."

"We all ran those risks, son," Enoch said. "And we all plan on splittin' the money with you and your ma."

I told Vince, "There's no point in arguin'. We all talked about it when you weren't around, and that's what we decided to do. We probably wouldn't have done this if the railroad hadn't cheated your ma." I couldn't help but grin. "And it was so much fun it was sure enough worth it!"

"Getting shot at was fun?" Vince asked.

Enoch said, "There's nothin' like the sound of a bullet goin' past your head to make you feel alive."

He was right about that. I nodded in agreement and said, "When we get back to the ranch we'll divvy up the money. You'll need to take the part that goes to you and your ma into town and give it to her. She can't put it in the bank, though, at least not right away and not all at once. That would make folks too curious about where she got it. Tell her to wait a little bit and then deposit some. She can say that relatives back east sent it to her, or some such."

Vince nodded.

"I understand," he said. "She's doing some work as a seamstress, too. She can use some of the money and claim she earned it that way."

"There you go. Now you're thinkin', son."

"I'll leave all of my part with her," he went on. "I don't need it. With that much money, she might be all right from now on."

I knew he was wrong about that. Money has a way of running out, no matter how much of it you have. I've heard people say that they have more than they could ever spend, but I don't believe it. You can always spend more money.

Bert said, "So we won't have to do this again, will we?" I thought he sounded a little disappointed.

"You mean nobody has to risk their lives again," Vince said.

"We'll see," I told them. "You can't ever tell what might come up."

That drew some odd looks from the three youngsters. Enoch and Gabe just smiled a little, and the vaqueros remained impassive.

As for me, the wheels of my brain were spinning around so

fast they were about to run away from me. In Enoch, Gabe, Santiago, and the Gallardo brothers I had the core of a tough, competent bunch. Randy, Vince, and Bert were raw as they could be, but they didn't lack for courage and they were smart enough to listen and remember the things I told them.

The possibilities were downright intriguing.

I knew I couldn't go any further with this, though, unless I told them the truth. They deserved that much. They deserved to know what they would be getting into.

I turned that over a few dozen times in my mind on the ride back to the ranch. By the time we got there I had reached a firm decision about what I was going to do. It could wait until after we handled a few other chores first, like dividing up the loot from the train robbery.

Night was falling as we rode in. Gabe said, "If one of you boys will take care of my horse, I'll get some coffee boilin' and rustle us up some grub."

"I'll tend to your horse, Gabe," Randy volunteered.

Gabe headed for the cook shack while the rest of us unsaddled and rubbed down our mounts, then made sure they had plenty of water and grain. The horses had done gallant service today, and they deserved some rest and good treatment.

I carried the money pouches in and set them on the table. An air of eagerness hung over the room, and I knew the boys wanted to gaze on those greenbacks. It wouldn't be right to do it without Gabe, however, so we waited until he brought in the coffee.

"Stew'll be ready in a while," he told us. "Let's go ahead and have a look at that dinero."

I unfastened the strap on one of the pouches. Just before I upended it to dump the contents on the table, the thought crossed my mind that ol' Carl might have lied to me. I didn't think so, but what if something besides money poured out?

Luckily, that wasn't the case. Banded bundles of cash fell onto the table as I turned the pouch upside down. The other pouch held more of the same. The men standing around the table stared avidly for a moment at the scattered loot. I knew that for some of them, at least, it was more money than they had ever seen in one place in their whole lives.

Then Bert reached out and started stacking the bundles in neat piles. He liked things orderly and organized.

"I've been thinking about what you said a while back, Bert," I told him. "About how this robbery was like something Jesse James or Butch Cassidy would pull."

"Yes, sir," he said, looking up at me in surprise. "I didn't mean any offense by that."

"None taken, son," I assured him. "In fact, I'm sort of honored by the comparison to Jesse James."

"But not by the one to Butch Cassidy?" he asked with a puzzled frown.

"Well, I can't rightly be honored to be compared to Butch Cassidy," I said.

Grins began to spread over the faces of Enoch and Gabe.

"You see," I went on, "I can't be compared to him because I am him."

Bert looked more confused than ever. He shook his head and said, "Who?"

"Butch," I said as I let my gaze sweep around the table at all of them. "You see, boys, I *am* Butch Cassidy."

CHAPTER 30

See, I told you I'm fond of dramatic moments. That bold declaration sure as hell was one of those moments. It caused the three youngsters to stare at me in shock, and even the normally stolid vaqueros seemed surprised. Javier and Fernando's bushy eyebrows went up at exactly the same time like they'd practiced it. Only Enoch and Gabe didn't look at me like I'd totally lost my mind.

Nobody said anything for a long moment before Randy finally spoke up.

"That's not possible," he said. "Butch Cassidy must be dead by now. He dropped out of sight a long time ago."

"Yeah," Bert chimed in. "I read about him in a magazine I found in the train station. I think it said he was hanged somewhere."

I asked, "Would that have been an issue of the *Police Gazette*, Bert?" I chuckled. "Hate to tell you this, son, but everything they print in that rag ain't always the truth. Sometimes it's nowhere close."

"I don't believe it, either," Vince said. "No offense, Mr. Strickland, but I'm not sure Butch Cassidy was even real."

I tried not to look forlorn as I said, "Now, you ought to know better than that, Vince. I'm as real as can be. I'm standin' right in front of you, ain't I?"

The three of them all started talking at once. Enoch listened to it for a few seconds, then raised his voice and said, "Hush!"

They all stared at him, sort of like they had stared at me a couple of minutes earlier when I told them the truth.

Enoch went on, "You sound like a bunch of chickens squabblin' in a farmyard. Of course Butch Cassidy's real. I seen him with my own eyes, years ago."

"Is that true?" I asked him. "We've met?"

"Not exactly. But we were in the same livery stable one afternoon in Winnemucca, almost fifteen years ago. You rode in on a big white horse with a couple of other fellas."

"I remember that horse," I said. "Fast as greased lightning he was."

Enoch nodded and went on, "Nobody around there knew who you were then. But when the bank was robbed a couple of days later, they all figured it out, sure enough. You were havin' a look around the town before you and the rest of the Wild Bunch hit the bank, weren't you?"

I shrugged.

"I always liked to know what we'd be gettin' into," I said. "So you saw me one time in a livery stable and never forgot it?"

"I'd already done considerable hell-raisin' myself by that time. Fact of the matter is, I wouldn't have minded ridin' with you boys back then. But no, I didn't recognize you right away when you came up to us in the saloon in Largo. I just knew you looked a mite familiar. Didn't think nothin' of that, since I've been a heap of places and seen a heap of people. But when you started talkin' about robbin' a train, that day in Winnemucca came back to me."

Gabe added, "And I knew you'd been an owlhoot, even if you were tryin' to go straight now. You'd get that faraway look in your eyes, like you could feel the wild, lonesome trails callin' to you."

"Why, Gabe," I said with a grin, "that was almost poetical."

Randy said, "So the two of you believe him? You think he's really Butch Cassidy?"

"Why shouldn't we believe him?" Enoch said.

"Because Butch Cassidy and the Sundance Kid are dead!"

I sighed.

"Bring back bad memories, Jim?" Gabe asked. "Sorry, that's what I'm used to callin' you."

"Jim's fine," I assured him. "I've been usin' it for a while. Ever since last December, when I came on a poor fella who'd been gut-shot—." I stopped and shook my head. "I'll tell you boys the whole story, but Gabe, you've got stew simmerin' and need to tend to it. How about we wait until after supper for me to explain everything?"

"That's not fair!" Bert said. "You can't just tell us that you're Butch Cassidy, then expect us to sit around and wait for the story!"

"I'll talk better on a full stomach."

"We can wait," Enoch said. "Butch Cassidy's been dead for a long time. He can stay dead for a little while longer."

The three youngsters didn't like it, but they didn't argue. Gabe went to check on the stew, saying, "You can count the money while I'm gone. I trust you to divvy it up right."

So that's what we did. Those pouches had $8,260 in them. That was $920 apiece, minus a couple of dollars on each share. For simplicity's sake the eight of us, not counting Vince, each kicked in $450, making a kitty of $3,600. With Vince's share put in, that made a little more than $4,500 to give to his ma.

He warned us, "She's liable to guess where it came from and refuse to take it. She's always prided herself on being an honest woman."

"After what the railroad did to your pa and then to her, she's liable to decide she's got it coming, even if she does figure out where you got it," I said. "It's only fair."

"We'll have to wait and see."

"She won't turn us in, will she?" Randy asked worriedly.

Vince glared and said, "Damn it, Randy, if we weren't friends, I might have to take a poke at you for that. My ma would never do such a thing."

I hoped he was right about that. But it was a chance we had to take.

After supper, the nine of us found places to sit. I was in one of the armchairs, with Scar curled up on the floor next to my feet. I reached down from time to time and scratched one of his ragged ears as I commenced telling them what they wanted to know.

"I'll start off by sayin' that I'm not gonna give you a lot of details about some parts of this. They're still too painful for me to dwell on, even after all this time. But I'll tell you that there came a time when Harry and me—that's Harry Longabaugh, my best friend, him who folks called the Sundance Kid—there came a time when the two of us went to South America along with a female acquaintance of ours who was Harry's particular ladyfriend."

Back in those days, when I was telling the story to the boys on the Fishhook, the general public didn't know about the whole South America business, about how Harry and Etta and I went to Argentina and tried to make a go of it as honest ranchers. It was a number of years later, when somebody wrote a story about it in another magazine, not the *Police Gazette*, that that part of our lives came to light for most folks, although friends and family knew where we'd gone at the time, of course. I had written letters to some of them to tell them about it.

Sitting there in the ranch house, I told my new friends about how the ranching hadn't worked out and how Harry and I had fallen back into our old, larcenous habits, especially after Etta fell ill and had to return to the States. With just the two of us knocking around down there on the loose, the temptation was too much to resist.

So we drifted over into Bolivia, robbed a few banks, and stuck up a mine payroll. When I got to that part I looked at the neat stacks of bills still sitting on the table and thought about how there are cycles in all our lives, patterns that repeat themselves again and again, sometimes right out in the open and sometimes so subtle you can't even see them unless you know to look for them.

"Hitting that payroll turned out to be a mistake," I said. "The army was lookin' for us, and when we stopped in a little village called San Vicente to rest our horses and fix something to eat, the soldiers caught up to us. Somebody in the village pointed to the abandoned hut where we were stayin' and told the capitan we were in there. He and his sergeant marched up and tried to arrest us, and Harry and me . . . well, we didn't want to be arrested."

Even though it was nighttime and we were indoors as I was telling the story, I seemed to feel the hot sun on my face again. I heard the shots booming, smelled the sharp tang of powder-smoke in my nose, relived the shock of a bullet hitting me.

I could see as well the bright splash of blood on Harry's shirt. He was wounded a lot worse than I was, even before he made an unsuccessful dash for the rifles we'd left outside and was hit several more times.

The afternoon we spent holed up in that hut had seemed like a year instead. It's a hard thing to watch your best friend dying by inches. For years afterward, I sometimes woke up at night in a cold sweat, having dreamed that I was back there sitting on that dirt floor with my back propped against an adobe wall, while across from me the light slowly dimmed in his eyes.

I didn't say much about that to Enoch and the others, just told them that we traded shots with some soldiers and then took cover inside the hut.

"That evening Harry died," I said simply. "If he had been able to hang on until they charged us, I would have stayed there with him and died beside him. That was the kind of pards we were. But with him gone there was no point in it. I managed to slip out in the dark, which is what I knew he would've wanted me to do." I sighed. "I heard talk later, while I was still in South America, about how they found us both dead in there and buried us in a cemetery close by. My hunch is that they didn't want to admit I'd gotten away, so they buried one of the soldiers who'd been killed in my place. But I don't know if that's right, and I don't reckon anybody ever will know for sure. The only thing that's certain is that Harry Longabaugh, the Sundance Kid, died there, and I didn't."

I paused for a long moment, overcome by the memories.

When I didn't go on, Bert leaned forward on the sofa, where he was sitting with Vince and Randy, and asked eagerly, "What happened then? How did you get from there to here?"

"Oh, a lot of things went on that weren't very interestin'," I said. "I was hurt and laid up for a while. Some of the Indians who lived down there took me in and cared for me until I got well enough to travel. There was nothin' left for me in South America, so I went to Europe. Knocked around there for a while. I finally came back to the States because I wanted to see some of my kinfolks again, and because I knew I needed to talk to Harry's ladyfriend and let her know the truth about how things ended up down there. I didn't want her hearin' any rumors and not knowin' the straight of things.

"I didn't spend a lot of time thinking about that part of it, either. Etta and I had been good friends—might have been more than that if she hadn't been with Harry—but she was hurt by the news I brought her and told me she didn't ever want to see me again. I had honored that request, even though it pained me at times.

"Since then I've just traveled around the country, visited family now and then, done a little gambling, worked at jobs when I had to. Honest jobs, mind you. I thought my outlaw days were over. I even got a laugh now and then when I heard that some fella somewhere was claiming to be me. That happened several times. I always thought, well, if that so-and-so is really Butch Cassidy, then the law should arrest him and send him to prison for all the things Butch did."

"Bet he would've changed his story in a pretty big hurry if that happened," Enoch drawled.

That made me laugh. I nodded and said, "I expect you're right."

"So if all this is true," Randy said, "how did you wind up here on the Fishhook?"

"That's a whole other story," I said, and I gave it to them, starting with finding Abner Tillotson in that gully and then settling his score with the Daughtry brothers for him.

When I was finished, Randy frowned and said, "I suppose it could have happened that way. The part about Butch Cassidy, I mean."

Vince said, "I believe you about the Daughtrys. They were a bad bunch. Probably everybody in this part of the country had heard of them. And most were glad when it looked like they pulled up stakes and moved on."

"Then this ranch is legally yours?" Bert asked.

"I've got the deed and a bill of sale signed by Abner," I assured him. "It's legally mine, all right."

"And yet you risked it to help me and my mother," Vince said.

"Ride for the brand," I said. "That goes both ways."

They let that sit there for a few seconds, then Bert turned to Enoch and asked, "Do you believe Mr. Strickland is really Butch Cassidy?"

Without hesitation, Enoch nodded.

"I do," he said. "I'd bet this old hat of mine on it."

"So do I," Gabe added. "His story rings true as far as I'm concerned."

"Sí," Santiago said. His cousins nodded in solemn agreement.

"Well, I'm not convinced," Randy said, "but it doesn't really matter, does it? The train robbery is over and done with. Nobody got hurt, and Vince's mother ought to be all right now. It's over. Finished."

"Well . . . ," I said. "I'm not so sure about that."

They all looked at me, and Enoch asked slowly, "Just what did you have in mind, Jim?"

"That money's gonna come in mighty handy for Vince's ma, no doubt about that. But that wasn't the only reason we decided to do this. What those fellas Kennedy and Milton did, cheating Mrs. Porter and havin' Rutledge spread those ugly rumors about Vince's pa bein' drunk, those things are just flat-out wrong, and they deserve to pay for 'em."

"The holdup's got to be embarrassing for them," Vince said.

"One holdup's not all that embarrassing."

That was true enough, but there was more to it than that.

Today I had felt more alive than I had in years. It hadn't been a bad life since coming back to the States, I suppose, but all of it sort of blended together. Today—that moment when I'd leaped from the bank onto the boxcar, the feeling of a gun in my hand, even the whine of a bullet past my ear—those things would never be a blur. They would always stand out sharp and clear in my mind.

"What are you saying, Mr. Strickland?" Randy asked.

I gave him a straight answer. I said, "I think this new Wild Bunch of ours ought to ride again."

CHAPTER 31

Nothing much was said after that. Enoch and Gabe weren't shocked, of course, and I couldn't tell about Santiago and his cousins. Bert, Vince, and Randy seemed to have a lot of trouble believing I had actually suggested such a thing. It had been a long day, and I could tell they were going to have to mull it over, so I suggested that we all turn in. That would give them a chance to sleep on it.

Since it was late, Santiago, Javier, and Fernando spent the night rather than returning to their spread, bedding down in the barn. The next morning nobody seemed to want to bring up the subject, and I thought it might be wise not to push the issue. I was confident that once they had a chance to get used to the idea, they'd all come around to my way of thinking.

Vince needed to take that money to his mother, but I didn't want him riding all the way to the county seat by himself while he was carrying that much loot. So after we'd eaten breakfast and the vaqueros had headed for home, taking their shares with them, I said, "Vince, why don't you and Enoch and I ride to town today? Gabe and Bert and Randy can hold down the fort here."

Vince gave me a suspicious look and asked, "Why do you and Enoch need to go?"

"Nobody knows that we had anything to do with that train robbery," I said, hoping that was true. "But even so, you might run into trouble carryin' that much money. There are road agents who are always on the lookout for a fella travelin' by himself."

"Maybe there used to be," he said. "I'm not sure there are anymore."

"Well, you don't ever know. I'd just feel better about it if you weren't ridin' by yourself."

Vince thought about it for a second and then shrugged.

"All right," he agreed. "I'd like to get that money to my ma and have a talk with her about it, and I probably *would* get a little nervous about riding that far with it by myself. What you're saying makes sense, Mr. Strickland."

"All right, then. We'll saddle up and ride."

We started out early enough to make it to the county seat by early afternoon. The idea of riding right into Sheriff Lester's bailiwick like that might've given pause to some folks, but it didn't really bother me. I didn't see how Lester could have recognized any of us the day before.

The sheriff could count, though, or at least I assumed he was smart enough to since he'd managed to get elected, and if he had noticed that there were nine of us, that might put some thoughts in his head. He knew that the Fishhook crew had totaled nine during roundup.

Having thoughts in your head was a far cry from proving anything, though. I was willing to run that risk. The truth is, knowing that Lester might suspect us just sweetened the pot that much more and made me look forward to that visit to the county seat.

We didn't stop in Largo but headed straight on to town. When we got there we went to the Porter house, where Vince's ma seemed surprised to see him. She gave him a hug, though, and nodded to me and Enoch.

"Mr. Strickland," she said. "Mr. Cole. What brings all of you to town?"

"I've got something for you, Ma," Vince said. We had fixed up a money belt for him out of a piece of blanket so he could wear it under his shirt. He pulled it out now and set it on the dining room table.

"What in the world is that?" Mrs. Porter asked.

"What the railroad owes us," Vince said.

His mother's eyes got big. She said, "All everybody in town is talking about this morning is that train robbery. Tell me you didn't have anything to do with that, Vincent. Please."

Vince didn't say anything. After thirty seconds or so, Mrs. Porter groaned and put her hands to her cheeks. She sank down in a wing chair with a lace doily on the back.

"Vince, no," she said. She looked like she could barely comprehend the situation. "You shouldn't have done such a thing."

"It was the only way for us to get what's rightfully coming to us, Ma," he told her.

"Only way for the railroad to get what it had comin', too," Enoch added in his dry drawl.

"What they're doing is wrong, but this . . . this isn't right, either," Mrs. Porter insisted.

I said, "Maybe not in the eyes of the law, ma'am, but I'll tell you . . . it's justice. None of that money came from the passengers, or from the mail sacks. No innocent person will suffer from losing it. The railroad will have to make it good, and it's the railroad's greed that cost you your husband. I'd say they could pay for a long time to come without squarin' that debt."

She looked at me and asked, "Mr. Strickland, was this your idea?"

I wasn't going to lie to someone who'd suffered like she had. I said, "Yes, ma'am, it was. So don't blame your boy. We pretty much forced him to go along with us, didn't we, Enoch?"

"That's not true," Vince said before Enoch could answer. "Well, the part about Mr. Strickland coming up with the idea is, but nobody forced me to do anything. I wanted to go along. I want Kennedy and Milton to have to answer to their bosses and try to explain how that payroll was lost on their watch."

Mrs. Porter clasped her hands together in her lap, looked down, and shook her head. I thought she was going to be stubborn about the whole thing, but then she looked up and I saw a hint of a smile on her lips.

"I imagine that was pretty awkward for them, all right," she said.

That made me grin. I said, "Yes, ma'am, I bet it was."

She looked at the makeshift money belt on the table.

"I don't feel right about this," she said. "But to tell the truth, Bob's death really left us in a bind." She thought about it some more. "I suppose I could take just enough to get by for a little while . . ."

"You need to take all of it," Vince said. "My part, too. I don't need it."

He went on to explain to her what I'd told him about not depositing the money in the bank just yet. She seemed to grasp the idea. She protested a little more about taking the loot, but I could tell she really wanted to and knew that in the end she would. It wasn't really a matter of the money. She just wanted to get back at Kennedy and Milton, as well she should have.

Finally, after it was all settled, she said, "You have to promise me, Vince, that you'll never do anything this foolish again. You could have been hurt, or even killed!"

He glanced at me, then said, "I promise, Ma. I'll never again do what I did yesterday."

That seemed to satisfy her. She asked, "Can you spend the night?"

Vince shook his head.

"We have to get back to the ranch," he told her. "But I'll come to town for a visit again just as soon as I can."

I could tell she was disappointed that he wasn't staying, but she didn't try to talk him into it. Instead she hugged him, shook hands with Enoch and me, and said, "Any time you gentlemen are in town, I'll be expecting you to stop by."

"I reckon there's a good possibility of that, ma'am," Enoch told her.

"I'm going to make sure of it," she said. "I baked some sugar cookies this morning. I'm going to wrap them up and let you take them with you."

Vince practically licked his lips at that, so I knew the cookies would be good. I said, "We sure won't turn down that offer, ma'am."

We had to go by the train station on our way out of town, and as we did I saw Sheriff Lester standing in front of the door talking to three men I recognized as Rutledge, Kennedy, and Milton. All of them looked upset, and I felt a real satisfaction from seeing that. Lester didn't seem to notice us, and we didn't linger in the neighborhood of the depot. I didn't see any point in reminding Lester of our existence if we didn't have to.

We had gone a few miles along the dirt road that led to Largo when I spotted something up ahead. An automobile had pulled off to the side and stopped, and one of the flaps that opened on the front of it was lifted. Somebody wearing a long duster was bent over looking under the flap. Obviously, something had gone wrong with the contraption and it wouldn't run.

I reckon the smile on my face must've been pretty smug when we rode up. I was thinking that this was just one more example of why a man was a lot better off with a horse. Of course, a horse could go lame or throw its rider, leaving a man afoot just like this poor gent was. But I didn't think about that at the time.

"Looks like you've got some trouble there, partner," I said in a mocking tone. "Need some help?"

The stranded hombre straightened up, turned around, and glared at me, and he was no hombre at all. He was a she, a fact that the long, shapeless duster had concealed. Her red hair was tucked up under a straw boater that was tied on her head with a scarf, so I hadn't had that clue, either.

"No, I don't need any help," Daisy Hatfield said with a defiant jut of her chin. "In fact, I'm just fine, Mr. Strickland!"

CHAPTER 32

There haven't been very many times in my life when I was rendered speechless, as they say, but that was one of 'em.

Of course that flustered condition didn't last but a second or two, and then I said, "Beggin' your pardon, Miss Hatfield, but if that automobile won't go and you're afoot out here miles from town, you ain't fine."

"Nonsense," she said without missing a beat. "I'll simply walk back to town and find someone to assist me."

"You got three someones right here."

"You mean you know how to repair an automobile?"

Well, she had me there. I looked at Enoch and Vince, and when they both shook their heads, I said, "As a matter of fact, we don't." Bravado prompted me to add, "But I'd be glad to take a look at it and see if I can figure it out."

She stepped back and waved a slender hand at the workings underneath the flap.

"Be my guest," she said.

I swung down from the saddle, but it took me only a moment to realize I had gnawed off a lot bigger hunk than I could chew. I looked at all the wires and hoses and metal rods and knew it was hopeless. None of it made sense to me.

Admitting defeat went against the grain, though, so I asked, "What does it do?"

"Nothing. That's the problem."

"No, I mean, it was runnin', wasn't it? You got this far, so it must have been."

"Yes, it was running," Daisy said. "But then it just sputtered a couple of times and the engine stopped running. It rolled a few more feet and I was able to get it over here on the side of the road, but that's all."

From horseback, Enoch rubbed his jaw and said, "Does it have any of that foul-smellin' stuff it runs on in it?"

Daisy's eyes widened. She put a hand to her mouth and said, "Oh, my word. I forgot to put gasoline in it, and I'll bet Father must have, too."

"Preachers' daughters shouldn't gamble," I said.

"That's not what I meant." She sounded pretty upset as she went on, "What am I going to do now?"

I had already started thinking about that. I said, "We could tie our ropes to it and pull it, I suppose. Three horses ought to be enough to get it rollin'."

"Could you take me back to town?"

I didn't particularly want to go back to the county seat. That would take the rest of the day and force us to spend the night in town. I said, "Why don't we just take you on to Largo? That's where you were headed, wasn't it?"

"Well . . . yes. But it would be closer to go back, wouldn't it?"

"Never go back when you can go ahead," I said.

Enoch added, "Davy Crockett said, 'Be sure you're right, then go ahead.'"

"Oh, all right, you've talked me into it," Daisy said with a sigh. "Once we get there I can put gasoline in the tank with the new pump at Mr. Farnum's store."

That was what I had thought, too.

Like all self-respecting cowboys, we never went anywhere without our lassos. We tied them securely to the front of the automobile, then dallied them around our saddle horns.

"Where am I going to ride?" Daisy asked.

"You can ride in the automobile," I said, pointing to it. "It'll go almost as fast with us pullin' it as it does under its own power, I expect."

"Why don't I ride with you?" She opened the duster to reveal that she was wearing trousers. "I'm dressed for it, after all."

"I'm surprised your pa would stand for a female relative bein' dressed in such scandalous fashion."

She had to smile at that. She said, "I told him it was necessary in order to operate the machine properly. He's still frightened of it, so he didn't question me."

It would have been more apt for her to ride with Vince, since he was closer to her own age, but once I was in the saddle, I held my hand down to her and took my left foot out of the stirrup. We clasped wrists, and she stepped up and swung a leg over the horse's back like she'd been doing it all her life.

"I used to ride when I was a little girl," she said, almost like she had heard my thoughts. "I always loved it, but I haven't been on a horse in quite a while."

"Come out to the ranch sometime," I told her. "We'll go ridin'."

"That's not a bad idea," she said as she slipped her arms around my waist to hang on and settled herself against me.

I told Vince to get in the car and steer. Enoch could lead his mount. Side by side, we urged the horses forward. The ropes tightened, and the car started to move, its wheels turning fairly easily on the hard-packed dirt.

"If your pa doesn't like automobiles, why'd he get one?" I asked once we were moving along at a steady walk.

"He thought it would allow him to cover more ground in his missionary work," she said. "He says we have to spread the word about the church in Largo."

"Is that what you were doin' in town? Spreadin' the word?"

"No, I went in to pick up some boxes of Bibles and hymnals that were delivered on the train yesterday. They're in the back of the car." She paused. "Thank goodness those terrible men who held up the train didn't take them, too."

"Yeah, you know how owlhoots are about stealin' hymnals," Enoch drawled.

I couldn't see her, but I suspected Daisy either glared at him . . .

or stuck her tongue out at him. From Enoch's chuckle, I couldn't tell which.

"Seriously, it's the talk of the town," she went on. "Imagine, an old-fashioned train robbery in this day and age. I suppose some things never change. It's just human nature for some men to be greedy."

That made me stiffen. I said, "It's just human nature for some men to want to see justice done, too."

"How could there be any justice in robbing a train?"

"If you'd ever had very many dealin's with the railroad, you might know the answer to that question."

I was getting mighty close to saying too much, but I felt compelled to defend what we'd done. With most folks, I wouldn't give a hang what they thought, but Daisy's opinion mattered to me, for whatever reason.

Despite that, I thought it might be a good idea to change the subject, so I asked, "How's the church-buildin' comin' along?"

She sighed and said, "Not very well, I'm afraid. Father says that raising funds is always a challenge. But if it was easy, it wouldn't really be worth doing, would it?"

"He can afford to buy an automobile and a shipment of Bibles and hymnals, but he can't finish buildin' the church?"

That was sort of a rude thing to say, and I knew it as soon as the words were out of my mouth. Daisy didn't seem offended, though.

"He's always had trouble managing money," she said. "Numbers don't mean as much to him as words do. To be fair, though, he had ordered the car and the books before he knew he would run into difficulty raising the funds to finish the church."

That might be true, I thought, but Reverend Hatfield should have anticipated that not everything would go smoothly. I really wasn't in a position to sit in judgment on anybody, though, so I didn't say anything else.

The conversation put an idea in my head. I filed it away to think about later.

Towing the car like that meant it was pretty slow going for us, but we made it to Largo by late afternoon. As far as I was concerned, we got there too soon, because I'd be lying if I said I didn't care for the way Daisy's body kept rubbing against my back as we rode. Her arms were tight around my waist and she rode pretty snug against me. It felt mighty good.

Nothing lasts forever, though. I'd proven that quite a few times in my life. When we reached Largo we hauled the automobile to the gas pump that stood to the side of Clyde Farnum's store. I saw the shell of the church at the edge of town, just the skeleton of a building at the present time.

Farnum must have seen or heard us coming. He walked out onto the store's porch and said, "Well, I'll swan. You run out of gas, Miss Hatfield?"

"It appears so," she said as she slid down from my horse. "The car wouldn't go anymore."

Farnum picked up a long, skinny stick that was leaning against the wall and came down from the porch. He went over to the automobile and unscrewed something on it. He slid the stick down into a hole, rattled it around, and pulled it out.

"Yep, dry as a bone," he said. "I'll fill 'er up."

"Thank you. And you'll put the cost on my father's tab?"

Farnum didn't look that happy about the idea, but he nodded and said, "Yes'm, I sure will."

He stuck a hose with a nozzle on it into the hole on the automobile, turned some sort of crank on the pump, and the sharp tang of gasoline filled the air as it ran into the tank. Vince got out of the car and untied our lassos from the contraption. I coiled mine and hung it on the saddle.

Daisy looked up at me and said, "Thank you for your help, Mr. Strickland. I don't know what I would have done if you gentlemen hadn't come along."

"You'd have figured out something," I told her. "I've got a hunch you're pretty resourceful."

"I've had to be," she said, and I knew she was talking about having to deal with real life while her pa spent most of his time with his head in the clouds of Heaven.

Vince mounted up again. I looked over at him and Enoch and said, "Why don't you boys head on out to the ranch? I'll catch up to you later."

"What are you plannin' on doin'?" Enoch asked.

"I thought I'd help Miss Hatfield unload those boxes of Bibles and hymnals."

She said, "Oh, you don't need to do that. I can handle it, and you've already helped plenty today. There's no need for you to bother."

"It's no bother," I told her with a shake of my head. "And it shouldn't take long. I don't mind."

"Well . . . all right," she said. "If you're sure."

Vince said, "It'd take even less time if we all helped—"

"The boss said get back to the ranch," Enoch interrupted him. "So we'd best get back to the ranch." He reached up and tugged on his hat brim as he nodded to Daisy. "Good afternoon to you, Miss Hatfield."

"Good afternoon, Mr. Cole," she said. "And to you, too, Mr. Porter."

Vince looked a mite confused, but he didn't argue. He just said, "Ma'am," and rode off with Enoch. I appreciated what the old gun-wolf had done, giving me some time alone with Daisy like that, whether he agreed with me taking an interest in her or not.

Farnum finished putting gasoline in the car. He took a pad of paper and a stub of pencil from his pocket and made a note of some numbers he got from the pump. I knew he was going to add the total to Reverend Hatfield's bill as Daisy had told him to.

"Want me to crank her for you?" he asked her.

"Yes, please," she said as she got behind the wheel.

Farnum turned the crank, bending over and putting some elbow grease into it, and after a minute or so the thing started with a sputtering blast of combustion. My horse shied away from it.

Daisy drove into the road and turned toward the boardinghouse. I followed her, wrinkling my nose at the smell coming from the automobile. I knew better than to think that the things were ever going away, but I hoped that they never got to where they were more common than horses.

When we reached the boardinghouse, the old woman who ran it was sitting in a rocking chair on the front porch. In the silence that followed Daisy shutting off the engine, she said, "Land's sake, child, that thing is noisy!"

"I'm sorry if it disturbs you, Mrs. Higgins," Daisy said as she climbed out and went to the back. She lifted a lid there and reached in to pick up a box. By the time she did, I had dismounted and looped my reins around the automobile's front bumper. I took the box from her and said, "I've got that."

"Then I'll take another," she said. "I'm not going to let anyone do all my work for me."

Since there was no point in arguing with her, I didn't try. I just smiled and helped her carry half a dozen boxes into the parlor, where we stacked them in a corner. I suppose Daisy's father had made arrangements with the landlady to store them there until the church was built.

Mrs. Higgins was still sitting on the front porch fanning herself when we finished with the chore. As we came outside, she said, "Your daddy asked me to tell you that he's down at the church, Daisy."

"I'm not surprised."

I suggested, "Maybe you'd better go down there and let him know you got back all right. He might be worried since the trip took you longer than you expected."

"My father has a tendency to lose track of time," she said with a faint smile. "He probably hasn't even given my absence a thought. But I suppose it wouldn't hurt anything."

"I'll walk down with you."

I knew I was just looking for an excuse to spend more time with her. I didn't want to leave. I'd enjoyed the afternoon too much.

"That's not necessary, Mr. Strickland."

"I don't know," I said. "Largo can be a rough place some-times."

"I don't think I'll be in any danger. The Comanches are long since tamed, aren't they?"

"Yeah, but there are outlaws around. You know what hap-pened to that train yesterday."

I had to make an effort not to grin at that one.

"I suppose you're right," she said. She had taken off her straw boater while we were unloading the books. Now she put it back on and tied it into place with the scarf. "It's a free country. I can't stop you if you want to walk with me."

I untied my horse and led it as we started toward the partially completed church. As we walked, I said, "I thought you were gonna call me Jim. You've been callin' me Mr. Strickland all day."

"I know. It just didn't seem—please don't make fun of me for this—it just didn't seem proper to be calling you that in front of other people."

I nodded and said, "I reckon I can understand that. But we're alone now . . . Daisy."

"We're also in the middle of the street in broad daylight . . . Jim. What do you expect me to do, throw myself in your arms and kiss you like that brazen hussy at the dance did?"

"I was sort of fond of that brazen hussy," I told her. I looked over at her and saw the flush that had crept over her face, but I also saw the pleased smile that curved her lips. Even in broad daylight, I wouldn't have minded kissing them.

Maybe it was a stroke of luck—whether good luck or bad is a toss-up, I reckon—but at that moment I heard loud, angry voices ahead of us, coming from the vicinity of the church.

CHAPTER 33

Beside me, Daisy caught her breath. She said, "Father . . ."

"Sounds like he's arguin' with somebody."

She shot a worried glance at me.

"He doesn't argue with people. That's not like him. But that doesn't stop other people from getting angry with him sometimes."

I took hold of her arm. She didn't pull away from me.

"We'd better find out what it's about," I said. I started walking faster toward the church. Daisy had to hurry to keep up with my long-legged strides.

Nobody was in sight in front of the framework, which had all four sides and the ceiling joists in place but was lacking the rafters and roof. I spotted several men behind the place, though, and one of them was Reverend Franklin Hatfield. The sun reflected off his mostly bald head as he stood there with his hands out, making conciliatory gestures toward the man confronting him.

That man was a stranger to me, a burly sort in work boots, khaki trousers and shirt, and a battered brown fedora. His sleeves were rolled up over brawny forearms. Two other men in work clothes were standing a few yards behind him, but they weren't taking any part in the ruckus, at least not yet. Off to one side was a truck with slat sides around the bed.

The big fella in the brown hat ignored whatever Hatfield was trying to tell him. He stepped closer, jabbed the preacher in the chest with a blunt finger, and said, "Excuses won't pay my bills. I don't care if you *are* a man of the cloth, you've got to pony up for that load of lumber!"

Hatfield said, "Please, Brother Nelson—"

"I'm not your brother! And I'm not my brother's keeper, neither. You'd better come up with the money you owe me right now, or else—"

"Or else what?" I said, moving so that I was in front of Daisy.

Nelson turned his beefy face toward me, looking startled and confused, and more than a little annoyed by the interruption.

"What?" he said.

"That's what I'm askin' you," I said. I waved a hand toward the framework. "What are you gonna do if you don't get paid? Looks to me like all those boards are already nailed together. Are you gonna pull all the nails, load up the boards, and haul them off? You won't be able to sell them for new anymore, and some of 'em will likely be too damaged from bein' pulled apart to be good for anything. So I'll ask you again . . . what are you gonna do?"

"Who the hell are you?" Nelson demanded.

Hatfield said, "Please, Brother Nelson, no intemperate language—"

Nelson shoved past him and took a challenging step toward me.

"I asked you who the hell you are."

"Seems like neither one of us like to answer questions much," I said. "But I'll go first. My name's Strickland. I'm a friend of the reverend and his daughter."

"You know good and well I'm not going to tear down that church, Strickland," Nelson snapped. "Although I might consider it if I'm pushed far enough. But you can damn well bet that I'll never bring any more lumber out here for this Bible-thumping deadbeat. Not only that, I'll spread the word through the whole county and make sure nobody else sells him any lumber, either. That church won't ever be finished!"

I didn't like the hombre, and he wasn't making me any

fonder of him by talking that way about Daisy's pa right in front of her. But I held my temper for the moment and asked, "How much money do you have comin' to you?"

"Five hundred dollars!"

I put my hand in my pocket. Daisy saw that and said, "Jim, what are you doing?"

I didn't answer her. Instead I pulled out a roll of bills. When I held out the money toward Nelson, he reached for it instinctively. I could have decked him then, but instead I slapped the roll down in his palm.

"I don't have that much on me, but there's a couple of hundred on account. I'll see to it that you get the rest. My name's Jim Strickland, and I own the Fishhook Ranch. Everybody in these parts knows me and will vouch for me."

Now, here's the odd thing. That was true. Despite all the disreputable things I'd done in my checkered past, I had become a respectable member of the community, at least as far as most folks were concerned. Of course, they didn't know about the train robbery . . .

"Jim, no," Daisy said.

Her father chimed in, "Mr. Strickland, that's very generous, but I can't allow you—"

I raised a hand to stop him.

"Just call it a donation, Reverend," I told him. "Folks donate money to churches all the time, don't they?"

"Yes, but this isn't really a church yet—"

"What's it say in the Good Book? 'Wherever two or more are gathered in my name . . .'? You and Miss Hatfield make two, I reckon, and there are plenty more folks around here who'll come to services once the church is finished."

Nelson looked at the money in his hand, then glared at me.

"Are you saying you'll pay the preacher's debt?" he asked.

"I think you must've been out in the sun too long, amigo," I told him. "That's exactly what I'm sayin'."

"Well, then . . . all right." He clearly didn't want to stop being mad, but with money in his hand he didn't have much choice.

"It looks to me like the reverend could use another load of lumber out here," I went on. "You figure out what he needs to finish the church, deliver it, and leave the bill with Farnum over at the store. I'll pick it up next time I'm here and settle up with you. Do we have a deal?"

I could tell he didn't trust me, but he didn't want to miss out on selling that lumber, either. After a moment he nodded, shoved the roll of bills in his pocket, and said, "It's a deal."

I held out my hand. We shook on it.

"All right," I said as I smiled. "Just so we're clear on that, in front of witnesses."

"What the hell do you mean by that?"

"I just don't want you tryin' to back out on it when I do this."

I punched him in the jaw.

The wallop caught him flat-footed. I put a lot into it, too. He staggered back, out of control, and probably would have fallen on his ass if the two men with him hadn't caught hold of him.

He blinked at me and yelled, "What the hell was that for?"

"You shouldn't'a been talkin' to a preacher that way," I told him, thinking about that 'Bible-thumping deadbeat' comment. "You had no right to call him names. And you cuss too much in front of a lady. You had it comin'."

Obviously, he didn't see it that way. He jerked his arms free and charged at me, roaring in fury.

I've seen several bullfights in my time, and that's sort of what it was like as I pivoted aside and let Nelson charge right past me like an angry bull.

Problem was, Nelson was at least a little smarter than a bull, and when he realized he was going to miss me, he flailed out with a hand and snagged my shirt. His momentum jerked me after him, our feet tangled up, and we both wound up falling to the ground in a welter of dust.

We broke apart and rolled away from each other. My hat had gone flying off my head, and so had Nelson's, revealing his thinning brown hair. As he came up on one knee, he waved the other men back.

"This is between me and Strickland!" he bellowed. "Stay out of it!"

One of the men shrugged, and they both moved back to give us room. I figured they worked for Nelson, and if he wanted to fight this battle by himself, that was his business.

Daisy and her father both looked anxious. Hatfield said, "Gentlemen, please, this is going to be the Lord's house. It's no place for brawling—"

Nelson and I didn't pay any attention to him. We surged to our feet and went at it.

Nelson was a big, tough hombre and was in no mood to give quarter. He had a couple of inches and probably thirty pounds advantage on me.

But I wasn't in a very forgiving mood myself, and I was considerably quicker than he was. I ducked away from his punches and stepped in to pepper his face with a series of quick jabs. His head rocked back from those, and blood spurted from his nose when my fist landed on it the third time. While he was a little off balance from that, I swung my right and buried it in his gut as far as it would go.

Unfortunately, that wasn't very far because there was a solid slab of muscle across his midsection. Still, the blow staggered him a little more and gave me the chance to throw a left hook that caught him on the chin.

He swung a backhand faster than I thought he could and his fist smacked into my jaw. It knocked me a step to the side, and the advantage swung back to Nelson for a second. He hammered a vicious blow to my chest. It seemed to paralyze my heart and lungs so I couldn't draw a breath. Dizziness caused my vision to spin around crazily.

He rammed into me, and I was reminded again of how much like a maddened bull he was. My feet left the ground, and I knew he planned to drive me down and land on top of me. I remembered how Bert had used that move on his opponent in the saloon fight, and that fella had wound up with broken ribs. I had to act fast to keep that from happening to me.

Nelson had wrapped his arms around my waist—which wasn't near as much fun as having Daisy do it, let me tell you—but my arms were free. I brought my hands up and clapped them over his ears, cupping them to catch more air. Nelson howled in pain and stumbled. I got my feet down and braced them to stop his charge. It wasn't easy with the weight advantage he had on me, but after a second we skidded to a halt.

He looked disoriented. I lowered my head a little and butted him in the nose, which was already bleeding. He yelled again, let go of me, and reeled back.

I didn't give him a chance to catch his breath. I hit him in the belly again with a left. It was a little more tender this time. He bent forward just enough to put his head in perfect position for the roundhouse right I threw next. The punch whistled around and smacked into his jaw with a sweet sound. He folded up and went straight to the ground.

I turned around quick-like, fists still clenched, as I tried to locate the two men Nelson had with him.

I didn't have to worry about them. They were still staying back, and as I turned toward them, one of the men lifted his hands, palms out, and said, "Take it easy, Strickland. The boss said this was between you and him, and we'll be happy to leave it that way."

I was breathing too hard to say anything, which reminded me that I was getting too old for things like this, but I gave them a curt nod.

Daisy and her father stood to the side the other way. Hatfield looked horrified that such violence had taken place so close to the church he was building. Daisy looked worried and excited at the same time. She took a step toward me and said, "Jim, are you all right?"

I summoned up enough breath to answer her with more than a nod.

"Yeah, I'm fine. He didn't hardly lay a hand on me."

That was true. Nelson had landed only a couple of good punches. But those had been enough to leave me shaken.

I forced a smile onto my face and went on, "I couldn't let that fella get away with talkin' ugly like he was."

"That doesn't matter," Hatfield said. "Words are no excuse for such brutality—"

"Look out!" Daisy said.

I turned around to see that Nelson was climbing to his feet. When he made it upright he spread his legs a little, planted his boots so he wouldn't sway, and dragged the back of his left hand across his face, smearing the blood that had leaked from his nose. He looked at the blood and suddenly grinned.

"Is it broken?" he asked.

"More than likely," I told him.

"Think you can set it?"

I shrugged and said, "I'll give it a try."

From the corner of my eye I could see how mystified Daisy was. She didn't know that the fight was over. I did. I went over to Nelson, took hold of his nose, and pulled on it. Something crunched inside it and he let out a howl, but when I let go and stepped back, his nose was reasonably straight again.

Tears streamed from his eyes. He blinked rapidly to clear them and said, "Thanks. I was ugly enough already without making it worse." He pulled a bandanna from his back pocket and used it to wipe away more of the blood from his face. "You're a handful, you know that? I haven't lost a fight in a long time."

"I'm not surprised. You got a punch like the kick of a mule."

He grunted and went on, "I'll have another load of lumber out here tomorrow, and if the reverend needs more, he can just let me know."

"I'll see to it you get paid."

"No hurry," Nelson said with a wave of his bloodstained hand. "I know you're good for it." He paused, then added, "I'll cut the price a little, seeing as how it's for a good cause."

"I'm obliged to you for that. Can't speak for the Good Lord, but I figure He might be, too."

Nelson nodded and went over to the Hatfields. He said, "Sorry for the rough talk, Reverend. I'm used to dealing with men who try to cut corners and take advantage of me. I should've known you weren't like that."

"That's . . . that's all right, Mr. Nelson," Hatfield said. I could tell he was baffled by the abrupt change in the man's attitude. "Thank you for your . . . consideration."

Nelson nodded and waved to his men, saying, "Let's go." One of them climbed into the truck cab with him while the other went to the front of the vehicle and turned the crank to start it. Then he hopped into the back, and Nelson drove off, leaving a cloud of dust behind him.

"What in the world just happened here?" Daisy asked.

Her father thought he had figured it out. He said, "Mr. Nelson changed his tune because he was afraid of Mr. Strickland." He didn't sound like that was a particularly good thing.

I shook my head and said, "Hate to disagree with you, Reverend, but Nelson wasn't scared of me. He respected me, and that's what made the difference. I treated him with respect, too, and didn't rub it in his face that I'd whipped him. He'll be a friend from now on."

"I'll never understand men," Daisy said.

I often felt the same way about womenfolks, but I didn't see any point in saying that.

"I really can't allow you to pay the expenses for this church," Hatfield said. "It's not fair to you."

"They say the Lord works in mysterious ways, don't they, Reverend? Well, just consider me one of those mysterious ways."

"But how can you afford such a thing?"

"Don't worry about the money," I told him. "Any time I need money, I know more than one way to get it."

CHAPTER 34

Daisy wanted me to have supper with them and spend the night in Largo. I refused the offer as politely as I could, reminding her that I'd told Enoch and Vince I'd catch up with them after I helped her unload the Bibles and hymnals.

It was probably too late for me to do that, but if I didn't show up at the ranch until the next day, they and the rest of the crew would probably start to worry.

It was after dark before I reached Fishhook. Scar heard me coming and ran out to meet me, barking furiously. He hushed when I called to him and he recognized my voice.

Lamps were lit in the bunkhouse, so it didn't surprise me when the fellas heard Scar's carrying on and came out to see what the commotion was all about. Randy, Vince, and Bert were in the lead. Enoch and Gabe hung back a little, and they had their right hands resting on their gun butts. It was hard to break the habits of a lifetime, and they both knew that trouble often came to call after dark.

"Hello, the camp!" I called. That drew a chuckle from Enoch, as he was probably remembering a lot of cold camps on dark trails.

"Figured you wouldn't get in any hurry helpin' that gal with her Bibles and hymnals," he said.

I swung down from the saddle and handed the reins to Randy.

"There was a little more to it than that," I said.

"You ain't engaged, are you?"

"What? Of course not!" The thought of getting married to Daisy hadn't really crossed my mind. For one thing, I was too old for her, for another she was a preacher's daughter, and for yet another, I was a train robber. Those things seemed to make holy matrimony an unlikely prospect.

"Then what happened?" Vince asked. "I thought you said you'd be right behind us. Enoch told me not to worry, though."

"This doesn't have anything to do with the sheriff, does it?" Randy wanted to know. He was still pretty jumpy when it came to the law and might always be that way.

"Come on in the house, all of you," I told them. "I'll explain in there. We've got some things to talk about, but we might as well be comfortable."

Once Randy had put up my horse and we were all inside and settled, I told them about the fracas with Nelson and the preacher's money troubles. Enoch was canny enough to know what was coming, but the others looked surprised when I concluded by saying, "So I think we ought to pitch in and help get that church built by holdin' up another train."

The younger ones looked at each other. Bert was the one who finally spoke up.

"Putting those two things together sort of doesn't make sense, Mr. Strickland," he said. "One of the Ten Commandments says 'Thou shalt not steal.' "

"Don't the Bible also say something about robbin' from the rich and givin' to the poor?" I asked.

"That's Robin Hood," Randy said. "That's just something from a storybook."

"Maybe so, but you got to admit, there's something to be said for the idea. We were already talkin' about hittin' another train—"

"You were talking about it, Mr. Strickland. Not us."

Enoch said, "It sounds like a mighty good idea to me."

"You just want an excuse to rob trains!" Randy accused.

"It sounds to me like we could do a lot of good," Enoch countered. "There's bound to be plenty of folks besides the preacher who could use some help, too. If we gave most of the loot to people who really needed it, I don't see how El Señor Dios could be too upset with us."

"I'm willin' to put it to a vote," I said. "Santiago and his cousins ain't here, so we'll have to see how they feel about it later, but right now, who amongst us thinks it would be a good idea to hold up another train and use the money to pay for Reverend Hatfield's church?"

I lifted my hand. So did Enoch and Gabe. I'd been pretty sure I could count on them. I was a little surprised when Bert's hand went up as fast as it did, though. The boy must've decided he liked being a desperado. Vince looked at him, shrugged, and lifted his hand, too.

"I don't care that much about the church," he said, "but I've got no reason to love the railroad."

"What about the promise you made to your ma?" I asked him. "I wouldn't want you to go against that and then be sorry about it later."

A smile tugged at his mouth as he said, "I promised her I'd never again do what I did yesterday. So you can't have me holding the horses again, Mr. Strickland."

I had to chuckle at that.

"You were usin' your head there, son," I told him. That just left Randy. I looked at him.

He sighed and said, "You've already got a majority, Mr. Strickland. I suppose I might as well go ahead and make it unanimous." He raised his hand but shook his head as if to say he wasn't sure it was a good idea.

"I don't think you'll regret it, Randy," I told him. "We'll need to leave somebody here, like we planned to before, and you can have that job. Only you'll really stay this time, because I think we'll be gone for a few days and I don't want to leave the place unattended for that long."

"Plan on goin' out of Sheriff Lester's bailiwick for the next job, are you?" asked Enoch.

I nodded and said, "I think it would be a good idea. We don't want anybody to track us down, so I figure we'll spread the jobs out far and wide."

"Jobs?" Vince repeated.

"This'll be just the start, boys," I said. "Why, in the old days Sundance and me, along with the rest of the bunch, ranged all over. That's the way to do it. Never let the law pin you down. That's the way it was in the Hole in the Wall days."

Saying that brought back bitter memories of how the law—or rather, the Bolivian army, which was the same thing down there—had pinned us down. Maybe we'd gotten careless. We'd gotten away with so much for so long, Harry and me, it was understandable how we might start feeling that the law couldn't ever touch us.

Or maybe our luck had just run out at last. It happens, and sometimes there's not a blasted thing in the world you can do about it.

But that wasn't going to happen here, I told myself as I shoved those memories away. This was a new century, a new era, a new Wild Bunch.

And our ride into legend was just beginning.

CHAPTER 35

A couple of weeks later, I was waiting on horseback behind some massive boulders about fifty yards north of the railroad tracks. On the other side of the tracks rose a steep cliff, and as I took off my hat and edged my head around the big slab of rock so I could peer up at the top of that cliff, I spotted Bert standing there looking down at the boulders. I waved my hat at him, and he waved his to let me know that everything was all right up there.

I pulled back behind the boulders, put my hat on, and checked my pocket watch. If the train was on schedule, right about now it would be starting the long climb up a slope to the east of our position. It would have to slow down to make that climb, and that was vital to our plan. If the train had been high-balling along, it might not have been able to stop in time.

We were more than a hundred miles west of our usual stomping grounds around Fishhook. Once we were committed to the idea of robbing another train—an idea that Santiago and the Gallardo boys had gone along with quite happily, by the way—I had done quite a bit of scouting before settling on this location. It was far enough away from the ranch that it wouldn't draw suspicion on us right away, and it was a place where we could stop the train without wrecking it.

Earlier that day Santiago and I had gone up on the cliff with Bert and Vince and showed them where to plant the dynamite.

A lot of train robbers could have been mining engineers if they'd turned their efforts in that direction. It sure helped to know quite a bit about blasting.

The two youngsters had the job of setting off the explosion that would dump twenty tons of rock on the tracks and force the train to stop. Also, from that vantage point they could pitch in with some rifle fire if we got in trouble and needed somebody to cover our retreat once the job was finished.

I heard the train in the distance. It was right on schedule, or close enough for government work, anyway. Not that what we were doing was government work. When it came to large-scale thievery, a hundred Wild Bunches couldn't match even a fraction of the larceny that the politicians in Washington pull off on a daily basis.

"Better get ready, fellas," I told the five men with me. We all pulled our bandannas up over our faces. Santiago, Javier, and Fernando were all wearing regular cowboy clothes and Stetsons today, as well as long tan dusters, instead of their vaquero garb and sombreros. That might help deflect suspicion from them later, I thought.

The noise of the locomotive grew louder as the train continued its steady approach. The boulders concealed us well enough that the engineer and fireman wouldn't be able to see us.

But we couldn't see the train, either, and that made me a little nervous. A lot was riding on Bert and Vince carrying out their part of the job right on time. We had gone over and over the plan, but when you're using dynamite, there's really no way to practice. You get one shot, and that's it.

I had measured off the distances as best I could. A quarter of a mile up the track, I had gathered some rocks and stacked them into a small cairn that would be visible through binoculars from the ridge. Vince's job was to watch that cairn, and as soon as the locomotive's cowcatcher passed it, he was to signal Bert, who would push down the plunger attached to the dynamite. I estimated that the train would have time to stop before it crashed into the resulting avalanche, but not by much. We had to cut it that close so the engineer couldn't stop the train and then try to reverse before we closed in on the cab.

Without being able to see, I didn't know if Vince was watching the cairn or how close the train was or whether Vince had already given the signal and the dynamite hadn't gone off like it was supposed to . . .

I didn't know anything.

But then the world shook as the peaceful afternoon was shattered by an explosion, and then a rumble swept across the West Texas landscape that dwarfed the sound of the locomotive and drowned it out completely.

I let out a whoop and shouted, "Come on!" I kicked my horse into a run and we broke out from behind the boulders.

It didn't matter if anybody on the train saw us now. Events had been set in motion, and there was no way on earth to stop them.

As we left the shelter of the rocks I saw a huge cloud of dust and smoke boiling up from the top of the cliff. Great chunks of rock and dirt had broken off and were sliding down the slope toward the tracks. More dust rose as the small-scale avalanche crashed down and swept across the steel rails, covering them completely.

I glanced at the cliff top again. I couldn't see Vince and Bert because of all the dust. At least, I hoped that was the reason. I had tried to position them well away from the blast site, but dynamite is tricky stuff. Right now I could only hope that we hadn't used too much and blown them to kingdom come, too. I would never forgive myself if that had happened.

There was no point in worrying about that until later, though, when I could actually check on them. For now we had to concentrate on the job at hand, which meant galloping toward the tracks and the onrushing train. I knew the engineer had seen the rock slide blocking the tracks, because I could hear the unholy screech of the brakes clamping down on the rails. It sounded like the howling of all the demons in hell.

We split up the same way we did on the first job, Gabe and me heading for the engine while Santiago and his cousins took over the passenger cars and Enoch dealt with the conductor in the caboose. The cowcatcher was just shuddering to a halt about twenty feet short of the first slabs of rock across the tracks as we swung down from our saddles.

The fireman yelled a curse and started to lift his shovel threateningly. I sent a bullet over his head.

"Drop it!" I ordered as I pointed the Remington at him. "Climb down from there, both of you!"

With Gabe and me covering them, the engineer and fireman didn't have any choice. Gabe herded them away from the engine and said to me over his shoulder, "I got 'em. You can go on about your business."

I hurried along the train. I was just passing the first of the passenger cars when a pair of shots blasted inside it. I scrambled up onto the platform and burst through the door. Men were yelling and women were screaming inside. The smell of powdersmoke hung in the air.

Santiago stood at the head of the aisle running between the bench seats. A man in the blue uniform of a conductor sat on the floor about halfway down the aisle. His cap had fallen off. He clutched his right shoulder with his left hand. I saw the bright red flash of blood between his fingers.

"You all right?" I asked Santiago as I motioned for quiet with my revolver.

"Yeah," he said. "He pulled a gun and opened fire on me. I had to stop him."

"I'm glad you didn't have to kill him. You've got this under control?"

"I don't think anyone else will cause any trouble," he said with a note of tense humor in his voice.

I clapped a hand on his shoulder for a second and went back out. It wasn't too surprising that he'd encountered the conductor in one of the passenger cars. Conductors had a habit of moving around their trains. The outcome could have been a lot worse, I told myself.

Enoch was already waiting for me outside the express car. He said, "The conductor wasn't in the caboose."

"I know. One of our boys ran into him in the first passenger car."

"Anybody hurt?" Enoch asked worriedly. "I thought I heard some shots."

"The conductor's got a bullet hole in his shoulder, but he'll be all right."

Enoch nodded and said, "That's good. I'd just as soon nobody died."

I felt the same way. The express messenger didn't need to know that, though. I hammered on the door and yelled, "Open up, or it'll go mighty hard for you when we get in there!"

I heard the latch being unfastened on the other side of the door and nodded to Enoch. We stepped back, moving in different directions so we flanked the doorway, just in case the messenger tried to come out shooting.

Far from it. Instead he tossed out a shotgun, followed by a small-caliber revolver. He called, "There's nothing in here worth dying over. Don't shoot, all right?"

"Climb down out of there, son," I told him. "We'll hold our fire as long as you don't try anything foolish."

"No chance of that," he said as he lowered himself to the ground. He was young, not much more than twenty, and looked more scared than angry.

I glanced toward the engine. Gabe had the engineer and the fireman turned around so that their backs were to us and they couldn't see what was going on, and we were far enough away that they probably couldn't hear the conversation, either.

"Keep him covered," I told Enoch. Then I holstered my gun and picked up the shotgun. The express messenger started to look more nervous. He licked his lips and watched me with wide eyes.

I pointed the shotgun into the air, angling it away from the train, and fired off both barrels, first one, then the other. The twin explosions made the messenger jump a little each time.

As I tossed the empty weapon back on the ground, I said, "There you go. When your bosses ask you about what happened, tell 'em you put up a valiant fight. Both barrels of that Greener are empty to prove it. But after that the outlaws overpowered you. Got it?"

He looked confused now, but he nodded.

"Yeah, I guess so. But why would you worry about what my bosses think of me?"

"Because there wasn't anything else you could have done here except die, and like you said, there's nothin' in there worth dyin' for. A man doesn't deserve to lose his job just because he's bein' sensible."

"Well . . . all right," he said, still uncertain. "I appreciate it, I guess."

"Tell you what we'll do," I went on. "We'll even blow open the safe so you won't have to open it for us. I saved a stick of dynamite for that."

"Thanks," he said. He was warming up to the idea now. "Can I say that I threatened you and told you that you won't get away with this?"

I grinned and said, "Why, sure, son. Tell 'em whatever you want. Hell, there won't be anybody around to contradict you, will there?"

Enoch kept the youngster covered, just in case, while I climbed into the express car and blew the door off the safe. I had performed that little chore often enough in the past that I knew how to do it so the contents weren't destroyed.

There was no big money shipment this time, but I found some assorted packets of bills and stuffed them in the inside pockets of my duster. I left the mail pouch alone. Individuals sent money through the mail; companies shipped it in the safe. They could force the railroad or Wells Fargo to make good on the loss. Of course, you could argue that that hurt the folks who were stockholders in the railroad, but it was such a big business I doubted if anybody would ever notice.

With that taken care of, I hopped out of the car and nodded to Enoch.

"We'll be leavin' now," I told the messenger. "Pleasure doin' business with you."

"Thanks again, mister," he said. "I hope if a train I'm on is ever robbed again, it's you who does the holding up."

I laughed and said, "Another testimonial from a satisfied customer." I gestured with the Remington in my hand. "You stay right there, hear?"

"I won't budge from this spot," the youngster promised solemnly.

I let out a rebel yell as Enoch and I hurried to our horses. That was the signal for Gabe and the three vaqueros to light a shuck, too. We all leaped into our saddles and got out of there as quick as we could. Up on the cliff, Bert and Vince were watching us go, I hoped, and would meet up with us later at the rendezvous point, a rugged hill five miles north.

I worried about those two until I saw them come trotting up an hour or so later. They'd had to circle around to get down from the cliff and avoid the scene of the robbery, so their route had been longer than ours. It was sure good to see them, and I told them so as there was hand shaking and back slapping all around.

"Everything went just perfect, Mr. Strickland," Bert said. "Just like you told us it would."

"I've been doin' this for a while," I said with a nod. "Robbin' trains is like anything else: you've got to practice to do it right."

"How much did we get?" Vince asked.

I had already counted the loot, so I had the answer ready when he asked the inevitable question.

"A whole $1,708!" I told them. That was less than $200 per man, but in those days even that sum represented several months' wages for a cowboy. Anyway, it didn't matter, because we'd all agreed that most of it would go to Reverend Hatfield for the church in Largo. Santiago and his cousins would have preferred if it had been a Catholic church instead of Methodist, but they'd gone along with the rest of us.

Satisfied that we'd done a good day's work—and that the law wasn't after us at the moment—we turned our horses toward home.

CHAPTER 36

The next few months were the happiest I'd been since the early days in Argentina with Harry and Etta. We hit five more trains, traveling as far as New Mexico to hold up one of them. The take was never less than two grand, and one glorious day it was almost $28,000.

We had to fire a few warning shots here and there, but the conductor Santiago had been forced to wound on the second job remained the only casualty, which pleased me considerably. Some people would probably say that I didn't have a conscience, but I knew that I did, and it stayed fairly clean as long as we didn't kill anybody.

The fact that we gave away so much of the money probably helped with that, too. The First Methodist Church of Largo, Texas, was finished now, with its white-painted walls, its towering steeple, and its bells that sounded the call to worship every Sunday. I usually attended the services, sitting in one of the front pews with Daisy and sharing a hymn book with her as we sang along with the rest of the congregation.

Her father had bought a small house in Largo to use as a parsonage, and of course the money from the holdups paid for that, too, although the reverend would have been horrified if he'd known.

Franklin Hatfield wasn't the only one we helped, of course. Clyde Farnum hit a rough patch when one of the companies that had been supplying the groceries he carried was sold and the new owner called in all the debts. Farnum needed a loan to tide him over, and I supplied it, telling him to just pay me back when he could and not worry about it. I didn't know if I'd ever see any of that money again, and I didn't care.

Santiago knew several Mexican farmers who were about to go bust, and we slipped them enough money to keep going. I did likewise with several small ranchers in the area who'd had financial reverses. When Tom Mulrooney needed a new forge for his blacksmith shop, I made sure that he got it.

Every time I helped somebody, I told them to keep to themselves where the assistance came from, but I suppose word got around anyway, at least to a certain extent. I couldn't go anywhere without folks nodding to me and smiling, and I figured I knew the reason why.

That was skirting on the thin edge of danger, and I knew it. The Fishhook was a good spread, but it wasn't any better than a lot of others and there was no reason it ought to be more prosperous. I knew Sheriff Emil Lester was a relatively smart man. If he heard that I was handing out money right and left, he might start to wonder where it was coming from.

The thing of it was, running that risk made the whole thing even sweeter for me. What's the use of living if you don't take a chance now and then?

I took chances with Daisy Hatfield, too, and that did sort of trouble me. She would rent a horse from Mulrooney and we would meet out on the range to ride together, or I would come to her father's house in Largo when he was off in the far corners of the county doing his visitations. We were careful about those meetings. Daisy claimed she didn't care all that much about her reputation, but I did. I wanted to protect her as much as I could, and that included not letting ugly rumors spread about her.

But I couldn't stay away from her. I argued with myself up one way and down the other that I was too old for her. I said that very thing to her on a number of occasions, and every time I did she got almost spittin' mad at me.

"I've told you that I'm older than my years, Jim Strickland," she'd say to me, "and you're younger than yours. That way we sort of meet in the middle. Anyway, there are plenty of couples in my father's congregation where the husband is in his thirties or forties, and the wife is barely out of her teens!"

She was right about that. Such matches weren't unusual in those days, especially when the husband had been married before and his first wife had passed away.

"I'm twenty-four years old," Daisy went on. "I'm practically an old maid!"

She had a point there, too. Most women didn't reach that age without being married. A lot of them had several kids by then. But as she admitted, she had spent her life taking care of her father and helping him with his calling. Now she wanted to do something for herself, and I couldn't really blame her.

It was a struggle, but we kept some boundaries in place. She was a decent woman . . . but she kissed like an indecent one. A man would've had to be made out of mighty stern stuff not to be tempted once he had that warm, sweet bundle of womankind in his arms, and I'd never been what you'd call good about resisting temptation. Somehow we managed, but it wasn't easy for either of us.

That was how it went, that summer of 1915. Was there trouble elsewhere in the world? Sure there was. Over in Europe folks were fighting a big war. We heard about that even in West Texas. But it didn't seem to have anything to do with us, and I never gave it much thought. My world was Largo, and the Fishhook, and the range around it, and as long as Daisy and my pards were there, that was plenty big enough for me.

One day when we were out riding, we stopped on top of a rise that looked down a long valley stretching for miles between low, rolling hills. Fishhook was at the far end of that valley. I couldn't see the ranch buildings from here, but I knew they were there and that put a good feeling inside me.

Daisy had brought along a blanket and a picnic basket. She spread the blanket on the grass and we sat down to eat while our horses grazed. The sun was pretty warm, so I was grateful for the shade of a cottonwood tree. Dappled patterns of light and shadow played over us as we ate. Daisy was lovely in a white blouse and dark green riding skirt. She had worn that dang straw boater of hers while we were riding, but when we sat down to enjoy the picnic she took it off and set it aside. The changing light made different shades of red shine from her hair.

I had never seen anything so pretty in my life.

After a while she blushed and said, "You're staring at me, Jim."

"Am I? I was just wonderin' how a beautiful young girl like you wound up with a worn-out old varmint like me."

"Stop that," she said. "You say things like that nearly every time we're together, and I don't like it. You know that's not the way I feel about you."

"There's no gettin' around the facts," I told her. "When I was born, George Custer was still nine years away from meetin' up with the Sioux at the Little Big Horn. By the time you were born, the West as I first knew it was almost gone. The little bit that's left is fadin' away with every day that passes."

She looked at me and shook her head.

"How can you be so melancholy on such a beautiful day?" she asked.

"I'm not tryin' to be. It's just that sometimes I think maybe I'm fightin' a losin' battle, tryin' to hold back time."

"Isn't that what we're all doing, though? Looking for happiness even though we know by its very nature that it's fleeting and doomed to end?"

I laughed and said, "Shoot, now I've made you gloomy."

She scooted closer to me and said, "I know a good antidote for doom and gloom that will work on both of us. Kiss me."

"That sounds like good medicine, all right." I put a hand under her chin, cupping it as I lifted her face. "Let me have a sample." When I took my mouth away from hers a couple of minutes later, I said, "I don't know if it works or not, but it tastes a whole heap better than castor oil."

"I think you need to increase the dosage," she murmured.

"Better too much than not enough . . ."

Well, we carried on like that for a while, and that riding skirt of Daisy's worked its way up her legs until they were bare to the knees. If she had been like some of the other women I'd known in my life, I would have put that blanket to even better use, but there came a point when Daisy started trying to straighten herself up and I didn't object, even though I wanted to. The last thing in the world I wanted was for that gal to do something she would regret later on.

We finished what was left of the picnic, put everything away, and folded the blanket. As we were about to mount up, Daisy paused and gazed off down the valley for a long moment. Without looking at me, she sighed and said, "Do you sometimes wish that the world could stay just the way it is at a particular moment, Jim? That the good things could just go on and on the way they are just then?"

"That's a mighty pretty thing to think about, all right," I told her.

But it was impossible. Nothing stayed the same for long, especially the good things. There was always a snake slithering into the garden somewhere.

In this case, that snake was named Simon Barstow.

CHAPTER 37

The railroad was not happy with me.

To be specific, Lewis Kennedy and Albert Milton weren't happy with me. Every time I went to Farnum's store, I picked up the newspaper from the county seat, as well as the papers from San Antonio, and every time after we pulled a job, Kennedy and Milton would be quoted spouting off to reporters about how outraged they were by the robberies and how this wave of crime and degradation would soon come to a halt. They took turns promising that the thieves would soon be apprehended, and they stopped just short of saying that when we were caught, we'd be strung up . . . after having a bullwhip taken to our backs. Hell, if it had been up to them, they would have dipped us in boiling oil.

And each time, they sounded more embarrassed, more desperate, and more scared for their own jobs than they had the time before.

That was fine with me. I intended to keep it up long enough to get those two no-account buzzards fired. Even that was a better fate than they deserved.

Desperate men are dangerous, though, and Kennedy and Milton, despite all their blustering, really did intend to put up a fight. They couldn't do it on their own, though. They had to have help.

That's why they sent for Simon Barstow.

Understand, I didn't know all this at the time. I'd never even heard of Barstow. He had risen to prominence in the Pinkertons while I was in South America and then in Europe. He'd made a name for himself catching bank robbers back east, and it stood to reason that eventually the Pinks would send him west. He'd busted up a gang in Iowa and another in Missouri. It was while he was in St. Louis that he'd gotten his first crack at train robbers. He chased them all the way to Pine Bluff, Arkansas, and caught up to them there. With half a dozen other Pinkerton detectives, he'd raided the gang's hideout and wiped them out in a fierce gun battle, recovering most of the loot they had stolen. I read all about it later on. According to the newspapers, Simon Barstow was Nick Carter, Old Sleuth, and Wyatt Earp all rolled into one.

You can look him up if you want. His picture is in newspapers and magazines from those days. He was a handsome man, with dark hair, piercing eyes, a strong nose, and a thick black mustache waxed to sharp points on the tips. Kennedy and Milton must have been as impressed as all get-out when Barstow strode into Kennedy's office in San Antonio, gave them a firm handshake, and promised to bring to justice the scoundrel who was causing them so much trouble—namely, me—and if I resisted, Barstow intended to send the villain straight to hell by any means necessary.

Meanwhile, blissfully ignorant, I started planning our next holdup. Reverend Hatfield's church had a piano to play along with the hymn singing, but I thought it would be nice if there was an organ, too. Some of those church songs just sounded better when they were played on the organ. I figured God could hear 'em better, all the way up yonder in Heaven.

I hadn't settled on a time and place to pull the next job when we got word that John Hamilton had died down in the county seat. He had battled that gut rot, as he called it, longer than anybody expected him to. Vince's mother called Farnum's store, since that was where the only telephone in Largo was located, Farnum told Reverend Hatfield, and the reverend drove out to the Fishhook to break the news to Vince, since Hamilton and

Vince's dad had been best friends. I thought that was mighty nice of the reverend, who had gotten the hang of driving that automobile, sort of. It still jerked and lurched quite a bit when he was behind the wheel.

"I ought to go to the funeral," Vince said. "Mr. Hamilton was like an uncle to me."

"I'll ride down with you," I told him. "Hamilton seemed like a good fella, and he stuck by your dad's memory when there was all that trouble, that's for sure."

Bert wanted to go, too. Since the funeral was going to be held the next morning, the three of us started for the county seat that afternoon, intending to ride well into the night to get there.

Vince told us his ma likely would be offended if we didn't spend the night there, so that's where we headed. Mrs. Porter was glad to see Vince, and she made me and Bert feel welcome, too.

"I was hoping you'd come," she said to Vince as we sat in her parlor. "Your father would have wanted you here to help say good-bye to his old friend."

"That's what I thought," Vince said.

Mrs. Porter got up and went over to a little table with a drawer underneath it. She opened the drawer, took out an envelope, and handed it to Vince.

"He left this for you," she said.

"Who?" Vince asked with a puzzled frown. "Mr. Hamilton?"

"That's right. It was in his room with his other things. The sheriff brought it over this morning."

I saw that the envelope was sealed and had Vince's name written on it. He tore it open, unfolded the piece of paper inside, and started to read. I could tell by the way his eyes widened and the muscles of his face got tight that the words written on the paper shocked him.

He did a good job of covering it up, though. When his mother asked him if something was wrong, he shook his head and put the letter back in the envelope. As he slipped it into his pocket, he said, "No, Mr. Hamilton just wanted to tell me again not to believe any of the things that were said about Dad."

"That was thoughtful of him, to do something like that while he was on his deathbed."

"Yeah," Vince said. I could see how distracted he was, even if his mother couldn't.

Vince was staying in his old room, of course. The house was small and didn't have a guest room, but there was a sleeping porch at the back with a cot. Bert would stay there, and Mrs. Porter made up the sofa for me. I was about ready to turn in when Vince came into the room, quiet-like, carrying the envelope with the letter from John Hamilton.

"Boss, you'd better look at this," he said as he held it out to me.

The only lamp in the room still burning had been turned down low. I turned it up again, brightening the glow until I could make out the words scrawled on the paper in the shaky writing of a man on his deathbed.

Vince—I know what you've been doing, son, you and your friends from that ranch. Don't worry, I'll soon take that secret to my grave. I would never betray you. But before I go, I want you to know something. My friends from the railroad and from Wells Fargo still visit me, and one of them let something slip the other day. Next Friday afternoon's westbound train will be carrying a shipment of gold bullion headed for the federal reserve bank in El Paso. Sixty thousand dollars worth. You can take it at the same place you took that very first train.

I looked up at Vince and asked, "Do you believe this about the gold bullion?"

"Yeah, I do," he said. "Before he had to retire because he got sick, Mr. Hamilton was in charge of freight operations for this whole section of the line. He knew everybody, and they all trusted him, with good reason. He was as honest as they come."

"But he's tellin' us to hold up that train."

"Keep reading," Vince said.

The only reason I'm telling you this is because of those greedy, cold-hearted bastards Kennedy and Milton. Losing that gold shipment will be the last straw for the railroad. Kennedy and Milton will be fired, and it's a fate they well deserve. You and your friends have done a lot of good for others, Vince. Think of the good you can do with that much money.

Something else occurred to me as I read the words with narrowed eyes. I pointed at the letter and asked, "Are you sure this is Hamilton's handwriting?"

"Yes, sir. I saw it on the chalkboard in the station often enough."

"And you trust him? This couldn't be some sort of trick?"

"I can't imagine him doing that. Not after he and my dad were friends for so long. You've got to understand, Mr. Strickland, my father was a brakeman. Mr. Hamilton didn't work with him. They didn't have to be friends. But they were, because they genuinely liked and respected each other."

I looked back down at the letter and read, *If I've guessed wrong about you and your friends being responsible for those train robberies, I hope you'll forgive me. Consider it just a figment of a sick old man's imagination. But if it's the truth, then take what I've told you and do with it what you will. I know I can count on you to do the right thing, son.*

Your friend, John Hamilton.

"Well," I said slowly as I lowered the paper. "That's mighty interestin'."

"What I can't figure out is how he knew what we've been doing."

"A good guess, I'd say. I just hope the sheriff doesn't make the same guess one of these days."

"A job like this," Vince said with a nod toward the letter still in my hand, "if we pulled that off, we could afford to stop. We'd have enough money to help anybody who needed helping, and the Fishhook could just be a ranch again."

"I don't know . . . ," I said.

"It's been really exciting and we've done a lot of good, but it had to come to an end sooner or later, Mr. Strickland. I'm just a kid and I know that."

I frowned, not liking it very much that somebody his age was lecturing me. I was the one who was supposed to be all grown up, not him.

But I'd had that trouble all my life, I suppose. Growing up, settling down, living a respectable life, it all sounded fine when you were just talking about it, but when the time came to do it, I'd always balked. Back home in Utah, down in Argentina, now here in Texas, I'd had my chances, and every time I'd grabbed the first excuse I could find to go back to hell-raisin'.

Maybe it was different now. Maybe with Daisy in the picture, I really could settle down, and as that thought crossed my mind the idea of getting married followed it. Yeah, I was older than her, but we could still have a long life together, and when I was gone, I could leave her a fine ranch, maybe even some kids, as my legacy.

I handed the letter back to Vince and said, "I'm not makin' any promises . . . but we'll look into it. And if it works out, you're right, son, we can go back to bein' honest citizens."

Not everybody on the ranch would like that. I could see Enoch and Gabe deciding to pull up stakes and drift on, rather than staying to spend the rest of their lives as mere cowhands. With Randy, Bert, and Vince, though, I'd have the makings of a good, permanent crew. Santiago and his cousins could still work for me at roundup time. They had pitched in enthusiastically enough when it came to the robberies, but I didn't think they would mind if we called that part of it quits.

The one who would really have trouble accepting it, I thought, was me. And I would have Daisy to help me get over missing the old days.

Time to look ahead instead of back, I told myself. Time to think about the future and stop trying to relive the glory days, the days of blood and thunder.

There was just one more thing we had to do first . . .

CHAPTER 38

When we got back to the ranch, I sent Enoch to fetch Santiago and the Gallardo brothers.

"What's this all about?" the old gun-wolf wanted to know. "You got a mighty serious look on your face, Jim."

"I'd rather just tell it once," I said, casting a warning look at Vince and Bert to keep their mouths shut for the time being. Vince had told Bert all about what was in John Hamilton's letter, of course.

When Enoch got back with the vaqueros, I gathered everybody around me in the house while I stood there with Scar lying on the floor at my feet and read John Hamilton's letter out loud to them.

When I was finished, nobody said anything for a long moment. Then Santiago asked, "What are you trying to tell us, señor? That we should stop being outlaws because this man Hamilton knew our secret?"

"That ain't what he's sayin' at all," Enoch spoke up before I could reply. "He's sayin' we ought to go after that shipment of gold bullion."

"Actually I'm sort of sayin' both of those things," I told them. "Damn right I think we should go after that bullion, but once we've got our hands on it, that'll be the right time to retire as train robbers."

Gabe said, "Sixty grand's a hell of a lot of money, all right."

"We wouldn't get that much out of it," I cautioned. "You can't just go into a store and spend a bar of gold. We'd have to sell it to somebody who can deal with it, and they won't give us the full value of what it's worth. But I figure we'll clear at least half, maybe more. We won't have to sell it all at once, either. We'll get more in the long run if we spread it out. But when all's said and done, it would still be a fine way to close out our train-robbin' career."

"Do we get to vote again?" Randy asked.

"I've never tried to make you fellas do anything you didn't want to do. You may work for me as ranch hands, but we're all equal partners in this other business. So yeah, sure, we'll take a vote."

"Then I vote yes," Randy said decisively, surprising me. When he saw my reaction, he continued, "I want to get this over with. And I want to be part of it this time, instead of sitting here on the ranch. I hate being stuck here, not knowing if you're all going to get shot full of holes."

"That ain't exactly what I'd call a vote of confidence," I told him with a smile, "but I'll take it. How about the rest of you boys?"

It took only a few seconds for all of them to chime in with their agreement. Once again it was a unanimous vote.

Enoch asked, "What do you think about Hamilton's suggestion that we hit the train at the same place we did that first one?"

"It might work," I said. "We've been ridin' pretty far and wide on these jobs. They might not expect us to circle back to where we started."

"It's closer to town and the ranch," Gabe pointed out.

"True. But if we take 'em by surprise, that shouldn't really matter." I folded the letter, replaced it in the envelope, and handed it to Vince. It belonged to him, even though Hamilton had sort of intended it for all of us. I went on, "We've got some time. I'll do some scoutin' and plannin'. That's been workin' out all right so far, so I don't see any reason to change."

With that settled, Santiago and his cousins went back to their spread. Santiago told me to let them know when we were ready to make our move.

That was a Tuesday, so Friday was three days off. I spent all day Wednesday riding through the countryside around the place where we had pulled that first holdup. That confirmed what I already thought. There wasn't a better spot to board and stop the train.

But that didn't mean we'd do things exactly the same way this time, I thought as I rode back east through that series of ridges to a spot a couple of miles away where the terrain dropped off fairly steeply to a broad flat. I reined in and sat there for several minutes while a grin spread slowly over my face.

The next day we all gathered at the Fishhook again to go over the plan I'd hatched. We talked it all out, up one way and down the other, and if anybody had any objections there were plenty of chances for them to voice those complaints. Nobody did, but the discussion helped get the whole thing straight in everybody's mind. When the time came, we'd all know what to do.

It seemed to be Friday afternoon in the blink of an eye, and suddenly there I was again, stretched out on top of that ridge the same way I'd been several months earlier, waiting for the train to rumble past my location. Life had come around in a big ol' circle, I thought, the way it always seemed to with me.

This time would be different, I told myself. That circle of outlawry wouldn't just keep running around and around from now on. The difference was Daisy. She was going to break me out of the same pattern that had ruled my life up until then.

I had to push all that musing out of my mind. I couldn't afford to be thinking about the future beyond the next half hour or so. I had to concentrate on the job at hand.

Because I heard the train coming in the distance.

Time had seemed to fly past until this point, but now it slowed down to a crawl. I waited and waited for the train to get there, and it seemed that it never would. Finally, though, the rumble of the locomotive got louder until it drew even with my position and then passed me.

I wasn't alone this time. I looked over at Santiago and nodded. We would do this together.

As I came up on my feet, Santiago did likewise. He had never done anything like this before, so he had to be nervous about jumping onto a moving train. I'll give him credit, though. He didn't hesitate even for a second. He sailed off the top of that cutbank right along with me.

I landed on top of one freight car, and he landed on the car right behind it. I grabbed hold and steadied myself, turning my head as I did so to make sure he had landed safely. He was spread-eagled in the center of the next freight car's roof, holding on for dear life, but after a moment he lifted his head and gave me a nod to let me know he was all right.

I waved at him and got to my hands and knees and then climbed to my feet, keeping my legs wide apart to brace myself. It was a shame Santiago hadn't been able to practice this part ahead of time, but I had told him everything I could about it, based on my own experience. I looked over my shoulder and saw that he had made it to his feet, too. We started toward our respective destinations, me going toward the engine while he headed for the caboose.

I wanted to turn around and watch Santiago, but I couldn't afford to take my eyes off what I was doing. It took me only a couple of minutes to reach the coal tender and start working my way along the ledge on the side of it. I was making better time now than I had during the previous holdup. The locomotive was just emerging from the cut when I swung around into the cab and covered the engineer and fireman with my Remington.

"Hands up, boys!" I called. "You're makin' an unscheduled stop!"

Funny thing, they didn't seem particularly surprised by my sudden appearance, and that was the first thing that set off warning bells in my head. But there was no turning back now, so I gestured with the revolver and told the engineer, "Stop the train now!"

He reached for the brake lever without arguing. The brakes squealed and the train began to slow.

It came to a stop about fifty yards short of the wash where the rest of the boys had waited last time. They weren't there today. That was the first difference in the plan.

I kept the engineer and fireman covered as I leaned back to look along the right side of the train toward the caboose. I spotted Santiago standing beside the express car. He snatched off his hat and waved it at me to let me know that his part of the plan had been completed successfully.

The fireman chose that moment, when I was sort of distracted, to make a move. He jumped at me, even though the engineer yelled, "Zeke, no! You're not supposed to—"

He didn't have time to say more. I could have blasted a hole through the fireman, but I still didn't want to kill anybody. I twisted aside from his rush and walloped him on the back of the head with my gun. He pitched out of the cab and landed sprawling on the edge of the roadbed, rolling over a couple of times before he came to a stop.

I pointed the Remington at the engineer's face and told him, "Reverse! Now!"

I knew something was wrong, but the plan was underway and all we could do was keep following it and try to cope with whatever happened.

The engineer gaped at me. I drew back the Remington's hammer, mostly for effect, and repeated in a quieter and more dangerous tone, "Reverse."

The engine still had enough steam up for what I had in mind. With the muzzle of that Remington only a few inches from his nose, the engineer had no choice but to do what I told him. He started backing the train along the tracks. It gradually built up speed.

The line ran pretty straight through the ridges. The train was going only about half as fast in reverse as it had been going forward, but that was fast enough for our purposes. I kept one eye on the landmarks sliding past, and when I knew we were in the right spot, I yelled, "Stop!"

Instinctively, the engineer hauled back on the brake lever. With a violent lurch the train began to slow again. Since it wasn't going as fast it didn't take as long for it to stop this time.

"Turn around," I told the engineer.

"Please, m-mister," he said, his voice shaking with fear, "don't kill me! I got a wife and kids!"

"I will kill you if you don't turn around," I warned him. With his hands in the air and a terrified expression on his face, he swung around so his back was to me.

I reversed the Remington and tapped him on the back of the head with the butt, hard enough to knock him out for a few minutes without doing any real damage. Then I leaped down from the cab as the drumming of hoofbeats echoed against the ridges.

Enoch loomed up, coming in from the west leading my horse. I swung into the saddle like an old Pony Express rider. My mount never even slowed to a complete stop before I was on its back, finding the other stirrup and leaning forward over the horse's neck.

Along the tracks to the east, I could see the express car and caboose still rolling freely on the steel rails. Santiago had uncoupled them from the rest of the train after taking over the caboose and knocking out the conductor. Those two cars had been pushed along with the rest of the train while the locomotive was backing up, but once the locomotive stopped, they kept going. The cars were almost at the top of the slope, and as Enoch and I galloped after them, I saw them speed up even more as gravity caught them and started pulling them down the hill.

It was a pretty sight, because it meant my plan was working. I didn't have time to feel too pleased about it, though. At that instant, as we started to ride past the passenger cars, the glass in the windows exploded outward and I heard the soul-numbing chatter of a Gatling gun.

CHAPTER 39

Of course it was a trap. I'd suspected that possibility all along. Vince had been convinced that John Hamilton was trustworthy, though, and I had felt the same way about the man.

So either someone had gotten to Hamilton and convinced him to write that letter on his deathbed—or forced him to write it—or else it was a forgery good enough to fool Vince.

Either way we were in the same amount of trouble, so it didn't really matter. As bullets smashed the windows in the passenger car and clawed through the air at me and Enoch, I yelled, "Stay down!"

I was practically laying down on my horse's neck. I felt the heat of several rounds passing close to my head. Then the horse lurched and went down.

I kicked my feet free of the stirrups so that I sailed through the air in front of the mortally wounded animal as it collapsed. When I slammed to the ground it knocked the breath out of me and seemed to paralyze all my muscles.

Enoch leaned down from the saddle and extended a hand toward me. I forced my arm to work and lifted it. His hand slapped against mine and we clasped wrists. I yelled in pain as it felt like my arm was jerked right out of its socket. I came off the ground, Enoch hauling me upward with all the strength in his leathery frame.

I kicked my leg upward and got my foot over the back of the

horse. Hooking it against the far side of the saddle, I pulled myself up even more and settled down on the horse's back behind Enoch. For the last few seconds I'd been so concerned with not falling and getting trampled, I hadn't had a chance to notice we'd made it past the car where the Gatling gun was set up.

That didn't mean we were out of the woods, though. The deafening roar of pistols and rifles pounded against our ears, and slugs whipped through the air all around us.

You might think it was impossible for us to gallop through such a fusillade without being killed, but really, it's mighty hard to hit a fast-moving target, even up close. And the old saying about a miss being as good as a mile, well, it's even more true when you're being shot at. They can't hurt you if they don't hit you.

We were stretching our luck mighty thin, though, and abruptly it ran out. I felt a bullet slice across my upper right arm at an angle. The impact jolted a grunt from me.

"You hit?" Enoch yelled over his shoulder.

"Just keep goin'!" I told him.

He did, making that horse flash along the train. Even though the animal was carrying double, Enoch got every possible ounce of speed out of him.

The bullet wound numbed my arm at first, but that lasted only a few seconds before it started burning like hell. I gritted my teeth against the pain and hung on. The passenger cars were behind us now. I halfway expected the doors of the freight cars to roll back and reveal a danged army hiding in them, but nothing of the sort happened. I guess the fella who set up this trap figured a Gatling gun and a couple of passenger cars full of armed guards would be enough to settle our hash. He was wrong about that. Luck and quick reactions had saved us . . . so far.

The train sat there on the tracks behind us. I glanced back and saw riflemen jumping out of the cars. As soon as they landed, they started firing at us again. Enoch juked that horse back and forth, though, and the slugs whistled around us but didn't find their targets.

We reached the top of the slope and plunged over it. That risked the horse falling as we began to descend at breakneck speed toward the flats below, but thankfully the critter was sure-footed and stayed upright, even though he slid a little every now and then.

The express car and the caboose still rolled across the flats, although they were beginning to slow down now that they were back on level ground. I spotted Santiago leaning out from the platform at the rear of the caboose. Off to the left, dust boiled up as the rest of the boys galloped to intercept the two cars. One of the Gallardo brothers led Santiago's horse.

Unfortunately, that meant we were one horse shy since mine had gone down. And I wasn't sure Enoch's mount could keep up with the others carrying both of us.

I was willing to bet that the express car held more armed men and no gold bullion. As soon as it stopped rolling across the plains, the door would pop open and those boys would come out shooting. I shouted in Enoch's ear, "Wave off the others! Let 'em know it's a trap!"

Enoch nodded grimly. He pulled his Colt from its holster and fired three times in the air to get the others' attention. Then he pouched the iron and jerked his hat off. He started waving it, motioning for them to stay away from the train.

We had gone over what to do in case of trouble, so the boys seemed to understand the signal. They immediately split up and veered sharply away from the railroad tracks, scattering in different directions so pursuers would have a harder time tracking them.

Except for Javier or Fernando, whichever brother it was who was leading Santiago's horse. He kept going. He wasn't going to abandon his cousin.

Santiago leaped down from the platform and ran to meet the rider. He stumbled and I thought for a second he was hit, but he righted himself and started running again, just as fast as before. If he was wounded, it wasn't bad. After a few more steps he slowed, half-turned, and threw some shots back at the express car, just to discourage any guards who might be in there, I figured.

The Gallardo brother reached him, and Santiago leaped into the saddle. They turned and galloped away.

By now Enoch and I were almost to the bottom of the slope. He angled his horse away from the tracks, too. There was no rendezvous point this time. In the event of trouble we were all supposed to ride far and wide, away from each other, and eventually make our way back to the Fishhook.

Instinct made me look behind us again. I bit back a curse as I saw a cloud of dust rising in the air from the place where the train was stopped. That meant a lot of riders.

"There's already a posse on our trail," I called to Enoch.

"How can that be?"

"They probably had horses hidden in the boxcars. Lawdogs have pulled that trick on me before!"

I sensed a brain smarter than that of Sheriff Emil Lester behind this. Lester was canny enough, but he was a plodder. He would follow a lawbreaker to the ends of the earth before he'd think to set a trap for one. That told me the railroad had brought in someone else to go after the gang, more than likely the Pinkertons.

I tapped Enoch on the left shoulder and pointed.

"Head for those rocks over there!"

"We're gonna make a stand?" he asked.

"Not you! I am!"

"The hell with that!" he responded without any hesitation. "We'll get away together or we'll die together!"

"This horse can't outrun a posse carryin' both of us. Damn it, Enoch—"

"You got a gal to go back to," he interrupted me. "I don't."

"You've got friends—"

"It ain't the same thing, and you know it. You take the horse, and I'll fort up in the rocks and slow the bastards down!"

We were almost there. Arguing was just going to waste time. But I would have done it anyway, if I hadn't seen movement behind the boulders. For a second I thought it was another trap, until a rider spurred out into the open and I recognized Randy.

"Damn it!" I shouted at him as Enoch reined in. "You were supposed to get out of here! It was all a trick, and now there's a posse after us!"

"We figured that out," Randy said. He seemed to be pretty calm, although his eyes were big. "I saw the two of you riding double and knew you must have lost your horse, Mr. Strickland. That's why I came back. You can have mine."

"No way in hell I'm leavin' you here," I said. "Either of you."

"You don't have to," Randy said. "I weigh quite a bit less than you, Mr. Strickland. Enoch's horse can carry him and me."

The youngster might have a point there, I realized. He was pretty skinny, and so was Enoch. I've always been a little chunky. It might work, I told myself, especially with one more little wrinkle thrown in.

"All right," I said as I dismounted. "Let's swap, and we'll all get out of here."

Enoch didn't object. He gave me a narrow-eyed look, though, like he thought I might be up to something.

I was, of course, but I wasn't going to take the time to explain it to them. Instead I swung up on Randy's horse, ignoring the pain from my bullet-creased arm. Blood had soaked a good-size patch on my shirt sleeve, but I couldn't afford to worry about that now.

"Go!" I called to them. "I'll be right behind you!"

Enoch heeled his horse into a gallop again. I was counting on the thunder of its hoofbeats to keep them from realizing what I was doing until it was too late to stop me.

I burst out from behind the rocks and raced back *toward* the posse, which was now riding down the hill in the direction of the flats.

They were still several hundred yards away from me, so to be sure they didn't fail to see me, I pulled Randy's rifle from the saddleboot and cranked off several rounds in the posse's general direction. I wasn't deliberately trying to hit any of them, but if one of the bullets happened to find a target, I didn't figure I'd lose any sleep over it. Those hombres were all professionals, hired guns whose job was to kill me and my friends.

Having a Gatling gun open up on me had put me in sort of a bad mood, you see. Getting winged hadn't helped, either.

After firing those shots I swung due east, galloping parallel to the railroad tracks. A look over my shoulder told me that Randy and Enoch were nowhere in sight. Once Enoch had realized what I was doing, it would have been too late to stop me, and for them to turn back would just waste whatever sacrifice I made. I knew Enoch was enough of a hardheaded realist not to do that. I was counting on it, in fact.

Nothing was in front of me for several miles except open plains. No place to hide or give the slip to my pursuers. My life depended on staying ahead of them, and I had to hope that Randy's horse was capable of that. It seemed like a long shot. If the posse's horses had been riding in the boxcars as I suspected, they would be fresher than my mount.

But when there's nothing else you can do, you lower your head and keep going. Keep moving and hope for the best.

It was hours until nightfall.

CHAPTER 40

That horse gave it everything. I knew I was going to wind up killing it, and I hated to do that. It wasn't even my horse.

But I loved it anyway. It must have sensed how desperate I was, and with the huge heart that some animals possess, it set out to save my life, even at the cost of its own. Amazingly, over the next half hour, we actually widened the gap between us and the posse.

Then a thinner column of dust separated itself from the big cloud raised by the posse and started drawing closer and closer. I cussed bitterly every time I looked over my shoulder and saw what was happening. At first I thought the dust was coming from two or three riders who had pulled ahead of the others, but then I realized it wasn't horses' hooves kicking up that dust.

It was the tires of an automobile.

Muscle and bone, even teamed with a gallant heart, couldn't outrun machinery. Not indefinitely, anyway. I could only hope that one of the tires would blow or the engine would overheat.

It didn't appear that was going to happen. I could see the automobile now. Two men were inside it. I figured one of them had to be Sheriff Lester. Chances were the other man was the one who'd planned the trap.

A flash of white up ahead made me groan. We had come to a salt flat. It stretched for a mile or more north and south on both sides of the tracks, and there was no telling how wide it was. If I turned north, the two men in the car could angle that same way and cut me off. If I tried to go straight across, there would be nothing to slow them down and they would stand a good chance of catching up to me.

Well, it had been a good run, I told myself as I galloped out onto the blindingly white flat. It was a damned shame things hadn't worked out. I hoped the rest of the fellas would have the good sense to take the loot they had and light a shuck. Once the law identified my body, they would come looking for the men who'd worked for me.

I rode hard for another mile. The salt flat still stretched ahead of me as far as I could see. I looked back. The automobile was on the salt, too, roaring after me.

I reined in and turned the horse around so I was facing my pursuers. The horse stood there, trembling slightly under me as I took a box of cartridges from Randy's saddlebags and filled the Winchester's magazine.

"You did good, old son," I said. "I couldn't have asked for any more. I hope you come out of this all right, but I've got to ask you for one more thing." I levered a round into the rifle's chamber. "Let's go!"

I drove my heels into the horse's flanks and sent it leaping ahead. As we charged toward the automobile I brought the rifle to my shoulder and began to fire as fast as I could work the lever.

It was a crazy thing to do, of course. I remembered Etta talking about an old Spanish fella named Don Quixote who had a habit of charging at windmills with a lance, thinking they were monsters. He was a character in a book, and since she'd been a schoolteacher at one time in her life, Etta knew about such things.

What I was doing at that moment reminded me of old Don Quixote. I figured I had a little better chance than he did, though. I had a Winchester with a full magazine.

With both of us moving fast like that, we closed the gap between us in a hurry. The fella in the passenger seat leaned out and returned my fire, but I guess the front seat of a bouncing, weaving automobile wasn't any better for accurate shooting than the hurricane deck of a galloping horse. We burned quite a bit of powder before one of us scored a hit, and that was me.

The windshield shattered as one of my bullets struck it. Glass sprayed back in the faces of the two men. The car skidded hard to its left, sending a shower of salt into the air from the tires. I thought it was going to flip over, but it didn't. It spun around a couple of times, though.

The passenger jumped out. He must have been jolted around enough during that crazy skid to make him drop his rifle. He clawed a pistol from under his coat, though, and tried to draw a bead on me.

I didn't give him time to do that. I was almost on top of him. I swung the rifle and smacked him in the side of the head with the barrel. He went down.

I could have trampled right over him, but instead I pulled the horse aside just in time. Circling back, I covered both men with the rifle. Neither of them moved. The fella I had just walloped was a stranger to me, although I found out later he was a Pinkerton agent named Simon Barstow. The other man, who was slumped forward over the steering wheel, was Sheriff Emil Lester, just as I had figured.

I dismounted and hurried over to check on Lester, keeping one eye on the dust cloud from the posse while I was doing it. Despite the fact that the sheriff was determined to bring me to what he thought of as justice, I sort of liked the stubborn ol' cuss. He seemed to be out cold, and when I pushed him away from the steering wheel, I saw why. He had a big lump on his forehead, along with a few cuts on his face from flying glass. I knew he must have hit his head on the wheel while the car was careening around and he'd knocked himself out.

An idea occurred to me. I leaned the Winchester against the side of the automobile, reached in, and got hold of Lester under his arms. I dragged him out and stretched him on the salt. His breathing was all right, and I figured he would be fine when he came to, except for a headache.

The other fella was unconscious, too. I had just clipped his skull with the rifle barrel, I decided when I probed the bloody lump above his ear. The bone wasn't crushed, so he ought to be all right, too, I told myself.

Once I'd checked on him, I went back to Randy's horse. The posse wasn't far off now. I took the saddle off and threw it in the back of the car. A swat on the rump with my hat sent the horse galloping away.

The automobile's engine was still running, which was a lucky break for me because I didn't know if I could have gotten it started by myself. I climbed in and put the rifle on the seat beside me. I had been in these contraptions before. I had even tried to drive one of them a time or two. So I sort of knew what all the pedals and levers did. I took a deep breath and started trying to make it go.

I knew the car was my only hope of outrunning the posse, as long as I could keep it moving. It lurched forward and the engine threatened to stall. I held my breath, and it started running smoother again. The car rolled forward as I pressed my foot down on one of the pedals.

It probably looked pretty funny, the way I had that thing bumping and jolting along, but eventually I got the hang of it and started going faster. I headed north, and as I twisted my neck around to look behind me, I saw the posse in the distance. They would stop to check on Sheriff Lester and his companion, and that would slow them down some. I had a chance to outrun them now, a real chance.

As I drove, the excitement started to wear off, and my arm hurt more. When I looked down at my sleeve I saw that it was bloody all the way down to my wrist. I had lost quite a bit of blood, and I could tell that from the woozy feeling that began to come over me. I told myself as sternly as possible that I couldn't afford to pass out. If I did, I would probably wreck the car. Even if I didn't, it would stop moving without me being able to push down on the pedals, and then the posse would catch up to me. It would spell doom either way for me.

As I drove I tried to force myself to think. Randy's horse was the one he'd ridden in on that night, so it didn't have a Fishhook brand on it. Even if the posse found it—and it was possible they wouldn't—they probably wouldn't be able to tell who it belonged to. That was the reason I'd taken the time to remove the saddle and toss it into the car. The horse that had been shot out from under me at the train was one of the mounts that had been ridden by the members of Randy's former gang and not the one I usually rode into Largo, so there was nothing tieing it to the Fishhook or to me, either.

I'd still had the bandanna over the lower half of my face and my hat was pulled down when I charged toward the automobile. Throw in the glare off the salt flat and it was doubtful that either man had gotten a real good look at me while the shooting was going on. Then Lester was out cold from bumping his head. He might have recognized me if he'd seen me close up, even with the bandanna over my face, but he hadn't.

That left the letter that had lured us into the trap. It was a pretty damning piece of evidence, but I didn't think it actually proved anything. Somebody could have tried to rob that train without knowing there was supposed to be a shipment of gold bullion on it. Given my growing reputation in the area as a philanthropist, I thought there were plenty of people who would testify that I couldn't possibly be an outlaw. If it came down to a trial, we would just maintain our innocence and trust in a jury to believe us.

All that went through my head as I kept driving. I came to the end of the salt flat and continued north. I didn't know how much gasoline the automobile had in it or how long it would run, but every time I looked back the dust cloud from the posse was smaller. I was pulling steadily away from them.

When I got closer to some hills that lay in my path, I turned west. That took me toward Largo. I was getting dizzier and dizzier, and if I hadn't had the setting sun to steer by, I might have driven around and around in circles. I couldn't feel my right arm anymore. That was pretty bad.

Somewhere along the way, an idea came to me. Dusk settled down, and as the stars came out in the bluish-purple sky above me, I also saw the lights of the settlement twinkling in the distance. Just like the now-vanished sun, they were a beacon to me and seemed to pull me on physically. Now that it was dark, the posse couldn't trail me, and I became convinced that if I could just make it to Daisy's house, everything would be all right.

Looking back on it, if I'd been thinking straighter I would have stayed as far away from Daisy Hatfield as I could. The last thing I should have wanted was for her to get mixed up in trouble with the law.

But I was hurting and half out of my head, and a vision of her beautiful face seemed to float in the air in front of me, drawing me on as surely as the lights of Largo. Maybe I thought I was going to die. Maybe I just wanted to see her one more time before I crossed the divide. I don't really remember.

But I know I felt a keen stab of disappointment when the automobile's engine sputtered, coughed, and died, and the damned thing shuddered to a stop. I leaned forward and rested my forehead on the steering wheel, probably about the same place Sheriff Lester had whopped his head and knocked himself out.

Finally I sat up again. I could sit there until morning came, I told myself, but if I did there was a good chance the posse would find me as it resumed the search. The cool night air was better for walking, and I could still see the lights ahead of me so I wouldn't get lost . . . as long as I didn't start imagining things that weren't there. Largo was only a few miles away, I estimated. I could walk that far.

I climbed out of the car, taking the rifle with me. I didn't like the idea of leaving the saddle behind, but I knew I couldn't carry it, too. Nor was there a good place nearby to hide it. I settled for slinging the saddlebags over my shoulders and hoped the saddle itself didn't have anything on it that would identify it as belonging to Randy McClellan.

Just like the night I had traveled through that bitter cold wind to track down Abner Tillotson's killers, I don't remember much about my journey to Largo. I kept my gaze fixed on the lights and put one foot in front of the other, again and again and again. A few times I stumbled and almost fell, but I fought to stay on my feet because I knew that if I went down there was a good chance I'd be too weak to get up again.

It felt like a million miles, but gradually the twinkling dots of light got bigger and turned into yellow glows from windows. A quarter-moon rose behind me, and in the silvery wash of its light I spotted the church, even though I was still a mile away. When I got closer I had to stop and think about where the Hatfield house was in relation to the church. It wouldn't do to show up bloody and half-conscious on somebody else's doorstep.

I didn't think about what Reverend Hatfield might do. I suppose my thoughts were just so full of longing to see Daisy again that I didn't even consider her father. Anyway, there was no real law in Largo, so there wasn't much the preacher could do without heading for the county seat, and if he did, I would worry about that later.

After what seemed like an eternity, I found myself at the back of Daisy's house. I knew which window went with her bedroom, so I stumbled over to it and started tapping on the glass. The shape I was in, just doing that much seemed like a monumental effort. I got so tired I rested my head against the glass as I continued tapping quietly on it.

The window going up almost made me fall down. I caught myself with my good arm against the sill. Daisy leaned out and gasped.

"Jim! My God! Is that you?"

I lifted my head. I could feel a silly grin stretching across my face but couldn't stop it. I was just blasted happy to see her again, even if it turned out to be for the last time.

"Daisy . . . ," I said. She must have already gone to bed, because her hair was tousled around her head. It looked dark in the moonlight. I went on, "You're so . . . so beautiful . . ."

"Jim, are you drunk?" she asked sharply.

"Drunk on . . . love," I said.

I didn't get any more words out because the last of my strength deserted me then. I reeled away from the window, half-twisting as I struggled to maintain my balance. Daisy let out a soft cry of alarm when she saw my bloody sleeve.

I felt myself falling, but that was the last thing I knew. Utter blackness had swallowed me by the time I hit the ground.

CHAPTER 41

An unknowable amount of time later, I woke up. Pain flooded through me, followed almost immediately by relief. There's no getting around the fact that if you hurt, you're still alive. I thought about that instead of the misery in my arm and the pounding in my head.

Something soft and cool touched my face. I let out a moan. It might have been smarter to hide the fact that I'd regained consciousness—at that point I didn't know what sort of situation or how much danger I was in—but I couldn't help it. That sensation just felt so blasted *good*.

"You're awake," Daisy said. "Aren't you? Jim?"

Opening my eyes seemed to take as much strength as lifting a fifty-pound sack of grain would have, but somehow I managed. When the light struck them, I blinked, and my eyelids rising and falling felt and sounded like thunder booming in my head.

It really wasn't that bright in the room. It just seemed that way to me at that moment. Actually, the lamp on the table beside the bed was turned down low enough that it left the corners of the room dim and shadowy.

Once my eyes adjusted, though, I had no trouble focusing on Daisy as she leaned over me with a concerned expression on her face.

"I was afraid you were going to die," she said. "You'd lost so much blood."

My voice sounded hollow and far away to me as I whispered, "Reckon I must've . . . been hurt worse than . . . I thought."

"You were shot in the arm. You're fortunate the bullet didn't break the bone, but I don't think it did."

"I thought I'd just been . . . grazed a mite."

I've seen it happen before. The bullets start flying, and a fella gets desperate and is moving so fast he doesn't really know how bad he's hurt. Sooner or later it catches up to him, though. I was just lucky I'd been able to hold it off until I reached Daisy's house.

Lucky . . . or so damned mule-headed I wouldn't allow any other outcome.

Daisy continued wiping my face with the damp cloth she held. It felt about as good as anything I've ever experienced. She said, "You have a fever, Jim. I cleaned and bandaged the wound, but you really need a doctor."

"No . . . doctor," I said. I shook my head slightly, or at least I think I did. "Where's your . . . father?"

"He's not here. One of the members of the congregation is gravely ill. Father drove out to his house to sit up with him." She paused. "When I first heard the tapping on the window, I thought you knew somehow that Father was gone and had come to see me with something else in mind. I wasn't expecting to find you injured. What happened?"

I could have spun some yarn about dropping my gun and shooting myself by accident, I suppose. But I was half out of my head, remember, and while I'm not particularly proud of it, there's no point in covering up the truth.

I said, "I got shot while . . . the boys and I . . . were tryin' to hold up the train. You see . . . Daisy . . . I'm Butch Cassidy."

I could tell by the look on her face that she thought I was just raving. But slowly, in fits and starts because I was so weak, I spilled the whole story to her, starting with the night I'd run into Abner Tillotson. It never occurred to me that she might go to the law and turn me in. I guess I just trusted her because I loved her so much.

By the time I was finished, she might not have believed me one hundred percent, but at least she didn't think I was completely loco anymore. She was willing to grant the possibility that I was telling the truth.

"None of that really matters right now," she said when I was finished. "What's important is that you rest. You'll feel a lot better once you've had some sleep, I hope."

"Maybe. But I got to get . . . back to the ranch. The sheriff's liable to . . . show up there lookin' for me. If I ain't there . . . he'll want to know what became of me. He's always been . . . a mite suspicious of me."

"You don't have to worry about that," Daisy said with a faint smile. "If it comes down to it, I'll simply tell Sheriff Lester that you spent the night here . . . with me."

I stared at her for several seconds before I was able to say, "Good Lord, girl! You can't . . . you can't do that. It'd ruin your reputation . . . forever."

"Do you honestly think I care about something that unimportant, Jim? My reputation means nothing in comparison to keeping you safe."

I didn't agree with that at all, but I was too weak to argue with her. She went on, "In the morning, if you're stronger, I'll put you in the buggy and we'll go out to your ranch. The sheriff won't be able to prove you haven't been there all along."

"That's what I'm . . . hopin'," I said. I felt myself slipping away again. "Daisy . . . thank you . . . I can't tell you how much I . . ."

I couldn't finish what I was trying to say. It didn't matter, because she clasped my left hand in both of hers and whispered, "I know. I love you, too, Jim."

I had been about to say I couldn't tell her how much I appreciated her help, but I reckon "I love you" worked just as well. I was able to squeeze one of her hands to let her know I felt the same way.

After that I let myself drift off. I could tell that I was falling asleep this time, not passing out, so I didn't fight it. Maybe she was right. Maybe a good night's rest was what I needed most right now.

I just hoped that when I woke up in the morning, it wouldn't be to find that I had handcuffs on my wrists.

CHAPTER 42

With that thought in my head, the first thing I did the next morning was to try to move my arms. I was able to lift the left one, but the right refused to go anywhere. Thinking that arm might be shackled to something, I lifted my head from the pillow enough to take a look at it.

That set the room to spinning crazily, but after a moment it settled down. I didn't see any handcuffs. My right arm was heavily bandaged, though, and Daisy had rigged a sling for it and strapped it down to hold it still against my body. It hurt, but really not as much as I expected it to.

I was thinking straighter now that I was awake again. I seemed to remember telling Daisy all about how I was Butch Cassidy and how the crew from the Fishhook and I had been robbing trains for the past few months. Surely I hadn't been crazy enough to do that . . . had I?

The memory was pretty clear in my head, but I wouldn't be sure until she came in. I heard faint noises of somebody moving around the house and figured it was her, so I thought about calling her. Instead I spent a few minutes looking around the room. I had seen her bedroom before, but it seemed especially bright and cheery this morning with the sun shining through gauzy curtains over the window and setting off a warm glow from the yellow, flower-patterned wallpaper.

I noticed a pitcher of water sitting on the dresser, and that made me realize how thirsty I was. My mouth was like cotton. Once I thought about being thirsty, I was hungry, too, hungry enough to eat a horse.

I heard footsteps through the open door, and then Daisy appeared there, looking as fresh and pretty as her room. She smiled at me when she saw I was awake.

"Your fever broke a little while ago," she told me. "I was hoping you'd wake up soon. How do you feel this morning, Jim?"

"Better," I said in a rusty voice. "My arm don't even hurt too bad. I sure am hungry and thirsty, though."

"I'm not surprised," she said as she came over and sat down on the edge of the bed beside me. "I've hardly been able to get anything down you the past few days."

It took a second for what she had said to sink in. When it did, I asked, "What do you mean, the past few days? I came here last night."

Still smiling, she shook her head and said, "That was three nights ago, Jim."

I tried not to groan. The fellas at the ranch probably thought I was dead. That is, if they were worried about me at all, considering the likelihood that they were locked up.

But maybe not, I told myself. Enoch and Gabe were cunning old lobos. They would know the sheriff didn't have much hard evidence against them. They might have tried to brazen it out. They might have even been successful . . . so far.

I was willing to bet that the sheriff was mighty interested in my whereabouts, though.

"What about your dad?" I asked Daisy. "He's bound to be back by now."

She shook her head.

"He's been here and gone. Mr. Abercrombie is still sick, but he's hanging on. Father came in, slept for a night, cleaned up, and went back out to the Abercrombie ranch. He was so tired he never knew you were here." She laughed softly. "It was quite a dilemma for me. I was worried because you weren't waking up, but at the same time I didn't want you to wake up and call out while he was here. As it turned out, that didn't happen."

"We've got to make sure there's no chance of it happenin'," I told her. "I need to get out of here."

"Not until you've had something to eat and drink and I've changed the dressing on your wound. Then maybe we'll see about getting you in the buggy and taking you out to your ranch. Are you sure someone there can take proper care of you?"

I figured Enoch and Gabe had patched up a heap of bullet wounds in their time, but I didn't say that. I just nodded and said, "Yeah, I'll be fine."

She stood up.

"Then I'll go get you some breakfast."

"That's the best offer I've had in a long time," I told her.

"If you were stronger, I might make you an even better offer," she said. The blush that spread over her face before she turned away reminded me that I was in her bed. More than that, I was stripped down to the bottom half of my long johns, and she was the only one who could have done that, as well as tending to my other needs. I figured it was best not to dwell on that too much.

She brought back a cup of coffee, a cup of broth, and a biscuit. I wanted to gulp down the drinks, but they were hot so I had to take it easy and sip them. That was probably better for me anyway. It gave them a chance to brace me up and send strength flowing back into my body. The biscuit was so light and fluffy it was like biting into a cloud in Heaven.

While I was eating, neither of us brought up all the things I had told her the night I showed up at her window. But as she was changing the bandage on my arm, after announcing that the wound looked like it was healing well, she said, "Jim . . . or should I call you Butch?"

"Jim's fine," I said. "I haven't used that other name for a long time. I'd even started to feel like Butch Cassidy was dead and buried down there in Bolivia."

"I'm afraid I don't know what you're talking about. I've barely even heard of Butch Cassidy. All I know is that he was some sort of old-time outlaw . . . ?"

I grinned at her and said, "Now you understand how come I

kept tellin' you I'm too old for you, darlin'. That's what I am: a relic of the Old West."

"You're the most vital man I've ever known," she said. "You're hardly a relic." She paused. "It's true, then? About the train robberies?"

"It is. I reckon I've broken that 'Thou shalt not steal' commandment more than any of the others."

"But you said you did it to help young Vince Porter, and then, after that, to help other people. That doesn't make it . . . really . . . what you'd call . . ."

"It's still stealin'," I said when her voice trailed off. "And I can understand if you want to turn me over to the law."

She leaned back and her eyes got big.

"I could never do that!" she said. "Just because something's against the law doesn't mean that it's, well, wrong."

"To most folks that's exactly what it means."

She gave a defiant little toss of her head and said, "I'm not like most folks. I never have been, and I never will be."

She was right about that. She had her own way of doing things, her own path to follow. I had already figured out that she didn't want anybody to pigeonhole her. It made her mad when people tried to.

"All right," I told her. "I'm not one to argue morality with anybody. If you're willin' to keep quiet about what you know, I appreciate that. For the sake of the other fellas, as much as for my own sake."

"I can do more than keep quiet," she said.

I frowned a little and asked, "What do you mean by that?"

She had finished tending to my arm. She smiled but didn't answer my question. Instead she said, "I think you're strong enough to travel. Let me go see if I can find some of my father's clothes for you to wear."

I felt like telling her that nothing belonging to scrawny little Franklin Hatfield was going to fit me, but I didn't say anything. She got up and left the room.

When she came back she held up a shirt that looked way too big for her pa and said, "This is the oldest thing Father has."

"That shirt's big enough for two of him," I said.

"He used to be a much more . . . substantial . . . man than he is now. He went through a bout of illness and nearly died. Since then he can't seem to regain any weight. He says he's glad it happened, though. He claims it brought him closer to the Lord."

"I don't doubt it," I said. "Nearly dyin' has a habit of doin' that."

"I hope this is big enough that you can put your left arm in the sleeve and then we can just drape the rest of it around you. First, though, we need to get your trousers back on you. There wasn't too much blood on them, and I was able to wash most of it out. I had to burn your shirt, though."

"I understand. Just bring me the britches and I can put 'em on by myself."

She shook her head and said, "I don't think so. Not as weak as you are and with only one arm that you can use. I don't mind helping, Jim. I'm not a little girl." She added, "Besides, I'm the one who took them off of you."

"Yeah, I figured as much," I said. "You don't scandalize very easy, do you?"

She laughed and said, "Not at all."

We managed to get clothes on me. It took a while, the shape I was in. And while it was awkward physically, it wasn't too embarrassing, I suppose. Daisy deserved the credit for that, because she had such a practical, easygoing manner about her. There was a lot to like about that girl.

Hell, there was a lot to love about that girl.

I didn't care for the idea of her putting me in the buggy and starting out for the Fishhook in broad daylight, but there was no telling when her father might show up, and we couldn't count on him remaining blissfully ignorant of my presence in the house a second time. Daisy said she could pull the buggy right up to the back door and take me out that way. If she circled away from the settlement right from the start, we might be able to slip out of Largo without anybody seeing us. We had to take that chance.

When I stood up and tried to walk for the first time in several days, I would have fallen flat on my face if she hadn't been there to hold me up. We struggled to the kitchen, where she had placed a chair beside the back door. Grateful for the chance to rest, I sat down in it while Daisy went to fetch the buggy.

When she came back in, she said, "The other night I hid your rifle and handgun in the shed. They're in the back of the buggy now."

"We won't need 'em," I said, "but thanks for takin' care of them."

"We can hope we won't need them. But you never know."

That was true enough, I supposed. I couldn't handle the rifle with only one arm, but I was a pretty fair shot with a revolver using my left hand.

And I wouldn't have put it past Daisy that she could shoot a rifle like Annie Oakley.

By the time I was in the vehicle, that old shirt of her father's was drenched with sweat. We made it, though. I leaned back against the seat, breathing hard, and nodded to her that I was ready because I couldn't speak. She picked up the reins and got the horses moving.

It came as no surprise to me that Daisy was good at handling the team. She seemed to be good at whatever she turned her hand to. She had done a fine job taking care of me, and if it bothered her that she was nursing a train robber back to health, she never showed a sign of it. She was as cool-headed as any man I'd ever ridden with, including Harry Longabaugh.

She had gotten to know the area pretty well from the times she had gone riding with me, so I didn't have to tell her the way to the ranch. She didn't take the easiest, most obvious trail but rather swung far to the east to make anybody who noticed the buggy leaving Largo think that she wasn't headed for the Fishhook.

Actually, we were headed toward the old Daughtry place, I realized. Before we got there she could circle back to the west and go at the Fishhook from that direction.

"You know, people all over the county are talking about the train being held up," she said as she kept the two horses moving along at a steady clip. She didn't let them go too fast because that would jounce me around and maybe hurt my arm. "That Pinkerton detective Barstow has pledged to round up each and every one of you."

"Who?" I asked. That was the first time I'd ever heard Simon Barstow's name.

Daisy told me all she had heard about him from the gossip in Farnum's store, as well as the information she'd gleaned from the newspapers. From the sound of it, the story had spread all over the state of Texas in the past few days.

"Mr. Barstow is very angry that his trap failed," she went on. She glanced over at me. "He wouldn't have sent that letter to Vince to lure you in if he wasn't convinced that you were responsible for the robberies."

"He probably got that idea from Sheriff Lester," I said. "The sheriff's been suspicious of me right along."

"Why didn't they just come out to the ranch and arrest you? Why try to trick you into holding up that train?"

"Because they don't have any proof we pulled those other jobs. The loot we got from them is cached where they'll never find it. If they were to go into court and say we have to be the robbers because there are nine of us, a jury would never believe it. There might be a dozen ranches around here with nine hands workin' on 'em. And we made sure nobody ever got a good enough look at us to identify us."

"What are you going to do now? Aren't you worried that if you keep going like you are, sooner or later you'll make a mistake and get caught?"

"We'll lay low for a while," I said. "I'll have to talk it over with the boys and see if they want to quit entirely after what happened. If they do, I won't try to talk 'em out of it. It's always been their decision."

She drove along in silence for a few minutes, then said quietly, without looking at me, "I can understand why you'd want to put all that behind you. But if you were to stop now, it would be almost like you allowed that awful man Barstow to beat you."

That made me laugh. I said, "Why, Miss Hatfield, it almost sounds like you're encouragin' me to go out and hold up another train."

"No, not at all. I just think that in the end, everyone has to be true to himself . . . or herself. Knowing you has made me see some things differently, Jim."

I would have asked her what she meant by that, but I didn't get a chance. We were passing a little canyon that cut through a ridge to our left, and as we did a rider spurred out of it and lunged toward us. He had a rifle in his hands. The ugly whip-crack of sound as he fired over our heads made the buggy horses shy and dance around skittishly. Daisy had to saw at the reins for a minute to bring them under control and keep them from running away.

It might have been better if they had stampeded, because as the buggy came to an abrupt halt, the rider stopped about twenty feet away and leveled his rifle at us. I knew him right away. The last time I'd seen him, he had been unconscious from being walloped by my rifle, out there on the salt flats.

Simon Barstow had the drop on us.

CHAPTER 43

"Mr. Jim Strickland, I believe," he said as he smirked at us.

"What if I am?" I asked as I tried to control the anger that welled up inside me. I didn't like the fella because of the trick he'd tried to pull on us, and the arrogant look on his face rankled me even more. What really put a burr under my saddle, though, was the fact that he was pointing that rifle at Daisy, too, not just me. I went on, "Why don't you put that gun down? You don't need it."

"I think I'd rather not take that chance," Barstow said. "You have a habit of slipping away from justice, Strickland, almost like some of those old-time bandits."

Daisy was furious, I could tell that by looking at her. She said, "Sir, you don't know who—"

"You don't know what you're talkin' about," I broke in. Even as bad as the situation seemed at the moment, I didn't want to take a chance that she was about to tell Barstow I was really Butch Cassidy. There was no need for him to know about that. It might just make things go from bad to worse.

Daisy must have caught on, because she said, "Why have you stopped us, sir? Are you going to rob us?"

Barstow grunted in surprise at the question.

"Hardly," he said. "I'm not an outlaw. My name is Simon Barstow. I work for the Pinkerton detective agency. Your companion there is the lawbreaker."

"You're mistaken," Daisy said coolly. "Mr. Strickland is a well-respected cattleman. You can ask anyone in the area about him. They'll tell you what a fine man he is."

"People who didn't know any better said that Jesse James was a fine man, too," Barstow snapped. He looked at me. "What are you doing here, Strickland? The men at your ranch—the rest of your gang—swore that you had gone to San Antonio to negotiate a deal to buy more cattle."

That was a decent story. I figured Enoch had come up with it, but one of the others might have.

"How do you know I didn't?" I asked.

"You can't be in San Antonio and riding along with Miss Hatfield in a buggy at the same time, now can you? Not only that, you appear to have a wounded arm. Is that a bullet hole in it, perhaps?"

"My horse threw me," I said. I didn't believe there was any way to talk myself out of this. Barstow was too dead set that he was right about me. But it wouldn't hurt to try. "My shoulder's wrenched from the fall, and I think I might've tore a muscle. That's why my arm's all wrapped up."

"Of course it is," Barstow said, smirking again. He didn't believe me. Well, I hadn't expected him to.

"I walked on into Largo, since my horse ran off," I went on, "and Miss Hatfield was kind enough to offer to drive me back to the ranch."

"From what I hear, that's not the only thing Miss Hatfield has been kind enough to do for you. The two of you have quite the romance going on." Barstow got a disapproving look on his face. "You ought to be ashamed of yourself, Strickland. You're not only a train robber, you've robbed the cradle as well."

"You keep a civil tongue in your head," Daisy told him. "You clearly don't know what you're talking about—"

"That's enough," I said. If I'd ever wanted to charge right at somebody holding a gun on me, that was the moment. I couldn't argue with him calling me an outlaw. That's what I was, after all. But when he laid that nasty tongue of his on Daisy's reputation, I could barely contain my fury. "Leave Miss Hatfield out of this.

She never knew the truth about me until today. When I showed up wounded at her house, I forced her to take care of me, just like I'm forcin' her to drive me to the ranch."

She looked at me and said, "You—"

"That's right," I went on, overriding whatever she was going to say. "You got me, mister. I'll confess to all of it in court, includin' the way I kidnapped Miss Hatfield. Once she found out what I've really been doin', she didn't want anything more to do with me."

Barstow regarded me intently as a frown creased his forehead. He said, "I don't believe you. But if you're willing to confess to your crimes . . . *and* to implicate your accomplices in the process . . . I suppose we can leave out any mention of your illicit relationship with Miss Hatfield."

Daisy was looking at me like she was about to explode. I stared back at her coolly and hoped she understood and would accept that this was the way I wanted it.

I turned back to Barstow and said, "You've got a deal."

I was lying, of course. There was no way I would ever go into court and testify against the rest of the bunch. But I planned to make a break for it before we got to the county seat and force Barstow to kill me. With me dead he'd never be able to prove anything against Daisy or the boys from the Fishhook. To me, that was worth dying for. I'd outlived my time, anyway. No man's meant to cheat death as often as I had.

Daisy opened her mouth to say something, probably to argue, but I drowned her out again by saying, "Go ahead, take me back to the county seat." I reached for the reins. "Turn this damned buggy around, woman."

"Hold it!" Barstow said. He had allowed the Winchester's barrel to droop a little, but it came up again quickly and menaced us. "We're not going back to the county seat yet. Drive on, Miss Hatfield. There's the remains of an old shack up ahead a ways. That's where we're going."

The Daughtry place, I thought. Why in blazes were we going there?

Barstow answered that question after jerking the rifle barrel at Daisy and forcing her to get the buggy moving again. He rode alongside us and drew a pistol with his right hand while using his left to slide the rifle back into its scabbard. He could cover us easier with the handgun from that position.

"We're going to rendezvous with Sheriff Lester," Barstow said. "He's out here searching for you, too, Strickland. We knew you'd try to make it back to your ranch sooner or later from wherever you were holed up. I was convinced that Miss Hatfield was hiding you and wanted to break in there and search the place, but the sheriff refused. He seemed to feel that since Miss Hatfield is the daughter of a minister, she deserved the benefit of the doubt."

I knew there was a good reason I felt a little liking for Sheriff Lester. He was a decent hombre, in spite of being a lawman.

"We've been ranging back and forth between Largo and the Fishhook," Barstow went on. "You really should have continued to lay low. I might have gotten tired of searching and given it up eventually." An ugly laugh came from him. "Along about the same time that hell freezes over."

It was still a couple of miles to the Daughtry place, so I had a little time to satisfy my curiosity. I said, "What made you come after us in the first place?"

"Sheriff Lester put me on your trail," he said, confirming my earlier guess. "All he had were vague, unfounded suspicions, though. I launched a thorough investigation and discovered that the first holdup took place after the accidental death of a railroad employee whose son works for you. That might have given you a grudge against the railroad. I interviewed everyone I could find who witnessed the robberies, and although everyone told the story slightly differently, I determined that the average number of participants in the crimes seemed to be nine. That was the exact number of you and your crew, including the three Mexicans who work for you part-time."

"You couldn't find any other spreads that have nine hands?" I asked.

"None that had a connection to the railroad. With all that to go on, it didn't take long to find out that in the past few months you've been handing out quite a bit of money to what could be considered worthy causes and individuals. Did you have some idea that such charity made it all right to steal from the railroad, Strickland?"

I could see why he was considered a good detective, all right. He had put together a strong case against me and the fellas. But it was purely guesswork, without any proof.

When I didn't answer his question, he went on, "I knew you were the ones I was after, but I thought if I could catch you in the act, that would tie everything up neatly. So I set that trap and baited it with a letter supposedly from John Hamilton."

"What'd you do, browbeat a dyin' man into helpin' you? I wouldn't put it past you."

"Neither would I, but that wasn't necessary." Barstow sounded mighty pleased with himself as he went on, "You see, early in my career I handled several forgery cases, and I learned all the tricks of the trade employed by such criminals. I'm a pretty good forger, if I do say so myself. All I needed was a sample of Hamilton's handwriting, and it wasn't difficult to get that. Any inconsistencies would be put down to the fact that everyone would think he wrote the letter on his deathbed."

That tied it all up as far as I could see. Nice and neat, just like he'd said. And we were in sight of what was left of the Daughtry shack by now. It had decayed and fallen in even more. In another year or two, nobody would be able to tell that folks had ever lived here.

Barstow glanced up at the sun.

"Sheriff Lester is supposed to meet me here at midday. We'll wait for him and go back to the county seat together."

"You want to show off how smart you are, right?"

"Smart enough to catch you," Barstow said.

But not smart enough to keep me, I thought. I gathered my muscles, getting ready to make a leap from the buggy at him. I knew that as tightly wound up as he was, as soon as I made my move he would pull the trigger. I just had to make sure my body was between his gun and Daisy, so there wouldn't be any chance of her being hit. I knew that pistol of his wasn't big enough to shoot all the way through me.

It was big enough to kill me, though. That was exactly what I was after.

Butch Cassidy could finally go to his grave.

That was when Daisy surprised both of us. She came up halfway off the seat and said loudly, "Oh, my! My head . . . it's spinning! I'm going to—"

She fell forward, but as she landed on the floorboard she slapped the reins hard against the rumps of both horses and cried out to them. They lunged ahead, throwing Daisy and me both backward.

Pretending to faint like that had drawn Barstow's eyes to her, just like she thought it would, and that pulled his gun out of line. When he tried to jerk it back toward me and fired, the bullet tore through the back of the buggy's canopy instead.

I twisted on the seat and reached behind it with my left hand, searching for the coiled shell belt and holstered Remington that Daisy had put back there before we left Largo. Barstow kicked his horse into a gallop and came after us, firing his pistol.

"Stay down!" I yelled at Daisy as I continued fumbling for the gun. She was lying on the floorboard, bumping against my legs as she slashed at the team and kept them running.

I'd been ready to die to protect her. I figure she must have known that, and she sensed somehow that I was about to put my plan into action. So she had moved first, trying to give me a fighting chance, anyway.

More of Barstow's bullets tore through the canopy and whistled around my head. My hand closed around the Remington's ivory grips as the ridge against which the Daughtry shack was built loomed up in front of us. Daisy had to swing the buggy to the side to keep from crashing into it.

We were going too fast to make that turn. As I yanked the revolver from its holster, I felt the buggy tip. We were suspended like that for a sickeningly dizzy second before it went over and crashed to the ground in front of the shack.

I was thrown out when the buggy turned over. I didn't know what had happened to Daisy. When I slammed into the ground I landed on my bad arm, and it sent an explosion of agony through me. Momentum rolled me over a couple of times before I stopped. Somehow I managed to hang on to the gun in my left hand.

Dust roiled around me as I lifted my head and cried, "Daisy!" I couldn't see her, and I was desperate to know what had happened to her.

"You son of a bitch!" Barstow roared somewhere close by. "You won't get away from me again!"

"Jim!" Daisy screamed as Barstow loomed out of the dust, on his feet now instead of in the saddle, gun in his outthrust hand. A light-colored shape darted in between us from the side. "Mr. Barstow! Don't—"

I saw Barstow's face as he pulled the trigger. It was twisted in lines of insane hatred. He didn't care that Daisy was in the way. He just wanted to kill me no matter who else got hurt. Flame lanced from the pistol's muzzle. Daisy cried out and went down.

"Daisy!"

The Remington's roar all but drowned out my scream. It bucked in my hand as I fired again and again until the hammer fell on an empty chamber. All five rounds tore through Simon Barstow's body. One of them broke the wrist of his gun hand. Two more went into his belly, one smashed his heart, and the last one caught him in the middle of his forehead and blew a fist-size hole in the back of his skull as it burst out. He flopped to the ground, dead as a man could be.

By the time he landed I had forgotten all about him. I had already dropped my empty gun and started crawling toward Daisy, who lay sprawled a few feet away. I yelled her name at the top of my lungs.

She rolled over and looked at me. Her eyes were open. I didn't see any blood on her dress. She came up on her knees at the same time I did and threw her arms around me. My good arm went around her and held her tightly to me.

"I . . . I'm all right, Jim," she said in my ear. "I just tripped and fell while I was trying to shield you. I'm not hurt."

I was breathing hard as I said, "Don't you . . . don't you ever scare me . . . like that again, Daisy Hatfield."

She laughed and clung to me. After a moment she pulled back and asked, "What about you? Are you hurt?"

"Reckon my arm's bleedin' again," I told her. "But I'll live."

Damn right I would, I thought as she hugged me some more.

CHAPTER 44

"It was terrible," Daisy told Sheriff Emil Lester. "That awful man was hiding in that tumbledown shack. He came out and started shooting at us with no warning as soon as we drove up. Mr. Strickland was wounded right away. The man probably would have killed us if Mr. Barstow hadn't returned his fire and driven him off." She paused and sighed. "Unfortunately, poor Mr. Barstow was mortally wounded in the exchange of shots."

The sheriff just looked at Barstow's bullet-riddled body and grunted.

"Yeah. Mortally wounded and then some, I'd say." He stared at Daisy and me with narrowed eyes. "He was shot by some fella who was hiding in the shack?"

"That's right, Sheriff," I said. I was sitting on the ground, leaning against the overturned buggy. Daisy sat next to me, re-bandaging my bloody, apparently freshly wounded arm. "I figure he must've been that train robber Barstow told us he was lookin' for. When I mentioned this old shack to him, he said this was just the sort of place where an owlhoot on the run might hole up. So I offered to show him where it was."

"What happened to this . . . outlaw?" Lester asked through clenched teeth.

"I believe he was wounded," Daisy said. "With everything that was going on, I didn't really see what happened to him. He must have run off."

"Maybe he had a horse hidden in the brush," I suggested. "If you take a look around, Sheriff, you might be able to pick up his trail."

For a long time, Lester didn't say anything. He stood there looking at us, and after a while he lifted a hand and rubbed his chin as he frowned in thought.

Finally, he said, "I reckon that would be a waste of time. Whoever the fella was, he's long gone by now."

Lester had ridden up about fifteen minutes after the shootout with Barstow. That had given Daisy and me time to get ready for him. We had trampled all over the place, making sure that the tracks didn't tell any comprehensible story.

"Too bad about Barstow," the sheriff went on. "I got to know him a little the past few days. Never saw anybody who hated outlaws more than he did. It struck me that when he was after somebody he considered a lawbreaker, he might gun down anybody who got in his way, male or female, no matter who they were."

I shook my head and said, "I only just met him today, so I couldn't really say, Sheriff. But from what I saw of him, I think that's exactly what he might've done."

Lester took off his hat, ran his fingers through his hair, and slapped the hat back on his head. I could tell he was furious, but at the same time I had a feeling that his dislike of Barstow was genuine. But was that dislike strong enough to make him fail to carry out what he saw as his duty?

"You were on your way back to the Fishhook from a business trip in San Antonio?" he asked.

"That's right." I looked over at Daisy. "Miss Hatfield was givin' me a ride. That's where we were goin' when we ran into that Barstow fella."

"What happened to your horse?"

"Well, you see, he threw me and ran off when I was almost back to Largo. Got spooked by a rattlesnake coiled up under a mesquite. But I was able to hoof it into town and prevail upon Miss Hatfield here to help me out."

"Uh-huh." Lester turned his head, peered off into the distance, and chewed his mustache. I could tell his thoughts were eating him up inside. He didn't believe our story for a second, but he couldn't prove we were lying, not convincingly enough to take it to court, anyway. However, Simon Barstow had been a fellow lawman, whether Lester liked him or not, and every instinct in Lester's body was probably telling him that he couldn't let the person responsible for Barstow's death escape.

At the same time, he was a man, and he had just about openly admitted that Barstow was a sorry bastard who would shoot a woman if she got in his way. Given that, you might say that Barstow had gotten what was coming to him.

I could read the decision on Lester's face as he made up his mind. He said, "You're wounded, Strickland. We'd better get you back to town."

"We're a lot closer to the Fishhook, Sheriff," I said. "The fellas there can take care of me. If you'll just dab a rope on this buggy and use your horse to set it upright again . . . "

Lester sighed.

"Fine. I'll see to it that you get home, then I'll come back here for Barstow's body. His bosses won't be happy that he's dead. They're liable to send even more men after those train robbers, especially after the owners of the railroad get through yelling."

"You could be right, Sheriff," I said as Daisy helped me to my feet. "I think they're gonna have a long chase for nothin', though. My hunch is that those varmints have lit a shuck out of this part of the country. You might not ever see 'em again."

"Normally I wouldn't say this about a bunch of no-good outlaws . . . but there's a part of me hopes you're right about that, Strickland."

A little while later, as we were rolling along in the buggy while Lester rode ahead of us, Daisy said, "Were you telling the truth back there, Jim, when you said that to the sheriff about the train robbers never coming back?"

"If they've got any sense, that'd be the smartest thing for them to do," I told her.

"In a way, that would be a shame," she said. When I looked

over at her, she was smiling as she flicked the reins. "I was thinking that the real problem is the gang needs ten members instead of nine."

"And just where would that tenth desperado come from?" I
asked slowly.

She looked over at me and her smile widened.

I was going to tell her she was loco, but I knew it wouldn't do
any good. Daisy Hatfield had a mind of her own, she did, and
the only way to get that foolish notion out of her head would be
to make sure she didn't have any chance to carry it out.

I could see the ranch up ahead now. Somebody must have noticed us coming, because several of the fellas were riding out to
meet us. Enoch lifted a hand and waved. Scar bounded alongside the old gun-wolf's horse, barking his greeting.

"Just think about it, Jim," Daisy said. "That's all I ask right now."

"I will," I promised, but I already knew what my decision
would be.

My train robbing days were over.

And Butch Cassidy was finally dead.

Zephyr, Texas, 1950

"But that's not true, is it?" Nathan Tuttle said as he sat on the bench beside Hank Parker. "You weren't through robbing trains, were you, or banks, either?"

Parker looked at his empty soda pop bottle and said, "This ran dry a long time ago."

Nathan started to get to his feet, saying, "I'll get you another one—"

"Hold on, son. No need to do that. I'm dry, too. I'm done talked out."

Nathan sank back down onto the bench and stared at the old cowboy.

"You can't stop there!" he said urgently. "You've admitted that you're Butch Cassidy—"

"Now wait just a doggone minute," Parker broke in. "I never did no such thing."

"But . . . but Jim told his friends that he was Butch Cassidy. He even told Miss Hatfield."

"Maybe he did," Parker drawled. "That don't make it true. He could've just been makin' up a whopper of a lie to get folks to go along with what he wanted 'em to do."

"This is ridiculous!" Nathan said. "First you admit that you used to go by the name Jim Strickland, and then you say that Strickland was really Butch Cassidy, but now you're denying the whole thing."

Parker shook his head.

"I never said such, and I can't be held to account for anything ol' Jim might've said to anybody else, now can I? It's a *story*, son. Maybe some of it's true. Maybe all of it's true." Parker set the empty bottle aside, leaned back on the bench, and crossed his arms. "After all this time, what does it really matter?"

"Because I want to find out what happened!" Nathan said. "There were other things in my grandfather's papers . . . notes about Pancho Villa and a bank in Mexico . . . and something about Wyatt Earp and Bat Masterson . . . I want to know about that and all the other things he hinted about." The young man paused and drew a deep breath. "And what about Daisy? I don't recall seeing anything about her. If she was so important in Jim Strickland's life, why is there no mention of her in my grandfather's papers?"

"That's a good question," Parker said, his eyes narrowing as if he were looking at something far, far away. "Thing of it is, I don't have an answer for you. Not today, anyway."

Nathan seized on that, leaning toward Parker as he said, "Does that mean you might be willing to talk to me again?"

Parker uncrossed his arms, put his hands on his knees, and pushed himself to his feet. He grimaced and said, "Hear those old bones poppin' and creakin' when I get up? That's what livin' too long will do for you. Time you get to be my age, all you got left is memories and achin' joints."

He started toward the door into the grocery store.

"You didn't answer my question," Nathan said. "Will you talk to me again and tell me the rest of it?"

Parker paused with the door open and looked at him.

"I guess you'll just have to come back and find out." Amusement sparkled in the old man's blue eyes as he smiled and added, "I do like a dramatic moment."